IRRETRIEVABLY
BROKEN

USA TODAY BESTSELLING AUTHOR
Melissa F. Miller

BROWN STREET BOOKS

This book is a work of fiction. Names, characters, places, and incidents either are the product of the author's imagination or are used fictitiously. Any resemblance to actual persons, living or dead, is entirely coincidental.

Published by Brown Street Books.

For more information about the author,
please visit www.melissafmiller.com.

For more information about the publisher,
please visit www.brownstbooks.com.

Brown Street Books ISBN: 978-0-9834927-6-4

Cover design by Clarissa Yeo

Book Layout & Design ©2014 - BookDesignTemplates.com

For Sue and Jim,
with appreciation for their support and en-
couragement.

ACKNOWLEDGMENTS

Sincere thanks and appreciation to Curt Akin, Lou Maconi, Gavin Russell, Trevor Furrer, Missy Owen, Al Furrer, and Ashley Davis for reading the drafts and providing comments, suggestions, editing, and proofreading assistance. Any mistakes or errors that remain are mine and mine alone. Special thanks to David, my husband, who cheerfully fills the roles of first reader, child-wrangler, and personal chef when the Muse strikes. Thanks, too, to my children, who have somewhat less cheerfully accepted that when mom is writing, the office is off-limits.

1.

Monday

THE PHOTOGRAPH ARRIVED IN A white Tyvek mailing envelope bordered by green triangles. It was addressed in elegant script to *Charles Anderson Prescott, V*. Across the bottom half of the envelope, block letters advised that the contents were PERSONAL AND CONFIDENTIAL. It bore no return address.

Caroline Masters, personal secretary to Charles Anderson Prescott, V (better known as Cinco, but always Mr. Prescott in her mind), looked up at the courier. He leaned on her credenza, with his head bent over an iPhone, texting away.

As she scrawled her name on the clipboard he proffered, Caroline asked, "Do you know who sent this?"

He looked up and shook his head.

"There's no return address."

"I see that. That's why I'm asking if *you* know."

Surely, he had a record of the sender. How else would his company bill the person?

He shrugged. "I just deliver the packages."

He tucked the phone into one of the many pockets of his frayed cargo pants, jammed his earbuds into his ears, and returned the clipboard to his black canvas bag.

As he let himself out, Caroline considered the envelope. Her practice was to open and prioritize Mr. Prescott's business correspondence for him. She did not open his personal mail.

She wasn't quite sure what to make of this package. A good ninety-five percent of the mail addressed to the attorneys who worked at Prescott & Talbott—including hand deliveries—was delivered to the firm's mailroom to be logged and then distributed internally by the mailroom staff.

On rare occasions, a courier would hand deliver a package directly to an attorney if its contents were urgent or otherwise very sensitive. But that sort of delivery was usually prearranged; she couldn't recall ever having received one without a return address.

No one touched Mr. Prescott's phone or calendar except for her, so Caroline knew he was not expecting this package. And it *was* marked confidential. This was the sort of package she should take, unopened, into her boss's office and let him open personally.

And, normally, she would have.

But as the chairman of the largest law firm in Pittsburgh, Mr. Prescott was having a particularly difficult day. For the second time in less than a year, one of the firm's partners had been murdered.

Mr. Prescott was hunkered down with his inner circle, trying to craft a public statement. It would have to convey sadness and regret at the loss of Ellen Mortenson, for both her warm personality and exceptional legal skill. At the same time, it would need to reassure Ellen's clients that, as special as she had been, she was sufficiently fungible that any one of her talented colleagues in Prescott & Talbott's estates and trusts department could step in to take over her matters in a seamless manner. Caroline knew striking the right balance was no easy task. It had taken Mr. Prescott the better part of a day to come up with a statement when Noah Peterson had been killed.

In the meantime, the press, clients, and friends of the firm had been calling nonstop. Caroline's strong but polite offers to place callers in Mr. Prescott's voicemail had become stronger and less polite as the afternoon had worn on.

And, if her patience was thinning, then she assumed his was, too. The last thing she wanted to do was to interrupt him with a package that was probably unimportant while he was dealing with a crisis.

So she plucked her letter opener out of the crystal vase on her desk, slit open the thin envelope, and shook its contents onto her desk.

A five-by-seven print of three young women in formal gowns, smiling at the bright future ahead of them, fluttered out. She recognized them immediately, even though the picture was sixteen years old: Ellen Mortenson, Clarissa Costopolous, and Martine Landry, the first-year associates of the class of 1996. She even remembered the function. It was the firm's holiday party, black tie that year, and the three new attorneys had exuded glamour, excitement, and possibilities.

The photograph had been defaced.

A thick red X covered Ellen's face. Across the bottom of the photo, someone had printed in large, red, block letters "ONE DOWN."

2.

Tuesday

SASHA McCANDLESS STARED INTO HER empty coffee mug then checked the time. Twenty minutes until she needed to leave for her lunch meeting. Definitely enough time for one last cup.

Out of habit, she started toward the corner of her office where she used to have a coffee station, then caught herself and headed out the door. She poked her head into Naya's office across the hall.

"Hey, I'm getting some more coffee. You want anything?"

Naya looked up from the discovery requests she was reading and shook her head, her dreadlocks bouncing off her shoulders.

"You need to slow down with the coffee, Mac. For real."

Sasha looked pointedly at the pack of Marlboro Lights that Naya had mostly hidden under a stack of paper, but said nothing. She still couldn't believe Naya had finally left Prescott & Talbott to join her. Having a friend and experienced legal assistant to share the workload and the occasional happy hour cocktail more than outweighed the hypocritical nagging.

"Okay, be right back."

Naya had come aboard at the end of the summer, after her mother had passed away. Once she was no longer shouldering the home health care bills, she'd called to take Sasha up on her standing offer of employment.

The timing had been perfect. Back in April, a bizarre and highly publicized case up in Clear Brook County had landed Sasha on the front pages of Pittsburgh's two major newspapers and put her face on the evening news for weeks. Even now, months later, every time a local station ran a story on community disagreements over hydrofracking, they showed the footage of her coming out of the county hospital, splattered with someone else's blood. WPXI, at least, usually had the decency to follow that with a shot of her, clean and unbloodied, at the Governor's press conference announcing the indictment of the Attorney General.

As a result of her minor celebrity, the Law Offices of Sasha McCandless, P.C., were awash with prospective new clients. Naya's most important job responsibility was client intake: she weeded out the crackpots and determined whether the sane ones were relatively solvent and had actual legal matters to litigate. Surprisingly few people met all three criteria.

Better her than me, Sasha thought, as she hurried down the stairs for her free coffee.

Free coffee. The phrase filled Sasha with an undeniable joy. When she had approached the landlord about renting additional space for Naya, he'd informed her he was selling the building to a guy who planned to put in a coffee shop on the first floor. Eager to have a paying tenant while he got his business up and running, the new landlord, Jake, had readily agreed to Sasha's request for free coffee and had thrown in a ten percent discount on food. She wasn't costing him much in food, but she figured she easily drank her weight in coffee each month. Good thing for Jake she was just shy of a hundred pounds.

She walked through the cluster of college-aged kids gathered around the bulletin board, amazed that they still read flyers pinned to corkboards. Shouldn't they all be checking in on foursquare or something?

Kathryn, the Pitt student who worked three mornings a week, gave her pink-streaked hair a toss and laughed when she saw Sasha approaching.

"No way? You want more?"

"Last one, Kathryn," Sasha promised, putting her mug up on the counter.

"Last one for my shift, at least. I'm off at noon."

Kathryn filled the bright orange mug and slid it back to Sasha.

Sasha walked back up the stairs, sipping the hot coffee as she went. She wondered what Will Volmer wanted. He'd been unusually cryptic when he'd called and asked her to lunch. All he would tell her was he had a possible referral for her but he couldn't discuss it over the phone.

Will, the head of Prescott & Talbott's white collar criminal law practice, had represented her back in the spring when she'd given the grand jury testimony that had led to the indictment of Pennsylvania's Attorney General. Will's unflappable demeanor and quiet calm had seen her through the chaos of that scandal, so she figured she owed him one. She'd show up and listen to what he had to say, but she doubted she'd be interested in the case, whatever it was.

Despite the lack of qualified clients who walked in off the street, Sasha was busy. Really busy. Hemisphere Air—notwithstanding its decades-long relationship with Prescott & Talbott's litigation department—now used Sasha for all its Pennsylvania trial work. She supposed that was what happened when you saved the life of a company's general counsel. As the head lawyer at Hemisphere Air, Bob Metz wouldn't hear of anyone other than Sasha handling a civil matter in the jurisdiction.

In addition to the Hemisphere Air work, Sasha had a decent stream of work for current Prescott clients. They sought her out for corporate litigation matters that were too small to justify Prescott & Talbott fees but sufficiently complicated to require Prescott & Talbott quality. They stayed with Prescott for their larger matters and retained Sasha for the rest. None of those clients had been direct referrals from Prescott, though. Whatever Will had in mind was a first.

Back in her office, she stood in front of the window with her coffee and looked down at the foot traffic on South Highland Avenue. People—students mostly, judging by the flip-flops and pale, bare legs—strolled from shop to shop, enjoying the

Indian summer. Seventy degrees in early October was unheard of in Pittsburgh.

A thin guy with dreadlocks ran across the street arm-in-arm with a tall, red-haired girl and ducked out of sight. She heard them laughing as the bell on the door of the coffee shop below tinkled to announce their arrival to the staff.

She checked the clock: it was time to go. Will was famously punctual. She shrugged a pale blue cardigan on over her sleeveless dress, poked head into the next room to say goodbye to Naya, and headed out to the restaurant across the street.

~ ~ ~ ~ ~

Sasha arrived at Casbah before Will and asked the hostess for a table in the basement. Sasha wasn't surprised that she'd beaten him there, considering the restaurant was less than a one-minute walk from her office and a solid twenty-minute drive from his.

She'd offered to meet downtown, but Will had insisted on coming to her. Casbah's food merited the trip, but she'd gotten the impression that Will didn't want anyone to see them together.

The cloak and dagger business was decidedly not Will's style. He'd begun his career as a federal prosecutor, but the prospect of putting three sons through college had driven him into Prescott & Talbott's affluent arms. As the partner in charge of the firm's small, but lucrative, white collar criminal practice, Will hadn't had any trouble funding his boys' stints at Yale, Stanford, and Duke. He did, however, seem to have trouble fitting in with his partners.

Sasha's mentor, the late Noah Peterson, used to say that a stench of earnestness clung to Will. Every year, after the firm's holiday party, while his colleagues were being poured into cabs, Will boxed up the leftover food in the cargo space of his ancient Subaru and delivered it to the Jubilee Soup Kitchen downtown.

Will came hurrying down the stairs behind the hostess. Tension painted his lean face.

"Sasha, I'm so sorry to keep you waiting."

She stood and accepted his kiss on the cheek.

"Don't be silly, Will. I haven't been waiting long."

He bobbed his head fast, and sat down.

"Oh, good. How's Leo?"

"He's well."

"Has he taught you to boil water yet?"

Sasha smiled at the gentle jab but didn't bother responding. Will was making small talk but his mind was elsewhere, judging by the distracted frown he wore.

She waited until the hostess had handed him a menu and gone off to get them glasses of water.

Then she said, "You look worried, Will. Everything okay?"

Will's eyes came up from the menu and met hers. He closed the menu and folded his hands over it.

"Not really." He blinked and cleared his throat. "I didn't want to just launch into this without any niceties—" he trailed off.

"But?" she prompted.

"But maybe it's better if I just get right to it. This is weighing on me."

His hands plucked at the menu absently.

"What is?"

"Ellen Mortenson."

Ellen had been a partner in the trusts and estates department. She'd been at the firm for over fifteen years and was a newly-minted equity partner, having paid her dues—first as an associate and then as an income partner for several grueling years.

Over the weekend, Ellen had been killed. Her murder had been splashed all over the news. The media attention was to be expected: Ellen had been a successful lawyer at one of Pittsburgh's largest and oldest law firms. And her death had been grue-some. As the breathless KDKA reporter had put it, Ellen's throat had been slashed "ear to ear."

Will swallowed and went on. "Did you hear her husband's been charged?"

"I did."

According to what Sasha had read in the papers and picked up through Naya's still-active connec-tions to the Prescott & Talbott grapevine, Greg Lang, Ellen's husband, had found her body. At first, he hadn't been a suspect. Then it came to light that the two were estranged. Ellen had recently filed for divorce, and rumor was that the split had been nasty. As it turned out, Greg had no alibi and El-len's wounds were consistent with Greg's straight razor, which was found, smeared with Ellen's blood, in the trash bin. It wasn't exactly a shock when the grieving soon-to-be-ex-husband was ar-rested for homicide.

Will cleared his throat again. Then he said, "Well, Greg fired the attorney who represented him at his preliminary arraignment and has ap-proached the firm to represent him."

Sasha cocked her head and looked at him.

Will continued, "The partnership has grown very fond of Greg over the past fifteen years and considers him a friend, just as Ellen was a dear friend." His eyes dropped to the table.

Sasha said nothing.

He fussed with the edge of the tablecloth and said, "Of course, we had to explain that our criminal practice is limited to white-collar crime."

White-collar crime. It sounded so respectable. As if the fact that someone was wearing a suit while they looted their employees' pensions or bribed government officials to let them bring to market some medication with dangerous, unreported side effects somehow made the resultant devastation better.

She fixed him with a look. "I imagine you also explained it would be a conflict, not to mention in incredibly poor taste, to represent the man who killed one of your partners?"

Will winced but leaned across the table and forged on. "Sasha, Greg maintains his innocence. And based on what we know of his case, we believe him. Which is why we want to help him secure excellent counsel. That's where you come in."

Sasha signaled for the waitress and thought about her response.

The waitress came over, all smiles. "Yes, ma'am."

Not caring if Will judged her for it, Sasha said, "I need some wine. Just whatever merlot you have by the glass, okay?"

Not only did Will not judge Sasha for ordering a glass of wine, he one-upped her and suggested they get a bottle. Will Volmer. Drinking in the middle of the workday.

They sat in silence until the wine arrived.

Finally, after the waitress had taken their orders and retreated, Sasha said, "If the firm wants to help Greg Lang, as sick as I think that is, perhaps you should try to find him an attorney who has experience defending a homicide case—or, at a minimum, someone who's appeared in criminal court at least once."

Sasha's practice focused on business litigation, but she took on matters in other areas, with two exceptions: divorces and criminal cases. She didn't do divorces because, as far as she could tell, it was a practice area filled with nothing but misery and pain; she didn't do criminal cases because everything she knew about criminal law she'd learned from watching *Law & Order* reruns.

Will sipped his wine and considered his response.

"When I was a prosecutor, my biggest concern in the courtroom wasn't the celebrity criminal attorney defending some splashy case. It was the nervous junior associate from the big law firm who'd never set foot in court before defending some lost cause as part of his firm's pro bono program. You know why?"

Sasha shook her head.

"Because a seasoned criminal defense attorney is a realist—no matter the facts, he'll likely cut a deal if the client lets him. If the client insists on going to trial, he'll give it his best shot, but both the lawyer and the client accept that the deck is stacked against them," Will explained.

He paused and tore a chunk of bread in half. As he mopped it around the dish of olive oil, he continued, "But a big firm lawyer who hasn't been ground down by criminal practice? He'll charge ahead, maintaining the client's innocence. And he won't spend every day in court handling misdemeanors, entering pleas, or negotiating bonds in the weeks leading up to trial. He'll have the luxury of focusing on the trial exclusively, working hundreds of hours, and come up with arguments a prosecutor would never anticipate."

Sasha supposed that could be true. At Prescott & Talbott, the criminal pro bono program—through which lawyers provided free representation to indigent accused criminals or already-convicted criminals who wanted to appeal—was serious business. Associates who took those cases were told to treat them like bet-the-company civil litigation, and they did. As a Prescott associate, Sasha had pitched in on some appeal briefs for a death penalty case. Eventually, twenty-two years after the firm had taken the case, a team of Prescott attorneys had exonerated the defendant through DNA evidence and he'd been released from death row.

She said, "Maybe so, but I'm not a big firm associate anymore. I'm building a practice, Will. I can't ignore my caseload to give a homicide trial the attention it would need, even if I could figure out what I was supposed to be doing. "

Will took a longer drink before answering this time.

"I'm here on behalf of the partnership asking you to take this case as a personal favor to us. We believe Greg is telling the truth—he didn't kill Ellen. And, it's in the firm's interest that he be found not guilty. We're still recovering from the scandal surrounding Noah's death last year. Our partner was murdered by a former partner—an officer of a client, no less—to prevent the discovery of her plan to murder hundreds of innocent air travelers to make a profit. This situation with Ellen has been salt in that wound. Our clients don't care to see their attorneys on the evening news quite so much. To the extent publicity in this case is unavoidable, Greg's exoneration would at least bring some positive attention."

Will finished his speech; Sasha thought she saw a shadow of self-disgust cross his face.

She arched a brow. "I still don't get it, Will. Why me?"

Will flushed. "You, yourself, have attracted a fair amount of attention in the past year, both as a result of the Hemisphere Air fiasco and because of the murder of Judge Paulson up in Springport. You *were* appointed special prosecutor by the chief justice of the supreme court, Sasha. That has a certain cachet. I think the firm's management likes the idea of a former Prescott & Talbott attorney handling this, especially one who seems to thrive in the spotlight. Speaking personally, I hope you'll consider taking on the matter because I believe you can help Greg."

He met her gaze, unblinking, and she felt sorry for him. Leave it to Prescott & Talbott to send Will to carry its water. She wondered if the gobs of money he earned really outweighed the psychic cost of selling his soul.

She sipped her wine.

"Oh," Will said, like he'd forgotten a minor detail, "the partnership also voted to pay for Greg's legal defense out of what would have been Ellen's next guaranteed draw. We will, of course, pay your standard hourly rate, but given the costs involved in defending a homicide, we also have a retainer for you."

He reached into his jacket pocket and took out a check. He placed it in the exact center of the table with the type facing her so she could read it easily. It was made out to The Law Offices of Sasha McCandless, P.C., in the amount of three hundred thousand dollars.

3.

BACK IN HER OFFICE, Sasha stared down at the check, wondering what the hell she was thinking.

She had agreed to talk to Greg Lang and make her own assessment of his case. She'd told Will she'd be in touch to let him know if she was going to take Greg on as a client.

Despite what Prescott & Talbott might have thought of her ability, though, she knew she had no business even contemplating taking on a homicide case. A quick chat with Naya had only served to confirm that Sasha should stay far away from Greg Lang and his murder defense. Naya's immediate reaction had been that no good could come of dabbling in criminal work, especially given that a Prescott partner was the victim.

Sasha shook her head and slid the check into her top desk drawer. She didn't owe Prescott & Talbott anything. If she had wanted to be the firm's lapdog, she would have accepted its offer of partnership a year ago. But she did owe Will.

She stood, stretched, and looked out the window. The sun was gone now; the sky was gray and cloudy, thick with the promise of rain.

Just get it over with.

She picked up Will's heavy, linen business card and turned it over. He'd written Greg Lang's telephone number on the back in tiny, precise script.

Not only was the firm paying Greg's legal costs, it had also posted his $1.5 million bail. As a result, Ellen Mortenson's accused murderer and estranged husband was awaiting trial from the comfort of their marital home.

Doesn't matter. Just call him already.

Sasha jabbed the numbers into her telephone's keypad and hit the speaker button. She adjusted her neck, cracking it first on one side and then the other, while the telephone rang.

Four rings. And then a recorded message—startling because it was in Ellen's lilting voice:

You've reached the Mortenson and Lang residence. We're out and about, but leave a message for Ellen or Greg, and we'll be sure to call you back.

Sasha waited for the beep.

"This message is for Greg Lang. Mr. Lang, my name's Sasha McCandless. I used to work with your wife at —"

She stopped when the screeching sound of someone picking up the phone filled her ear.

"Wait, hold on! Let me turn this thing off!" A man's voice, agitated.

She cringed at the metallic shriek that followed.

Then the man said, "Hello? Ms. McCandless, are you there?"

"I am."

"Oh, good. I have to screen all the calls. Blasted reporters."

"I understand. This is Mr. Lang, correct?"

"Yes." His voice took on an accusing tone. "Am I on speakerphone?"

Sasha looked down at the phone on her desk.

"You are. But I'm alone in my office. I like to have my hands free in case I need to take notes."

"Oh. Okay, then." He said it reluctantly, as if he'd rather stay offended.

"As I was saying, I'm a former Prescott—"

Lang cut her off. "I know who you are, you're the tiny little girl. We've met at a few Prescott parties. Anyway, they told me you'd be calling."

Sasha invested considerable energy in *not* thinking of herself as a tiny little girl, but she had to admit the description was accurate. At just under five feet tall and around one hundred pounds, she was rarely anything other than the smallest person in the room, unless she was babysitting her nieces and nephews. And, even then, at eight years old, Liam was gaining on her.

She viewed her diminutive size as a competitive advantage, though. People tended to underestimate her. It was as though they expected her to be weak or childlike just because she was small. Opposing attorneys sometimes failed to adequately prepare when they squared off against her for the first time. They were always prepared the second time.

"That's me," she said, searching her memory to try to place Lang.

She had a fuzzy recollection of Ellen's husband as some type of scientist with no sense of humor. If she had the right guy in mind, Greg had trapped her date at one of Prescott & Talbott's cocktail parties and talked at length to him about polymers and the dangers of BPA.

Of course, her date had been partially at fault. Ben, a chronically underemployed independent filmmaker, had thought he was being funny when he'd answered Greg's question about what he did for a living by saying "I'm in plastics." Greg apparently had never seen *The Graduate* and hadn't gotten the joke.

"I'd like to come over and talk to you," she said.

"Of course," Greg said, all business now.

Sasha pulled her old Prescott & Talbott attorney directory from her top desk drawer and looked up Ellen's home address. The telephone number matched the one Will had given her.

"Are you still on Saint James Place?" she asked.

"Uh, yes, I'm keeping the house. For now."

"Great. I'll be there in ten minutes. Twenty, tops."

"You want to come here? Now? This isn't a good time. The house is a mess, and I have some errands to run this afternoon. Why don't I come to your office tomorrow?"

"Listen, Mr. Lang," Sasha said, "I'm trying to determine if I'm the right person to represent you. To do that, I need to meet with you. If you aren't interested in my services, that's fine. If you are, I suggest you reschedule your errands."

Although she halfway hoped he'd refuse to see her, thereby solving the problem of whether to represent him, she collected a notepad, pen, her wallet, keys, and mobile phone as she spoke and swept them into a light blue leather laptop case that matched her sweater.

Greg Lang huffed and puffed and then finally said, "Fine."

"Great. Goodbye."

She hung up and shut down her laptop. That went into the bag, too. Then she turned out the lights, locked the door behind her, and hurried down the stairs to the coffee shop.

The point of springing her visit on Lang was to see him on his home turf. Sasha believed she could learn a lot about a person from seeing him in his natural environment. She would have preferred to show up unannounced so that he wouldn't have time to clean up or hide anything, but that would have been unprofessional. The best she could do now was get over to his place quickly.

Sasha made it a habit to meet people at home. She'd started the practice after she'd stopped by the home of a well-regarded economist to drop off an expert witness report for her to review. Sasha's expert had answered the door at two o'clock on a Saturday afternoon in a bra and panties, expecting to find the male exotic dancer she'd picked up the night before, not the attorney who'd retained her to testify in a commercial dispute. Although Sasha didn't particularly care what Professor Robbins did in her spare time, she did think some discretion was in order considering she held herself out as an economic expert to the tune of seven hundred and fifty dollars an hour. The last thing Sasha needed during trial was to have to rehabilitate the credibility of a woman who, as it turned out, claimed her patronage of male sex workers was an effort to support and legitimize an underground economy.

Despite the threat of rain, she decided to walk. Greg's house was just about a mile away, and she could use the air. She confirmed there was a travel umbrella in the bottom of the laptop bag, then slung the bag across her chest diagonally, like a messenger bag, and headed toward Ellsworth Avenue.

She'd never been inside Ellen's home, but she knew the street from her running route through the neighborhood. Saint James Place was a short street that ran between Fifth Avenue and Ellsworth; the homes there could fairly be called mansions. Both sides of the street were lined by hulking hundred-year-old Victorians set back behind wrought iron fences. None of the homes on Saint James looked to be smaller than six thousand square feet, and several of them were considerably larger. Ellen and Greg had no children. Sasha tried to imagine what they did with all that space.

She crossed against the light, jogging through the intersection, although no cars were in sight. As she turned onto Ellsworth, the wind picked up and she pulled her cardigan tight. She stopped in front of a massive, pre-war apartment complex to check the time. It had been six minutes since she'd left the office.

A dime-sized raindrop splashed onto her arm. Followed by another.

She was a little more than halfway there. Options were to take out the umbrella and mince her way along the wet sidewalk in heels or to take off her shoes and run for it.

She ran for it.

The rain was cold on her face, but the fat drops were still long seconds apart. She felt as though she really were dodging them. She opened her lungs and her stride and sprinted, flat out.

She stopped in front of a painted lady Victorian done up in yellow, green, and pink. An iron gate with scrollwork detail cut into the six-foot fence was unlatched and hanging ajar.

This was it.

She squeezed through the open gate and hurried up to the wide, columned porch. She took her shoes out of her bag and put them back on, then shook the water from her hair and caught her breath. Then she wiped her hands on her sweater and stepped up to the door to ring the bell.

A shadow passed behind the stained glass transom window, and the door jerked open before she could press the doorbell button.

"Don't you have a car? Or an umbrella?" Greg Lang said.

He stood to the side and let her pass into the entryway.

He was the humorless scientist she remembered from the cocktail party. Tall and stooped, with a shock of red hair. Green eyes that might have been soft and kind at one time but were now bloodshot and dull.

Sasha ignored his questions and stuck out her hand, "It's good to see you, Mr. Lang, although I wish it were under other circumstances."

He shook her hand with a lazy grip, taking just her fingers in his hand.

"You might as well call me Greg. Can I call you Sasha?"

"Sure."

He led her over to a seating arrangement in front of a fireplace surrounded by green, black, and brown mosaic tiles. The chairs faced an enormous staircase carved from dark wood with thin, intricate spindles.

"Let's talk here in the sitting room," he said, taking a seat in a formal wingback chair covered in a dark green and brown paisley silk.

She lowered herself into its mate. They were in what was essentially a hallway. From her seat she could see solid wood pocket doors leading to three rooms. All three were closed off.

Greg reached for a cut-glass decanter that sat on the table between the two chairs. It held an amber liquid. "May I offer you a drink? Scotch? Something else?"

"No, thanks."

"Suit yourself." He shrugged and tipped a generous pour into a dirty-looking tumbler.

In fact, the entire place, majestic as it was, looked a little dingy. As if it hadn't been thoroughly cleaned in weeks. A musty funk hung in the air. It smelled like wet dog. She wondered about the condition of the rooms behind the closed doors.

"Thank you for seeing me on such short notice," she said.

He stared into his glass. "I suppose I should be the one thanking you for even considering to take my case. They say you're very good."

"I'm an experienced litigator, Greg, but I trust Will told you I have no criminal law experience."

"He did. I don't care. Ellen always said you were a superstar. I need a superstar."

His face didn't soften at the mention of his dead wife's name. He leaned forward and searched Sasha's face. "Will you take my case?"

"I don't know. Why do you need a superstar?"

He frowned. "What?"

"You're innocent, right? Why do you need a superstar lawyer?"

Anger flashed across his face, but he controlled his voice. "Don't be cute. I know how things look. The divorce proceedings, the razor. And ... I found her."

He looked toward the pocket doors that closed off the room to the right of the front door, staring at the dark wood.

Sasha followed his eyes. "Is that where she was?"

He nodded. Didn't speak. Dragged his eyes back to hers.

She stood and ignored the lump in her throat. "Walk me through it."

He sighed but didn't argue with her. He deposited his tumbler on the table with a heavy thud and led her over to the doors.

He slid the doors open, careful to push them into the recessed area of the wall, and stood back. From behind him, Sasha could see into the room. It was a good-sized square, with floor-to-ceiling cherry bookshelves on three walls. The outside wall housed a large window, with a built-in, cherry bench running its length beneath it.

The window looked out onto a flower garden that may have been a riot of color and beauty at one time. Now tall weeds choked the handful of late summer roses that were still in bloom, and the heather was drying from purple to brown. Rain drummed against the window.

Sasha waited for Greg to go into the room, but he stood rooted in place in the doorway. She walked around him and stood in the approximate middle of the room. She thought she smelled the metallic tang of blood, but that had to be her imagination. That smell would be long gone by now.

"Was this Ellen's office?"

"Yes." He cleared his throat. "Mine was—*is*—upstairs."

She'd assumed as much. Legal journals formed a neat stack on one corner of the desk, and law books lined at least a third of the shelves. There was one section devoted to biographies and another to literary fiction. Photographs displayed in silver frames in a mix of sizes were scattered on several shelves in a deliberately casual way, as if Ellen had had a designer's help. Ellen and Greg smiling on a ski lift. Ellen in a cap and gown, standing between a beaming older couple. A large black-and-white candid shot of Ellen and Greg sitting under a leafy tree; she was leaning against his chest, her eyes closed and her lips parted, her face upturned to the sun, and Greg had his arms wrapped around her, looking down at her with a tender expression. Sasha felt a lump in her throat at the obvious love they'd once shared and turned her attention to the next picture. It was a photo of Ellen, beaming, along with two other women, all dressed in ball gowns, their arms linked.

Sasha narrowed her eyes and reached for the picture. As she picked it up, Greg muttered something she didn't catch.

"Pardon?"

"I said, The Terrific Trio. That's Ellen, Martine Landry, and Clarissa Costopolous. At their first Prescott & Talbott holiday party. We weren't married yet."

Sasha recognized all the names, although the grinning, youthful beauties in the picture were a far cry from the serious power hitters in sensible suits they would become.

"The Terrific Trio?"

Greg nodded. "They were all in the same summer class. Someone on the recruiting committee named them that and it stuck."

Sasha returned the picture to its spot. A thin trail of dust curled up from the shelf.

"Clarissa is still at Prescott & Talbott. I know Martine by name, but she was gone by the time I got there."

Greg nodded again, "Martine made partner very quickly under the old system. It took her about five years. By then, she had had her first child and was working a reduced schedule when the firm elevated her to partner. When she was pregnant with her third, she and the firm agreed to part ways. She got her buy-in money back and a decent lump sum. I think she's teaching legal research and writing as an adjunct at Duquesne now."

"And, Clarissa is a new equity partner."

"Yes; after Martine left, the shine was off The Terrific Trio. Ellen and Clarissa started calling themselves The Tainted Two. It took them a long time to make partner; Ellen longer than Clarissa. And, of course, by then, there were two tiers of partner: income and equity. Ellen thought income partnership was just a way for the firm to delay making a real decision about its female lawyers until their childbearing years were over. I'm sure you know all this."

Sasha knew that partnership decisions were made primarily by men who had stay-at-home wives to raise their kids and run their households. But she wasn't interested in discussing gender equality and the glass ceiling with Greg.

"Sure. Okay, let's talk about what happened the night Ellen died."

Greg was still in the doorway, unwilling or unable to come into the room where his wife died.

He cleared his throat. "Uh, I came home around ten—"

Sasha looked up at him, surprised. "You were both living here? I thought Ellen had initiated divorce proceedings."

He reddened.

"She had, but yes, we were both still in the house. I was hoping we could reconcile. And, well, to be frank, I had been let go at work. Renting an apartment seemed silly until I found a new job. This place is huge," he said, sweeping his arms wide. "We more or less divided the house. I stayed on the third floor when she was home. But you know Ellen—she was always at work, anyway."

Sasha nodded. Ellen had probably been at the office from eight-thirty or nine every morning until well after eight at night. They wouldn't have had to interact much. In fact, she wondered if they'd interacted much before their marriage had hit the skids, given the realities of Ellen's work life.

"Okay, so you came home at ten in the evening?"

"Yes."

"From where?"

"Excuse me?"

"Where were you?"

Sasha walked over and sat on the cushioned window bench. She didn't really want to sit behind Ellen's desk, but she hoped moving to the far side of the room would draw Greg in from the doorway so she could see him better while he spoke.

Behind her, the rain continued to beat against the glass.

Greg came in and perched on the edge of a nubby, light green chair that had been pushed against the bookshelves at an odd angle. Probably by the police, she thought.

"I was out. Alone."

"Where? Maybe someone saw you."

"No one saw me. I was just out walking."

"At ten o'clock at night?"

Greg met her eyes and held her gaze. "Yes."

"Do you have a dog?" *Maybe he was walking a dog.*

"No, I was just taking a walk."

He crossed his arms and leaned back in the chair.

His body language told her everything. He was lying. She dropped it. For now.

"What happened when you came into the house?"

"I came in the front door," he said, pointing out into the hallway at the door. "It wasn't locked. But I had locked it when I left."

"When did you leave?"

"Around six. I had dinner at the Fajita Grill on Ellsworth, alone, at six-thirty. I finished up just before eight and then took a walk."

A two-hour walk.

He looked at her, waiting. She said nothing.

He continued. "The door was unlocked, so I knew Ellen was home. The office doors were closed, but I saw the light coming out from under the doors. I knocked. I wanted to say good night. Just, you know, out of courtesy."

Sasha wasn't familiar with proper etiquette for estranged spouses who lived together, so she assumed that was reasonable. "Go on," she said.

"Ellen didn't answer, which was annoying. I thought we could at least be civil, so I pushed the door open and ..." he trailed off, staring down at the bare wood floor in the center of the room.

He closed his eyes and gave his head one quick shake, then he looked up at Sasha, but she knew he was seeing Ellen. His eyes were dull and distant.

"She was lying there, on the floor. Well, she was on the rug, but the police took it. Evidence. It was covered in blood. She was covered in blood. Her face and neck were just ... red. She wasn't moving. I stood there for a long time. I don't know how long. Then I went to her. I felt for a pulse. She was warm; blood was still pouring out of her. It was pooling on the rug. I used the desk phone and called 911. Then I sat there, where you are. And waited."

"Did you touch anything?"

"No, just Ellen. And the phone."

Sasha shifted on the window bench. She wanted to leave. To get out of this room and think through Greg's story, away from him.

He was pale and shaking.

"Okay, let's get out of here."

They walked out of the office. He banged the pocket doors shut.

She led him back to the pair of chairs by the fireplace. He lowered himself into a chair and reached for the decanter with still-shaking hands. She took the other seat.

"How about a cup of tea? Or some water?" Sasha said.

So far, Greg wasn't the most likable person, and she was certain he wasn't telling her the whole truth. But she wasn't convinced he'd killed his wife, and there was no denying he was shaken by having to relive finding her body.

He responded with a snort and poured himself another glass of scotch.

He kept his eyes on his drink and said, "Are you going to take my case?"

She ignored the question. "Who do you think killed your wife?"

"I don't know, a random intruder?"

"With your straight razor? Which was where—in the second floor bathroom?"

"Actually, third floor. But I don't know that it was *my* straight razor. It was *a* straight razor."

He narrowed his eyes and threw back his head. He drained his glass in one long gulp.

Sasha's throat burned just from watching.

"Your razor was missing, though, when the police searched?"

"Yes."

"A random intruder killed your wife with a straight razor he brought to the scene, left it in the trash, and then took yours from the third floor bathroom?"

Greg stared at her for a long moment, started to speak, and then shrugged.

"Anything else missing?"

"No."

"Were either of you seeing anyone else?"

Sasha hadn't heard anything about an affair, but she was a step removed from the gossip. Maybe Ellen had had a boyfriend who wasn't wild about the fact that Greg was still living in the house.

"No."

"Are you sure she wasn't?"

He moved forward and put his thin face up to hers. "I'm sure."

She leaned back. "Why did Ellen want a divorce?"

He answered her with a question. "Why is that relevant?"

"It's relevant because the prosecution will paint you as enraged because your wife wanted to end your marriage. I'd like to know why it was ending."

He pursed his lips but said nothing.

Sasha stood. She didn't intend to play this game; if Greg wouldn't talk to her, he could find a different attorney. She dug around in her bag until she found her small, black umbrella. Then she slung the bag across her chest and turned to Greg, who remained in the chair.

"Thank you for meeting with me. I know it wasn't easy talking about what happened to Ellen," she said.

He looked up at her, no emotion on his face. "Will you talk to my divorce attorney if I ask her to call you?"

"What can she add?"

"I don't know. Maybe nothing. But I think she believes me."

"Will you authorize her to talk to me about the divorce?"

He narrowed his eyes but nodded yes.

"Okay, then have her call my cell phone. The number's on my card." She plucked a business card from her bag and placed it on the table beside his booze.

He nodded, glanced at the card, and then eyed the scotch again.

She let herself out.

4.

CINCO STARED OUT THE WINDOW. The rain had stopped, and he could see clear to the top of Mount Washington, where a vibrant red and orange home had been built into the side of the hill. He didn't know who had built the post-modern house or who lived in it, but he loved it. He loved it because it so clearly didn't fit in with the surrounding homes. They were all dignified, well-built family homes that signaled stability, a degree of prosperity, and good roots. Not the red and orange house. It screamed of whimsy and individualism. Cinco often thought he was that house.

He sighed and looked around the table at the three staid and serious Victorians looking back at him, unblinking, waiting to follow his lead.

"Who are we waiting for?" he asked.

"John Porter. He's debriefing Volmer. He'll be right up."

Cinco frowned, the smallest downturn of his mouth, to make sure the assembled men knew he was not happy about having to wait. The truth was Cinco didn't care how long they waited. He spent his days—every day—going to meetings at the law firm his great-great-grandfather had built. They just blended, one into the next, into one interminable meeting.

He wished his father, or at least his grandfather, had been as smart as the Talbott heirs, who had not followed their patriarch into the family business. Instead, they had used his money to fund ventures ranging from a decent Mediterranean restaurant to a Jeep dealership to a discreet, high-quality escort service. Instead, here he was, a lawyer, surrounded by a bunch of lawyers and all their endless *"on the one hand, on the other hand"* discussions.

The door opened, and John Porter hurried in, his open suit jacket flapping behind him like a tail.

"Sorry, gentleman," he said as he pulled out the last available chair.

Cinco's personal secretary uncapped her pen, ready to begin her note-taking duties, but Porter shook his head at her.

"Cinco, I don't think we need Caroline for this, do we?"

Cinco scowled. It wasn't Porter's place to dismiss his assistant.

He turned to her. "Mrs. Masters, there's no need to transcribe our first order of business, but you should stay, as I am sure other business will arise, and we will want a record of our discussion."

He turned back to Porter and eyeballed him hard, daring him to object. Porter said nothing.

Marco DeAngeles broke the tension. "Tell us, John. What did Volmer say?"

The five men assembled in the room were the firm's power hitters. They pulled down seven figures a year, regardless of how their own client billables shook out. As the top of the pyramid, they reaped the rewards and dealt with the headaches. And this business with Ellen Mortenson's husband was a headache they did not need. Not after the mess with Hemisphere Air.

Porter glanced at Caroline before he spoke, then he said, "Volmer gave her the check, but she hasn't agreed to do it. She wants to talk to Greg herself, then she'll let Volmer know."

DeAngeles slapped his hand down on the table, "I told you we should have sent someone other than Volmer! He's too wishy-washy. We should have sent someone convincing."

Cinco held up a hand. "Volmer was the right choice. We need a soft sell with Sasha. For crissakes, Marco, she *turned down* partnership."

That one still stung. It just didn't happen. Some lawyer wastes her twenties working twenty-five hundred hours a year, nights, weekends, holidays. No husband, no kids, no meaningful vacations. And then she says "no thanks" when they try to hand her the prize?

Sasha McCandless had not had a rational reaction. And Cinco was worried that they were pinning all their hopes on her. What if she said she wouldn't do it?

Kevin Marcus must have read his mind. "Gentlemen, do we have a plan B?"

He was answered by silence.

"Clearly not," Fred Jennings laughed.

The rest of them turned to him. At sixty-four, Fred was knocking on the door of the firm's mandatory retirement age. He was winding down his practice, offloading his clients onto junior partners, and, although he still showed up to every Management Committee meeting, he rarely spoke. Cinco had taken to calling him Justice Thomas in private.

Fred went on. "We best come up with one, fellas." Then he folded his hands over his belly and leaned back.

"Thanks for contributing to the discussion, Fred." Cinco worked to keep the sarcasm out of his voice.

"What about Clarissa?" Porter said.

"What about her?" Cinco answered.

It was Porter's turn to frown. Clarissa Costopolous was a partner in the antitrust department—Porter's fiefdom—and he felt some responsibility toward her.

"Do we tell her?" Porter said.

"Tell her what? There's nothing to tell her!" Across the table, Marco grew agitated again.

Cinco held up a hand. Sometimes he felt like a crossing guard. He said, "He's right, John. It'd be premature. Let's just wait and see what Sasha says."

Fred chuckled, "You guys sure seem certain you can control that girl. Not sure why."

Cinco decided he preferred it when Fred played the role of the silent justice.

Marco spoke up. "Maybe we can't control her, but we can control what information she has access to. We need someone resourceful enough to get Lang off without sniffing around the firm's private business. Our job will be to protect the firm's reputation; hers will be to defend her client."

Marco shrugged when he finished, as if the success of this harebrained scheme were a foregone conclusion.

Cinco scanned the others' faces; his gaze landed back on Kevin.

"She was in your group, Kevin. Will she do it?"

Kevin considered the question. "It's hard to say. If she believes he didn't kill Ellen, I think she will. If she's not convinced … I don't know. Frankly, I'm doubtful she's the right choice."

Cinco didn't like that answer. But then, he didn't like any of this.

~ ~ ~ ~ ~

Three floors below, Clarissa Costopolous sat behind her desk, a tower of paper threatening to shift and bury her, and hissed into the phone at her divorce attorney.

"Yes, I'm sure! Andy, we've been over this. I want to put it in the damn papers."

Andy Pulaski took his time answering.

Finally, he said in a gentle voice, "Clarissa, I know you're upset, okay? I get it. And trust me, your scumbag husband will get it, too. I just don't see the need to make such an inflammatory allegation in a court document. Do you understand?"

"No, Andy, I *don't* understand!" Clarissa tried to keep her voice down. "It's not an allegation, I saw the pictures. That girl cannot be eighteen! He's screwing a high school student!"

"Clarissa, we don't know how old she is. She could be in college. And the picture just shows them kissing."

"That doesn't make it better!" Clarissa screamed, her grip on the phone so tight that her knuckles turned white.

She drew in her breath. When she spoke again, her voice was strained but calm. "I have a client meeting to prepare for. Can we talk about this later?"

Her attorney spoke soothingly. "Of course. Whenever's good for you, Clarissa. Trust me, once you officially file, you'll feel like a weight has been lifted from your shoulders. Don't worry, I'm going to nail the bastard to the wall."

"You'd better, Andy."

Clarissa carefully returned the handset to its cradle, moved aside an article she'd been reading about the Lanham Act, then put her head down on her desk, and sobbed. Her best friend was dead, her marriage was over, she felt like crap, and Porter was hovering around her office nonstop, like he was going to fire her or something. What more could possibly go wrong?

5.

RICH STARED AT THE PICTURE of Clarissa's beaming face. She looked so young and vibrant. Out of the three whores, she came across as the warmest. Nice, even. Not at all like someone who would ruin his life like it was some kind of game.

But she had; there was no denying it. He could never get back all those lost years. And she had to pay for the damage she'd caused. Justice required it.

The photograph shook in his hands.

Cool it, he told himself. *Stick with the plan.*

The plan would work. He'd spent the better part of a year developing it, perfecting it, tweaking it. He'd been so patient for so long. Plotting. Watching. Waiting. He had put all his trust in his plan.

The plan had worked with Ellen. It would work with Clarissa. And, after that, Martine.

He just had to stay the course he'd set.

He took one last look at the picture, drinking in the joy and confidence that shone in Clarissa's eyes. Soon enough, he'd replace that joy: first, with despair and terror; then, with the blank-eyed stare of death. Soon enough.

Not that he relished the killing, because he didn't. But the only way to make them pay for what they had done was to ruin their marriages and then take their lives. He wasn't some kind of freak who got off on that sort of thing. He'd considered other ways to punish them for what they'd done, but nothing else seemed fitting. This plan was elegant.

In fact, the only small drawback of his plan was the fact that it set up their husbands to take the fall for their wives' deaths. That was an unanticipated, but understandable, result of destroying their marriages. After all, Rich had watched enough cop shows to know that it was always the husband. The estranged husband? Even better.

A twinge of guilt smacked him in the gut. His dad wouldn't like that part, and Rich was doing all this as much to honor his dad's memory as he was for his own satisfaction. But it was unavoidable. The husbands would have to take the blame. He told himself they were better off—even if they went to prison, at least they'd be rid of the heartless shrews they'd married.

He slid the photograph back into the envelope and fastened the clasp. Then he placed the envelope in its gallon-sized Ziploc bag, pressed down to force the air out of the bag, and zipped it closed. He returned it to its spot in the freezer, right under the bag of frozen peas. Everything in its proper place.

He checked the clock on the stove. Time to get back to work. His job was a critical component of the plan. He couldn't risk arousing any suspicion at the office. That could ruin everything.

6.

THE PHONE RANG WHILE SASHA was changing into her running clothes. She'd decided not to go back to the office after she'd left Greg's house but to go for a run instead. She hoped a long, hard run would bring her clarity. She didn't recognize the number that flashed across the display, but she picked up the call and squeezed the Blackberry between her neck and shoulder.

"Sasha McCandless," she said as she tied her shoes.

"Hi, Sasha. My name's Erika Morrison. I'm at Feldman, Morrison & Berger. I represent Greg Lang in his divorce."

The woman on the other end had a soft, cheerful voice.

Sasha checked that her double knots were tight and stood up.

"Hi, Erika."

"Is this a good time to talk? I should tell you, I only have about twenty minutes. My kid's in the elementary school play tonight, and I have to get out of here and get dinner on the table before we go."

"That sounds like fun. What's the play?" Sasha asked.

"Some propaganda piece about eating a healthful diet. Kieran is a stalk of broccoli." Erika gave a gentle laugh.

"I guess dinner needs to be in keeping with the theme."

They both laughed this time. Avoiding the topic at hand.

Sasha glanced at the time display on her microwave. It was almost four. She could hear what Erika had to say and still have plenty of time for a run and a shower before Connelly showed up.

Erika said, "Let me start by saying I don't believe Greg killed his wife. I don't *know* for sure that he didn't, but I just can't see it."

Sasha took out a notepad and pen from her bag and sat at the kitchen island.

"Do you mind if I put you on speaker?"

"No, of course not, but I do have to ask you not to take any notes."

Sasha looked at the pen in her hand. "Really?"

Lawyers take notes. That's what they do.

"Sorry. Ellen's divorce attorney is a real piece of work. If you end up not representing Greg, I don't want that jerk making a play for your notes, and, trust me, he will." Erika's tone was apologetic but made it clear the issue wasn't open to negotiation.

Sasha capped her pen and tossed it and the pad onto the kitchen island.

"Okay. Well, I don't practice family law, so here's a stupid question: isn't the divorce moot? Ellen's dead."

Erika sighed. "It should be. But yesterday, Ellen's attorney filed a motion to finalize the terms of the divorce, saying he represents the estate. Greg, of course, is the executor, because Ellen never revised her will. We're opposing that, but, long story short, it's just a mess."

It sounded ugly. And confirmed Sasha's belief that divorce law was a practice area to be avoided.

Erika's next statement made Sasha wonder if she was a mind reader.

"Let me step back, since you don't do family law. Divorce isn't usually like this. Not anymore. There's a serious movement toward collaborative divorce. Ever heard of it?"

"No."

"Okay. It's about twenty years old now. Collaborative divorce is an alternative to litigation. The parties and their attorneys work together to create a peaceful resolution to the marriage. Sometimes, especially if there are children, counselors or other professionals are on the team. It's intended to take away the nasty, vengeful piece of the experience."

"Does it work?"

"When the parties both want it. And when they both retain lawyers who are trained collaborative divorce facilitators, yes, it does."

"But not with Ellen and Greg?"

Erika barked out a short, bitter chuckle. "Oh, hell, no. I mean, Greg wanted to go the collaborative route. That's why he hired me. It's the bulk of my practice these days. So much more dignified for everyone involved than getting into a red-faced screaming match over who gets to keep the hutch, you know? As soon as I heard who was representing Ellen, I knew we were in for a fight."

"Why?"

"Ellen retained Andy Pulaski."

"Never heard of him," Sasha said.

"No reason why you would have, unless you practice family law or know someone who went through a bitter, messy divorce. Andy specializes in war. He actually advertises that way. Calls himself

'Big Gun,' and says something like, if you're going to go to war, make sure you have the Big Gun."

"Sounds delightful."

"He's something, all right. But it was strange, his taking Ellen's case. I've only known him to represent men. Usually, some rich guy who wants to trade in the old wife for a new model. That kind of guy would retain Andy to help him avoid having to pay alimony to the woman who helped him build his business from the ground up for forty years. That's the sort of thing Andy does."

"Why do you think he took Ellen on as a client?" Sasha asked.

"No idea. I mean, old Big Gun has rent and salaries to pay just like everybody else. Maybe Ellen came around when funds were running a little bit light. It surprised me. I had him pegged as a woman-hater."

Sasha considered what she knew about Ellen. A scorched earth divorce didn't seem like her style.

"Why would Ellen hire him? I didn't know her that well, but I knew her. She didn't strike me as a vindictive person."

"I can't answer that of, course," Erika said. "But Greg felt the same way. Even when it became clear this wasn't going to be a collaborative process, he kept saying she'd be fair to him. And, he was open about his desire to reconcile with her. He couldn't see how hopeless that dream was. I mean, Pulaski filed a fault divorce, for chrissakes."

Sasha summoned up from the recesses of her brain the little she knew about Pennsylvania's divorce laws. A couple could get a no-fault divorce by consent in as little as three months if both parties agreed that the marriage was irretrievably broken. Even without one party's consent, a court could find the marriage to be irretrievably broken after the couple had lived separately for at least two years. Fault divorce required proof of some horrible behavior on one spouse's part: adultery; extreme cruelty; abandonment—that sort of thing. It was harder to establish, messier, and more expensive.

Maybe Greg had refused to sign the affidavit for a divorce on mutual consent and Ellen hadn't wanted to wait two years. Under that scenario, Pulaski might have filed the fault complaint to force Greg's hand. It wasn't completely irrational.

"Was Greg not willing to consent to a quick no-fault?"

Erika sighed and answered carefully. "He was *willing* to. He didn't want to, of course, but after he lost his job, he decided a fresh start might be in order. Ellen did let him stay in the house—although they lived separate lives—and he was grateful for that. If she had come around on the no-fault issue, Greg would have signed the affidavit. But she, or at least Pulaski, wouldn't budge."

"What were the alleged grounds?"

If Ellen had alleged that Greg had abused her, he might as well plead guilty to murder charges now.

Erika rattled off the boilerplate language. "She alleged he imposed such indignities on her as to render her condition intolerable and life burdensome."

"Did she specify what these alleged 'indignities' were?"

"Not in the complaint, but Greg knew, of course. She was talking about the pictures."

"What pictures?"

7.

HE PICTURES, Erika had explained, before hurrying off the call to get home to her little broccoli stalk, had arrived in Ellen's office mail the Friday before Labor Day weekend.

Greg told Erika that Ellen had been waiting for him when he got home from work. It was so unusual for her to be home first that he knew something was wrong as soon as he saw her car in the driveway.

Ellen had been sitting at the dining room table. Six eight-by-ten glossies were fanned out in a half circle. Six photographs of Greg at The Rivers Casino. All time- and date-stamped. Six different weekday mornings when he should have been at work, but there he was, sitting at a poker table with a stack of chips in front of him.

According to Erika, Ellen had gone online and combed through their bank records while she'd been waiting for Greg to come home. So, in addition to the photos, she greeted him with bank statements detailing the tens of thousands of dollars he'd been slowly siphoning out of one of their savings accounts.

Sasha considered this information as she ran. The rain had stopped, and she headed up Fifth Avenue to Shady Avenue and its long hill. She pounded upward and thought about Greg Lang.

The fact that he hadn't told her about the pictures irritated her. It didn't surprise her, though. In Sasha's experience, clients never told their lawyers everything right out of the gate. It didn't matter how many times an attorney explained how important it was to know *all* the facts—good and bad—in order to provide the best advice, clients would withhold the embarrassing stuff in the misguided belief that it would never come out.

It always came out. And, most of the time, the effect was much worse than if they had just been upfront about it. But her clients were civil litigants. A criminal defendant who held out on his attorney was a different animal entirely.

She powered up the steep incline, looking forward to the plateau and the gentle decline as she looped around to Forbes Avenue. She wondered what else Greg had neglected to tell her.

She'd probed the divorce attorney about Greg's whereabouts the night of his wife's murder, but he'd told Erika the same story that he'd tried to feed Sasha—that he'd been walking around alone for hours.

She puffed out a breath in frustration that a man accused of murder would play the games Greg Lang seemed to be playing.

Her left elbow suddenly was jerked hard to the side, and she stumbled. She flew sideways, into the hedges that fronted a well-maintained, red brick house. Two arms encircled her waist from behind and tugged her backward into the bushes.

Her stomach lurched.

Stay on your feet, she told herself. The worst position for a street fight was on the ground. A street fight wasn't choreographed like a wrestling match. Grappling from a prone position was an excellent way to get killed.

Base out. She bent her knees and planted her feet wide.

Being attacked from behind meant she didn't know what, if any, weapons her assailant had. She went deeper into her crouch. Behind her, her unseen opponent tightened his grip around her middle with one hand and wrapped his other hand around her neck, squeezing.

She struggled to breathe.

Connect. She lifted her left elbow over her head and swung it behind her, smashing it into the side of his neck under his jaw. Twisted and swung her right elbow into the other side of the attacker's neck. Left elbow. Right elbow. Again.

His grip loosened just enough for her to maneuver, and she turned to face him, panting, fingers ready to jab him in the eyes.

"Not bad," Daniel said, dropping his hands from her waist and rubbing his neck.

She leaned against the elm tree in his parents' front yard to catch her breath.

"You went a little easy on me, don't you think?"

Her Krav Maga instructor smiled. "A little. Didn't want a repeat of last time."

The last time Sasha had been the subject of a surprise takedown, she had ended up with a cluster of large, dark bruises on her forearms that made her skin look like rotting fruit and had prompted her primary care doctor to ask a series of embarrassing questions about her fledgling relationship with Connelly.

Sasha should have realized that running past Daniel's parents' home was an invitation for him to ambush her. *Ambush* wasn't quite the right word, considering she had paid a nice sum for the out-of-class simulated attacks. She'd been taking Krav Maga classes for years and was proficient at the self-defense system. Her training had saved her life during the Hemisphere Air fiasco and had earned an oversized goon a trip to the hospital for reconstructive surgery. She had also fended off an attacker in Clear Brook County back in the spring. More typically, though, she used her skills to put a stop to her brothers' favorite pastime of picking her up and putting her on top of their parents' refrigerator. After the year she'd had, she figured keeping her hand-to-hand combat skills was at least as important as fulfilling her continuing legal education requirement.

Daniel's father stepped out onto his porch and yelled down to her, "Did you kick his behind, girlie?"

Sasha smiled and gave him a thumbs up sign.

He waved and made his way over to the glider on his porch, leaning heavily on his cane.

Sasha turned back to Daniel. "What's your dad up to these days?"

Daniel shrugged. "Driving my mother crazy, I guess."

Larry Steinfeld, now in his early seventies, had finally retired from the practice of the law. He'd worked for years in the Federal Public Defender's Office, before moving over to the ACLU. Sasha had heard him speak at several conferences before realizing he was Daniel's father.

Sasha checked her watch. "I gotta go."

"See you in class tomorrow?"

"Yep."

She gave Mr. Steinfeld a wave and jogged away to tackle the rest of the hill.

8.

SASHA STEPPED OUT OF HER steamy shower, wrapped herself in a thick, over-sized towel, and reflexively checked her Blackberry, while she was still dripping wet.

Prescott & Talbott required its attorneys to respond to e-mails and voicemails within sixty minutes of receipt. The policy held true in the middle of the night, on holidays, and during natural disasters and championship sporting events. Exceptions were made only for travel to remote areas.

It was no coincidence that the firm's attorneys had begun to opt for rugged, off-the-beaten track vacations in unheard-of locales. Their out of office memos began with sentences like, "At the Buddhist monastery where I will be on retreat, I can be reached via air mail, which is delivered once per week to the village at the base of the mountain and held for the monks until they visit the village to barter goods."

Although Sasha had removed her electronic leash nearly a year earlier, she had not yet broken the habit of checking her Blackberry. She was like one of those dogs that wouldn't cross the bounds of an invisible fence even when the power was out.

She looked down at the display: no e-mails; no voicemails; one missed call from the Prescott & Talbott main switchboard; and a text from Connelly: *Running late. Meet you @ Girasole.*

As she toweled off, Sasha wondered if Connelly had stopped by his apartment. Although he'd been working out of the Pittsburgh Field Office for about a year, as far as the Federal Air Marshal Service was concerned, it remained a temporary placement. So, in its customary fashion, the federal government was still paying for corporate housing in a complex out by the airport, even though Connelly was more or less living with her. She shook her head at herself in the mirror. A live-in boyfriend, practically, whom she'd been dating for eleven months.

Before Connelly, her longest relationship had expired in less time than a half-gallon of milk. She knew this for a fact, because on the way home from her first date with that guy—Vann, a surprisingly

funny butcher who worked at Whole Foods—
they'd stopped by his workplace so she could pick
up some milk. And, for almost a week after they'd
called it quits, she'd continued to drink that milk
with no need to even sniff the carton first.

~ ~ ~ ~ ~

Connelly was waiting when she walked into the
restaurant. He leaned across the cramped space in
front of the hostess station and kissed the side of
her head by her ear.

"Our table's ready," he said.

The friendly redhead who served as the hostess
and fill-in bartender gave a nod from the center of
the restaurant. One of the benefits of being regulars was that Paula always seemed to be able to find
them a table in the tiny dining room.

Sasha turned back to Connelly. The tight expression stretching across his face reminded her of
Will.

"Everything okay? You look a little tense."

"It's just ... work. We can talk over dinner." He
smiled, but it didn't reach his eyes.

Paula squeezed past a couple walking arm-in-
arm toward the door and plucked a pair of menus
off her station.

"Sorry, guys. Busy night," she breathed over her shoulder.

They followed her to a two-top squeezed into a dark corner. They hadn't yet spread their napkins on their laps when a waiter appeared to take their drink order.

Connelly, who usually limited his drinking to a glass of wine or two with his meal or a beer while he watched SportsCenter, ordered a vodka tonic.

"What's the occasion?"

Connelly didn't answer. Instead, he told the waiter, "She'll have the same."

Hungry after her run, Sasha turned her attention away from Connelly's odd behavior and to the menu. She debated between the squid ink linguine and the fish of the day.

She looked up to ask Connelly what he was having and found him staring at her.

"What?"

"Nothing. Sorry." He dropped his eyes to his menu.

She opened her mouth to tell him about Greg Lang, but he spoke first.

"No, that's not true. I've been offered a job in D.C.," he said, lifting his eyes and searching her face for a reaction.

Sasha tried to make sense of the words.

When she didn't say anything, he continued, "It's a pretty good offer. I'd be the chief security officer for a pharmaceutical company."

Sasha's heart hammered in her chest.

"D.C.?" she managed.

"Just outside, actually. In Silver Spring."

"You'd leave the government?" she asked, confused.

That didn't sound like Connelly at all. He was always going on about law and order, duty, and, well, other stuff that she generally tuned out. But still.

"At this point, the private sector has more to offer me, I think."

He was hunched forward over the table, waiting for her to respond.

"Oh. I'm just ... surprised," she said.

I didn't begin to cover it. She felt nauseated. Stunned. Dizzy. But he seemed to be waiting for her to say something more, so she added, "It sounds like a great opportunity."

Her words rang hollow in her ears, but they must have sounded convincing to Connelly. He reached across the table and took her hand in his.

"I think so, too," he said.

"When do you need to make a decision?" She tried to sound casual. She wasn't sure she succeeded.

"Very soon. By the end of the week."

"Wow. That's fast," she said, just to have something to say.

She wondered how long this change had been in the works and why she was only now hearing about it.

"It's only D.C. We can see each other on weekends, right?" he said.

"Sure." She forced a smile.

He sounded to her like a man who had already made his decision.

9.

"I CAN'T BELIEVE SHE'S DEAD," Martine said on the other end of the phone. Her voice was scratchy, like she had a cold.

Clarissa could hear Martine's kids squealing in the background, but it was faint. She couldn't tell if they were playing or fighting. Either way, she figured Martine had about ten minutes tops before she had to go break up a squabble, kiss a skinned knee, or help someone get a snack. That's the way it always was at Martine's house.

"Cee Cee, are you there?" Martine asked.

"Yeah, sorry. Me, either." Clarissa sighed, and then she asked, "Do you think Greg killed her? Really?"

"I don't know. Greg never struck me as the violent type, but things were pretty ugly. I mean, they

were getting a *divorce.* Ellen was admitting failure.
It *had* to have been bad."

It had been bad. Ellen had told Clarissa that
Greg was gambling again, but had asked her not to
tell Martine. Clarissa chewed on the ragged skin
near the fingernail on her left ring finger and let
her eyes drop to her wedding band. There was a
time when the three of them hadn't kept any secrets from one another, but after Martine had left
the firm and all its pressures behind, she sometimes seemed to forget what it was like to work
there, how it frayed the edges of a person's relationships, driving a spouse into a casino or, worse,
the arms of some slutty teenager.

Clarissa willed herself to put the picture of Nick
and that girl out of her mind.

"It was pretty bad," she said. Then, feeling guilty
that Martine didn't know, she blurted, "Ellen found
out Greg was gambling."

Martine let out a long, low whistle. "Oh."

"Yeah."

Clarissa instantly felt better. She was still keeping her own secrets from Martine, but what was
the harm in sharing Ellen's now?

"Was he in deep? Like last time?"

"I think it was more money, but, you know, they
could afford it. I guess he was just taking the

money out of their accounts, trying to take care of it behind her back."

The last time had been when the three of them were still junior associates. 1998. Ellen and Greg were engaged, and the wedding had been just four months away, when she'd broken down crying at a happy hour. Greg had been betting on football and owed his bookie thirty thousand dollars. To them, back then, that was a lot of money. Today, any one of them would have written a check for that amount without bothering to confirm the balance in the account, but they didn't have that kind of money in 1998.

Ellen had sold her engagement ring and emptied out the fund she'd set aside for the wedding and honeymoon; perhaps presciently, her parents hadn't been wild about Greg and had no intention of footing the bill for the reception. She'd been saving a chunk of her salary every month. But they came up eight thousand dollars short on the gambling debt.

Greg's attempt to negotiate the debt had earned him two cracked ribs and a busted nose, and Ellen was terrified he was going to be killed. Clarissa and Martine had each lent Clarissa four grand. They told themselves they would have spent that much on shower and wedding gifts, bridesmaid dresses, and other wedding-related hoopla if Ellen and

Greg hadn't canceled the wedding in favor of a quiet civil ceremony at the courthouse.

As a condition of going through with the wedding, Ellen had made Greg join Gamblers Anonymous. Grateful to her for saving his hide and afraid of losing her, he had thrown himself into the program. As he'd worked through his steps to recovery, he'd eventually made amends to both Clarissa and Martine and had repaid them the money they'd given Ellen.

And, as far as Clarissa knew, in the fourteen years that followed, Greg had never once broken his promise to Ellen that he wouldn't gamble. Until those pictures showed up.

Funny how she and Ellen had both gotten their pictures on the same day.

Unlike Ellen, though, she hadn't flown into a rage and confronted her husband with them immediately. Instead, Clarissa had deliberated, planned. She'd taken patient steps, beginning with retaining Andy Pulaski to ruin Nick's life.

Martine broke into her thoughts again. "I thought they were really a solid couple. You know? Like you and Nick or Tanner and me."

Clarissa swallowed her laugh, or maybe it was a sob. She couldn't tell anymore. Martine still believed she and Nick were solid. If she only knew.

Clarissa had a sudden urge to confide in her, now that Ellen was gone.

"Can you get away for a drink tomorrow night? In honor of Ellen?" she asked.

Clarissa could almost hear her ticking through a mental schedule of carpools, soccer practice, dinner, homework, and baths.

Finally, Martine said, "Sure. Let's do it late. Maybe nine-thirty? If I don't help the kids with their homework and get lunches packed before I leave, I'll have to do it when I get back. Tanner just gets so overwhelmed."

"Sure, nine-thirty's great. The bar at the William Penn?" It had been their hangout, way back when they were three single girls with a lifetime of glamour and excitement ahead of them.

"Where else?"

10.

Wednesday

SASHA WOKE WITH A HEADACHE, a furry mouth, and an empty bed.

From behind her closed bathroom door, she heard the shower running. She sat up and the room started to spin. She laid her head back down on the pillow as if her skull were made of blown glass and replayed the previous evening.

After Connelly's bombshell, they'd shared a joyless meal and then had decided to go for a nightcap. They'd started at a hip martini bar, stopped in a neighborhood saloon, worked their way down the food chain to a dive bar frequented by hard-core drunks and twenty-somethings looking to stretch their drinking dollars, and had ended the night at the Mardi Gras, a refuge for drinkers who'd been banned from other establishments and underage kids trying to pass off bad fake IDs. Its signature drink was a hellish version of a screwdriver, wherein the bartender squeezed the juice of half an orange into a glass of vodka.

The Mardi Gras. No wonder her head pounded.

She took three slow breaths and forced herself out of bed. She made her way to the kitchen, taking the stairs from the loft slowly, and steadied herself against the wall when she reached the bottom.

She poured herself a cup of strong coffee, thankful she'd apparently remembered to set up the coffeepot and turn on the timer the night before, and considered her options.

It was almost six o'clock. She looked out the window. The sun had not yet risen, but early light, gray and soft, streamed in. No rain. She could follow her routine: put on her running shoes and jog to Krav Maga class, then try to ward off punishing blows while her hangover attacked her from within. It didn't sound appealing. Or she could sip some more coffee, nibble a piece of dry toast, and try to get her legs back underneath her.

The shower turned off. She pictured Connelly wrapping a towel around his waist and combing through his black hair with his fingers. Next, he'd run the hot water in the sink and start his daily shaving ritual. A ritual that would be moving to D.C.

She put down the coffee mug and found her running shoes.

~ ~ ~ ~ ~

She returned from her class feeling almost human and found Connelly's used coffee mug holding down a note on her recycled glass kitchen island.

Hope you're feeling better than I am. I was thinking I'd make pho tonight? Love you, LC

Despite their respective Irish surnames, Sasha was half Russian and Connelly was half Vietnamese. Although she hadn't been able to sell him on borscht, he had gotten her hooked on the Vietnamese beef noodle soup.

Having spent eight years eating at her desk at the office, Sasha was not in the habit of buying groceries or preparing meals. Connelly had tackled that role with enthusiasm. Now he was leaving. Maybe she'd finally have to learn how to cook.

She poured a glass of ice water and drank it greedily. She knew rehydrating would help clear the remnants of her headache. But she wasn't sure what to do about the lump that rose in her throat every time she thought about Connelly leaving.

Her cell phone vibrated on the countertop. She checked the display, curious about who would call so early. Volmer.

"Hi, Will," she said, putting her glass in the dishwasher.

"Sasha, I'm sorry to bother you so early." Will's voice was grave.

"It's no problem, but I'm afraid I haven't come to a decision about taking on Greg's case yet."

She'd planned to bounce the idea off Connelly over dinner the night before, but, in light of his news, she hadn't gotten around to it. Although he wasn't an attorney, he was one of the most deliberate, analytical people she knew, and she valued his opinion.

Will cleared his throat. "I really hate to pressure you, Sasha—"

"Then don't."

He hesitated but picked up where he'd left off, "I must. Mr. Lang's constitutional rights are at issue here. The longer he goes without counsel, the less time he will have to prepare a robust defense."

"It hasn't even been twenty-four hours," she said. She felt irritation clawing at her.

"I know. I'm sorry, Sasha. I've been instructed to get an answer now."

Will sounded genuinely apologetic. She was sure someone higher up in the Prescott food chain was making him press her for an answer, but it didn't matter. She bristled.

She opened her mouth, intending to tell Will that Prescott & Talbott could find someone else to do its biding.

Instead, she heard herself say, "*If* I am going to represent Mr. Lang, we need to get straight what role the firm will have in that defense. Here's a hint: it'll be limited to writing the checks."

"Of course, of course." Will's answer was quick and soothing.

"No offense, Will, but I'd like to hear it from someone with the authority to say it," Sasha said.

Will sighed then said, "If I get you a meeting with the Management Committee, can you come in today?"

Sasha mentally scrolled through her calendar. "I'm free until lunchtime. The rest of the afternoon is blocked off."

Blocked off so that she could spend some time processing the fact that Connelly was probably leaving.

"I'll make it happen," he promised.

11.

WILL STOOD IN THE MIDDLE of Cinco's office, trying not to look at the painting of a nude woman's buttocks that hung over the white leather couch where Cinco sat. The painting, like the rest of Cinco's office decor, raised eyebrows. It also inspired a long-running rumor among the senior partners that Cinco's secretary had been the model.

Will doubted there was any truth to it; it was just the sort of salacious gossip that lawyers seized on to relieve the tedium of their workdays. He did have to admit, though, he had never looked at Caroline quite the same after he'd heard the rumor.

He cleared his throat and his mind and waited for Cinco to speak. He assumed Cinco hadn't offered him a seat as a way to drive home his displeasure. He toed the interlocking square pattern beneath his feet.

Cinco finally spoke. "I'm disappointed, Will. I thought John impressed upon you how important it was for Sasha to take on Greg Lang's defense."

"He did, indeed."

Porter had made it abundantly clear to Will that he had to get Sasha to agree. Will didn't see how he could be charged with such a task in the first place, given the existence of free will. And, to be honest, as talented as Sasha McCandless was and as much as he personally liked her, she had no criminal defense experience. Without taxing his memory, he could name at least a half-dozen young lawyers, formerly employed by Prescott & Talbott, who would be better suited to handling a homicide trial.

He said none of this to Cinco. Instead, he emphasized the positives.

"She hasn't said no. She just wants to meet with the Committee and get some assurances that we aren't going to micromanage her case."

Cinco rubbed his forehead. "I heard you the first time. But she hasn't said yes, has she? We don't have time for this, Will."

Will couldn't quite understand the urgency. When Marco had barreled into his office earlier

and told him to lean on Sasha, Will had tried to
explain why an ultimatum was the wrong tack to
take. But Marco had insisted.

Now, Will said, "I understand that. I think she's
reacting mainly to the pressure I applied this morning. I told Marco we shouldn't have tried to force
her hand—"

Cinco cut him off. "Don't fix the blame. Fix the
problem."

Just in time, Will stopped himself from rolling
his eyes. The partners often joked that Cinco used
a Successories catalogue of motivational posters as
his management manual.

"How do you mean?"

"How do I mean? I mean, get the meeting scheduled and get her in here. Now go."

Cinco dismissed him with a wave of his hand,
then he added, "Tell Caroline to come in on your
way out."

Will started to speak and thought the better of
it. He snapped his mouth shut and left.

As he sent Caroline in to see her boss, he
couldn't resist a quick peek at her shapely rear,
nicely displayed by her snug skirt.

12.

ASHA LOOKED AROUND THE TABLE, not quite believing she was sitting in the Carnegie Conference Room with Prescott & Talbott's five most powerful partners. And Will.

Marco DeAngeles, Fred Jennings, Kevin Marcus, John Porter, and Cinco. Their combined net worth had to have eight digits. Maybe nine. And each of them was usually more than ready to seize control of any conversation. They were assertive. Confident. Decisive.

Except they were none of those things right now. Right now, they were all looking at Will with varying degrees of hope and desperation in their eyes.

Will straightened his tie and swallowed, then he said, "Sasha, thank you for coming in on such short notice. As you know, the firm would like you to represent Mr. Lang, and we're willing to discuss the contours of that representation with you."

Jennings nodded along as Will spoke.

Don't let them intimidate you. Be cool. She thought of what Noah used to tell her: fake it if you have to.

Sasha arched a brow. "As it happens, Mr. Lang would also like me to represent him. And I spoke to him about an hour ago to tell him I would do so, subject to the firm's agreement not to interfere with our attorney-client relationship. Those are the contours."

She sat back and watched the heavy hitters defer to Will.

"As a criminal defense attorney myself," Will began, "I understand your concerns. You rightly don't want the firm to second-guess your advice or whisper in Mr. Lang's ear. But you have to understand, too. Two Prescott & Talbott partners have been murdered in the past year. We need to control the fallout from that fact. As a result, the firm has an interest in the outcome of Mr. Lang's case. We will want to be kept apprised of the case and consulted on strategy."

He flicked his eyes to Cinco, looking for confirmation that he'd delivered the right message. Cinco gave a little nod.

Sasha stared straight ahead at the painting on the wall. As befit Cinco's private conference room, it was a nude. There was no question that his secretary had not posed for this one. According to the brass placard hanging beneath it, it was the work of Philip Pearlstein, a native Pittsburgher and noted painter who specialized in nude models posing with unusual objects—in this case, a yoga ball.

She ran through a series of calculations in her head. When she'd spoken to Greg, he'd admitted that Ellen had filed for divorce because of his gambling. He'd also admitted he'd lost his job because he'd taken to stopping in at the casino on his way to work, which inevitably led to him not going to work. With with no income and Ellen's estate tied up in the divorce, Greg had told her that, despite his ritzy address, cash flow was a problem.

But Sasha simply wasn't willing to be at Prescott & Talbott's beck and call. Greg would have to figure out another way to pay her. She wondered if he had any space on his credit cards. Presumably, Naya could set arrange for her to accept credit cards. To date, all her clients had paid by wire transfer or check—yet another strike against dabbling in criminal law.

She pushed her chair back from the table and stood.

"Your proposal's not feasible. If Mr. Lang wants me to represent him, we'll work something out between the two of us. But I won't have you breathing down my neck and second-guessing me."

Sasha reached in her purse for the retainer check, prepared to throw it on the gleaming table as part of her dramatic exit. It had been a mistake to even consider taking the case. What she really needed was a clean break from her former firm.

Kevin Marcus leaned forward and said, "Wait. Please reconsider your position. I personally assure you that we won't interfere wth your work. We will, however, stand ready to give you any support you request in your representation of Greg Lang. I'm sure we can work through this."

His voice was strained, but he stopped just short of begging.

She remained standing but asked, "Why is this so important to the firm? And don't feed me some line about friendship with Greg Lang. I bet half of you couldn't pick him out of a lineup."

Kevin looked at Cinco. Cinco looked at Fred.

Fred spread his paw-like hands wide and leaned back in his chair. "Seems to us Ellen was killed and her fella was framed to make the firm look bad."

"You think someone killed one of your female partners and framed her estranged husband so you'd get bad press?"

"That's right."

Had Fred slipped into dementia without anyone noticing? His conjecture was insane. She looked around the table. Everyone else was nodding, like it was a reasonable theory.

"Assuming that were true, how exactly does it make Prescott look bad?" Sasha asked.

Kevin fixed her with a look. "Come now, Sasha. You know we got very low marks on the Mothers in the Law's last survey."

He tilted his head, as if he was wondering whether she had been one of the anonymous female lawyers who had responded to the survey by describing Prescott & Talbott as a place where relationships go to die.

She held his gaze and said, "I was single, not to mention childless, during my time here, Kevin, remember? I didn't pay any more attention to those surveys than I did to the mandatory retirement age issue. It wasn't relevant to my life."

Marco bobbed his head and said, "And that's why you were so damn good, Mac. No family, no kids. No whining about maternity leave and breast pumps and on-site daycare. None of that bullshit."

Cinco jumped in and said, "Although work-life balance issues weren't high on your priority list, Sasha, they are important to the new associates and law students." He paused and looked hard at

Marco, then he said, "And I mean the women *and* the men. They all want to know that they'll have time to raise their families."

Sasha shook her head. "Ellen didn't have kids."

"Well, that's true," Kevin conceded. "But you know, that survey also made a big point about the divorce rate for our lawyers. It's hovering at around eighty percent for the partners."

Sasha thought of Noah, who had died convinced that his wife was going to leave him. As it turned out, he'd been right. Feeling neglected because he was always working, Laura Peterson had been having an affair.

She looked around the table, meeting each of their eyes for several seconds, then she asked, "Do you have any actual support for your belief that Greg is being framed for Ellen's murder in an effort to sully the firm's reputation?"

John cleared his throat, but Cinco spoke first, saying, "Of course not. If we had proof, we'd have taken it to the district attorney the instant Greg was charged."

He sat back and waved both hands, gesturing to the men sitting around the table. "We may not have proof, Sasha, but we have, collectively, over a hundred years of solid legal judgment in this room. And, in our judgment, this is an act against the firm. Ellen and her husband, are——horrific as this may sound—collateral damage. Someone has committed this heinous crime in an effort to, as you say, sully our stellar reputation."

Sasha tried to ignore her rising nausea. Leave it to Prescott & Talbott to consider itself the true victim.

When Cinco finished his self-serving speech, she said, "Not to be cute, but who do you think would murder one of your partners so your firm ranking plummets? WC&C?"

Fred chuckled and covered it with a cough.

Whitmore, Clay, & Charles—or WC&C—was probably indistinguishable from Prescott & Talbott to the average Pittsburgher. And for good reason. They were both well-established, well-regarded law firms that had served the city since the 1800s. Both employed hundreds of attorneys, most of whom hailed from the very best law schools. Both had filled seats on the federal bench and in boardrooms of publicly traded companies with their former partners. Both charged rates that topped out around a thousand dollars an hour.

But if one were to suggest to an attorney employed by either firm that the two were interchangeable, one had better be prepared to duck. The bad blood between the firms was legendary. And long-lived.

The three attorneys who formed WC&C broke off from Prescott & Talbott in 1892, in the aftermath of the bloody Homestead Strike. The strike, one of the most violent labor-management disputes in the history of the United States, had resulted in a shootout between striking steelworkers and Pinkerton agents, who had been hired to provide security for the steel mill.

The Pinkertons had approached the mill from the river after dark. When they attempted to land their barges, the striking workers were waiting for them. In the end, several men were killed on each side of the gun battle; the Pinkertons surrendered and were beaten by a throng that was estimated to contain more than five thousand striking mill workers and sympathizers; the militia was called in; and the battle moved to the courtroom.

More than a dozen of the strike leaders were charged with conspiracy, rioting, and murder. Similar charges were filed against the executives of the steel mill. Eventually, the charges were dropped against both the workers and management. Prescott & Talbott, of course, represented the Carnegie Steel Company; its owner, Andrew Carnegie; and Henry Clay Frick, who was running the company.

Josiah Whitmore, a partner at Prescott & Talbott, was contacted by the Pinkerton Agency, who wanted to sue the steel company in civil court for putting its men in harm's way. Prescott & Talbott couldn't take the case because it would be a conflict of interest, but Whitmore saw it as his chance to strike out on his own.

Joined by Matthew Clay and Clyde Charles, two newly minted lawyers, he left the firm and opened WC&C. In the early days, the three specialized in suing Prescott & Talbott clients, which resulted in protracted, bitter courtroom battles, where Prescott & Talbott tried to have their opponents disqualified.

Despite the public enmity between the two firms, the arrangement had worked to their mutual advantage for more than a hundred years: both firms ran up their clients' bills fighting over every little thing, no matter how minor, and the attorneys at both firms could pound their chests about their take-no-prisoners battles.

Marco turned to Sasha and said, with no trace of humor, "I wouldn't put it past those bastards."

She was still formulating a response when Cinco frowned at Marco and said, "Of course it isn't WC&C. But I have no doubt that someone has murdered one of our respected colleagues—one of your former colleagues, I might add—in a deliberate attempt to smear the firm."

Cinco spoke with such self-assurance and conviction that she almost forgot his belief had no basis in fact.

Will cleared his throat and added, "Sasha, even if you aren't convinced that we're right, it's clear you aren't convinced that we're wrong. That means there's a chance Mr. Lang was wrongly accused. Imagine being charged with a murder you didn't commit."

She did as he asked. She put aside her own reaction to the man and to the firm's idiotic theory and put herself in Greg's shoes. She pictured herself finding Connelly's lifeless body and then being charged with his murder. Facing that fear in the middle of a sea of grief and despair.

She nodded.

Sasha walked out of the Carnegie with the retainer check and two new things: an agreement that she would defend Greg Lang and keep Volmer—and Volmer only—in the loop and the unshakeable feeling that she was being manipulated.

13.

EO TOOK A DEEP BREATH before he pushed open the door to Sasha's office building. The jangle of the bells over the door caught Ocean's attention, and she turned around from the chalkboard where she was writing the lunch specials in stylized bubble letters.

"Hey, Leo, you wanna cup?" she offered, with a wide smile.

Leo smiled back. "Not right now. Thanks, though. Is Sasha around?"

Ocean's shoulders rose in an exaggerated shrug and she said, "I haven't seen her. I just got here."

"Okay. Save me a bowl of that white chicken chili," Leo said, nodding to her half-finished menu.

He took the stairs by two and poked his head into Sasha's office. It was empty. Her screensaver—

an image of the Lady of Justice statue that graced the clock tower atop the Clear Brook County Courthouse—was on, so she'd been gone more than a few minutes.

Probably across the hall gossiping with Naya.

He rapped on Naya's door.

"Come in," Naya called.

He eased the door open and craned his neck to look in: no Sasha.

"Oh, it's you. I thought you were Mac," Naya said.

"Hello to you, too, Naya."

He strode in and flung himself into the cream-and navy-striped guest chair.

"Come on in and have a seat, fly boy," Naya deadpanned.

"Thanks."

Leo smiled at her. For all her prickliness, he knew Naya liked him. Or, he was pretty sure she did. Most of the time.

"Where is she, anyway?" he asked.

"She must still be at P & T."

"Prescott & Talbott? What's she doing there?"

Naya gave him a sharp look. "She didn't tell you?"

Leo shook his head. Their conversation the night before had centered on his job opportunity, before devolving into a trip down memory lane, as they recounted their year together over drinks—far too many drinks. She hadn't mentioned work at all, which, in retrospect, was unlike her.

Naya arched an eyebrow.

"What?" Leo asked.

She sighed. "They asked her to represent Ellen Mortenson's husband on his murder charges."

Leo shook his head like he had water in his ear. "I'm sorry, Prescott & Talbott wants Sasha to represent the man who's been charged with killing a Prescott partner?"

"You got it."

"That's ..." he trailed off, unable to come up with a word to describe the situation.

Naya had several, however.

"Insane? Ridiculous? Inadvisable? A terrible idea?"

"Well, yeah. She's not going to do it, right?"

Naya shrugged, with an exaggerated motion, as if to say, who knows *what* that girl will do. She narrowed her eyes, taking in his khakis and sweater.

"No work today?"

It was Leo's turn to give Naya a sharp look.

"Sasha didn't tell *you*?" he asked.

"Tell me what?"

"I've been offered a job in the private sector. Outside D.C."

Naya's dark eyes flashed, but she hid her surprise and said, "You're not going to take it, though."

He said nothing.

"Leo?"

He couldn't tell her. He didn't trust her not to tell Sasha.

The job offer was more like a soft landing that his supervisor had arranged. Apparently, the Department of Homeland Security had decided he was not a team player, as befit a special agent with the U.S. Air Marshal's Office. "Lone wolf," was what his supervisor had said, in describing his unofficial investigation into the Hemisphere Air crash and the role he'd played in the Marcellus Shale mess up in Clear Brook County.

Leo hadn't bothered to argue the decision. He'd been tagged as a problem. His impeccable record, past commendations, and indisputable effectiveness meant nothing now, as far as the Department was concerned. It was a stain that no amount of argument would remove. He supposed he should be grateful that he had enough goodwill left within the Department to get him the cushy civilian job with the six-figure salary.

But Sasha couldn't find out. She'd blame herself, even though he'd decided on his own to skirt the limits of his authority to help her. She'd never asked him to do anything. He'd wanted her to see him as indispensable. He'd wanted to be important to her.

Naya was still staring at him. Or glaring at him, actually. She was leaning forward in her chair like she was ready to spring at him.

"I don't know, Naya. It's an enticing offer."

Her glare grew even fiercer.

Leo felt the absurd need to make her understand. "Come on, Naya, Sasha knew my position here was temporary."

It was true. He'd been working out of the Pittsburgh field office for nearly a year with no real justification for it. Once it had become clear that no marshals had been involved in the Hemisphere Air disaster, he should have packed up and returned to D.C. Instead, he'd stayed because of Sasha. And, up until the powers that be had decided he was no longer wanted in the department, they'd been happy to let him stay indefinitely. But they could have called him back at any time, and Sasha had understood that.

Naya proved to be less understanding.

"Sure, right, Homeland Security could have told you to haul your butt back to D.C., but they didn't, did they? You went out and got yourself a better gig with no regard for Sasha or her feelings," she said, her voice thick with anger.

"It's not like that," he protested.

"Then what's it like?" she shot back.

Leo clamped his mouth shut and shook his head. It wouldn't matter what he said; Naya was on the attack now, like a mother bear.

14.

SASHA STARED INTO THE WHITE foamy water pulsing up from the Point State Park Fountain and shivered. The early October wind whipped through the water, sending a spray in her direction. Some time in the next few weeks, the Department of Public Works would shut off the fountain's pumps for the winter and the eight hundred thousand gallons that fed into the fountain from the underground river that ran under the Point would flow wherever it was they flowed.

She scanned the park. It was nearly deserted, except for her and a lone older man walking a white cockapoo on the far side of the park. Both owner and dog had their heads bowed, leaning into the wind. The dog yipped and yapped at the leaves that skittered by him.

She looked back to the fountain. Leo was going to leave. How could he not? A position as the chief security officer of a large pharmaceutical company was a great career opportunity.

Her chest tightened and her eyes stung.

Don't cry.

Growing up with three older brothers had taught Sasha innumerable survival skills. She could pitch a tent in a driving rainstorm, dress a good-sized wound without growing faint, and change her car's oil. But the skill she valued most was her ability to shut down her tears before they started flowing. It was just a matter of discipline.

Think about something else.

Like why the firm was so eager for her to represent Greg Lang. The partners couldn't actually believe Ellen had been slaughtered and Greg framed just so Prescott & Talbott would be dinged on work-life balance surveys. It was too crazy.

They were worried, deeply worried, about something. That much was clear from the cloud of fear that had hung over the conference room. As far as she could tell, Will didn't seem to know their real motivation, and the others would never tell her.

In the end, it didn't matter. She'd been retained to represent Greg, regardless of why Prescott & Talbott wanted her. They'd gotten her. Now what?

Did she have an innocent client? Did it even matter? She didn't know. What she did know was someone had taken pictures of Greg Lang at the poker table and sent them to his wife. Might as well start by finding out who and why.

~ ~ ~ ~ ~

Walking back to Prescott & Talbott's garage to retrieve her car, Sasha pulled up Naya's telephone number on her Blackberry.

Naya answered on the third ring.

"Where the hell are you, Mac?"

"I took a walk after my meeting on the Death Star. Why, is something wrong?"

Naya ignored her question and said, "Leo stopped by."

"Oh."

"Oh? *Oh?* Your boyfriend's thinking about moving. Doesn't that seem like the sort of thing you'd mention?" Naya's voice oozed irritation.

"We can talk about it later, okay? Did he mention what he wanted?"

"No. He was surprised to hear you were at P & T to meet with the partners about whether you were going to represent a killer," Naya said, still seething.

"Alleged killer," Sasha muttered, as she climbed the stairs to the fourth floor, where she'd left her car. Her heels clattered on the stairs but did nothing to drown out Naya.

She pushed the door open and, out of habit, scanned the parking garage. Saw nothing unusual.

On the other end of the phone, Naya was still griping.

"Whatever, Mac. Why's everything gotta be top secret with you? You don't tell me anything; you don't tell your boyfriend anything."

Suddenly, it hit her: Naya wasn't mad; she was hurt.

Sasha squeezed the phone between her shoulder and her ear, unlocked the car door, and tossed her bag inside. She exhaled, long and slow, and cleared her mind before she slid into the car and answered Naya.

"You're right. I'm sorry. I didn't tell you about Leo because I wasn't ready to talk about it. I didn't tell Leo about Lang because he dropped his news on me before I had the chance. I'm trying to process everything, okay? I'm not holding out on you," Sasha said in a soft voice.

Naya was instantly placated. Her tone shifted from annoyed to concerned. "Okay. How are you doing, Mac?"

"I don't know. Can we talk about Lang for a minute?"

While she waited for Naya to agree, she started the car and eased it out of the spot.

"Sure, of course."

"We're a team. If you really object to our representing Lang, we won't do it. But I think if you meet with him, you'll be on board. Especially because of those pictures. Somebody took them and mailed them to Ellen. That someone just might have killed her, right?"

"Maybe, but, Mac—"

"Just keep an open mind. Call him and set up a meeting at the office tomorrow morning. After that, I promise, I'll hear you out. Just hear him out first."

Naya sighed. "Fine. Are you coming back to the office?"

Sasha glanced at the dashboard clock. Almost four-thirty.

"Not unless I need to."

"No, you're cool. You need to read those discovery responses and give me your comments, but they're on the system. Do it from home tonight."

"Thanks, Naya."

"Sure. Take it easy, okay, Mac?"

Sasha accelerated as the garage ramp dumped her out of the garage and into the early wave of rush hour traffic. She had one stop to make before she went back to her condo.

15.

ASHA PARKED HALFWAY UP THE Steinfelds' long cement driveway. She rehearsed her pitch as she walked past Bertie Steinfeld's carefully tended chrysanthemum bushes and mounted the wide stairs to the porch.

The front door swung open while she was reaching forward to press the doorbell. Bertie stood in the doorway, wiping her hands on a red and pink Vera Bradley apron. Sasha recognized it because she'd bought one of her own, finding it cute and flirty. Connelly, it seemed, found it hilarious.

"Sasha, what a nice surprise," Bertie said, beaming. "Come in, come in. I'm making rugelach."

Sasha's blank face gave her away.

"It's a cookie, Cookie. I'll send you home with some. And the recipe, so your young man can make them for you if you like them."

Sasha forced a laugh as she stepped into the gleaming hallway, which smelled like lemons and sunshine. "Thanks, Bertie. Is Larry home?"

"Is he home? Does he ever leave?" She waved toward the closed study door to the right of the hall stairs. "He's in his office. Go ahead in, while I get my rugelach before they burn."

Bertie trotted toward the kitchen in the back of the house, tutting to herself.

Sasha knocked on the oak door.

"What is it, Bertie?" Larry yelled from inside.

Sasha eased the door open and stuck her head in.

"Hi, Larry. It's Sasha McCandless. May I come in?"

Larry looked up from the legal journal he was reading and peered at her over the top of his glasses.

"Sasha, how good to see you. Of course, come in."

He started to push himself up from the desk chair.

"Please don't get up."

He ignored her and straightened to standing until she'd taken a seat in the pineapple-patterned wing-backed chair in front of his desk. Larry—who had served in the Israeli Military as a young man, where he'd been trained in Krav Maga—refused to accept that he was aging. Except for his bad leg, he was strong and fit. He still swam laps at the Jewish Community Center every morning.

"To what do I owe the pleasure?" he asked, sinking back into his chair.

"I was wondering if you'd like to help me out with a criminal case."

"A criminal case?" Larry repeated. A glint of interest lit his brown eyes behind his glasses.

"Yes. I've been asked to represent a gentleman accused of murdering his wife."

Larry rocked back in his chair and said, "A homicide? That's not really a good way to cut your criminal law teeth, Sasha."

"I know," she agreed. "I don't know why he wants me to represent him, but he does. Well, actually, Prescott & Talbott does."

He leaned forward, eager and interested.

"What do you mean?" he asked.

"His wife was Ellen Mortenson. Recognize the name?"

"Sure. She's the gal who had her throat slit. Wasn't she a Prescott partner?"

"She was," Sasha confirmed.

"And they want you to represent the husband?" Larry said slowly.

"Right." She decided to skip the story about the murder being an elaborate scheme to make the firm look bad. "They maintain that he's innocent. And so does he."

Larry dismissed that notion with a wave of his hand. "Eh, so what?"

"So what?"

"That's right. So what? Rule number one: it doesn't matter whether your client is guilty or innocent. What matters is whether the state can *prove* he's guilty. And that's the *only* thing that matters," Larry said in a serious, intense voice. "Don't ever forget that."

Sasha nodded her understanding and said, "Will you help me?"

He looked at her for a long time before he answered. "I will. You're going to need all the help you can get."

The sound of clattering trays from the kitchen seemed to remind him of his wife.

He shook his head slowly and said, "Bertie's not going to like this one bit. Not one bit."

Sasha just smiled. She knew Bertie would put up a fuss about it, but she'd secretly be glad to have a little less together time with her recently retired husband.

16.

CLARISSA SLIPPED INTO THE Tap Room at the William Penn and waved to the bartender, a young, clean-shaven man she didn't recognize. She surveyed the room. No sign of Martine yet.

She took the booth in the farthest corner of the room and sat facing the door. The pub was not quite half full. Most of the patrons had their eyes glued to the World Series playoff game being broadcast on the two television monitors mounted over the bar. As usual, the Pirates' season was over, so she neither knew nor cared who was playing.

A heavyset, light-skinned waiter materialized with a glass of water and a dish of nuts.

"How you doing tonight, ma'am?" he asked in an interested voice.

"Fine, thanks," she answered automatically.

The truth was that she was exhausted. She felt sluggish and heavy. Like her brain and limbs were encased in maple syrup.

He smiled and waited for her drink order.

"I'm meeting a friend. She's going to order a vodka cranberry. When she does, I'm going to say I want the same, but just bring me a cranberry juice, okay? Bill me for the real thing, though," Clarissa said, feeling silly.

The waiter looked at her for a moment, then a slow smile spread across his face. "You got it, and congratulations!" he said.

"Excuse me?"

He laughed. "Father of four. I know all about keeping it a secret till you're sure it's gonna stick. That vitamin C will be good for the baby, anyway."

"Thank you." She smiled back at him, and her mouth felt stretched by the movement. She hadn't had much to smile about recently.

"You bet," he said, as Martine rushed through the door.

"Oh, here she comes now," Clarissa said, catching Martine's eye and giving her a little wave.

The waiter moved to the side to allow Martine to hurry into the booth.

"Sorry. Am I late?" Martine asked, while she piled her coat and tote on the booth and caught her breath.

"No worries, I was just saying we'd each want a vodka cranberry. That is still your drink, right?"

"Sure. Sounds good," Martine said.

"Very good, ladies," the waiter said, throwing Clarissa a wink.

"So," Martine said, once he'd left.

"Yeah."

They sat, not speaking, and stared down at the table between them. Clarissa was seeing Ellen's face—her crooked smile and the smattering of freckles across the bridge of her nose that had made her seem more like an imp than the detail-oriented estates and trusts attorney she was. Judging by Martine's long sigh, she had a similar picture in her mind's eye.

Martine broke the silence. "Have you heard anything about the arrangements for Ellen?"

"Yeah, Cinco sent around an e-mail. Her parents are having her cremated as soon as the coroner releases her body, but they don't want to have a memorial or anything. Not now, at least," Clarissa said.

The waiter returned with two vibrant red drinks and took care to place the one with the swizzle stick in front of Clarissa.

Martine raised her glass. "To Ellen."

Clarissa hefted her glass and clinked it against Martine's. "To Ellen," she echoed. Then she took a long swallow of the bitter juice and said, "I'm leaving Nick." The words sounded flat and far away.

Martine put her drink down fast, sloshing liquid over the top of the glass, and reached across the table for Clarissa's hand.

"Oh, Clarissa, no."

Clarissa nodded, not trusting herself to speak around the lump in her throat.

"Why?"

"He's cheating on me, Marti," she answered, using the nickname they'd given Martine a lifetime ago.

"Nick? Are you sure?"

"Pictures don't lie," Clarissa mumbled.

"You have *pictures?*"

Clarissa knew Martine was going to be hurt to learn that she and Ellen had been keeping their troubles from her, but she didn't care. She needed someone to talk to.

"Yeah. It's kind of funny, actually. Well, not funny. Strange. On the Friday before Labor Day, Ellen and I both received envelopes at work marked *Personal and Confidential.* Hers had pictures of Greg at The Rivers Casino, with a stack of chips in front of him." She stopped.

Martine asked, "And yours?"

Clarissa took a deep breath and exhaled, then said, "And mine had pictures of Nick and some woman—more like a girl, really—making out."

"Oh my goodness, Clarissa, that's *horrible*," Martine said in a dramatic tone that immediately irritated Clarissa.

It *was* horrible, of course. But was it any more horrible that the crushing boringness that Martine's husband displayed on a daily basis? Or Greg's gambling problem? Hadn't she known from the very beginning of their relationship that Nick had a roving eye? Why was it that when she and Ellen talked about their relationship problems, Clarissa had felt supported, and now she was feeling judged? Probably the hormones.

Martine, ever logical and analytical, had already moved on.

"Where did these pictures come from?"

"I have no idea," Clarissa said.

She and Ellen had tried to find out, of course. But the packages had been delivered to the busy firm mailroom on the afternoon of a holiday weekend; most of the support staff had already been permitted to leave early to get a start on the weekend, and those who remained were flying through their jobs in an effort to get out of work as soon as possible. The harassed mailroom supervisor could only tell them that the packages had been logged as having been hand-delivered. No messenger company name, no other information.

Besides, it had hardly been their biggest concern. More important than who had sent them or why, was what those pictures meant to their marriages. As they huddled together in shock and anger, Clarissa had suggested calling Martine and getting together for a drink to process what had just happened, but Ellen had been itching to get home and confront Greg.

After Ellen had left, Clarissa had hidden in her office, too embarrassed and raw to face anyone who might still be around, finishing up work. Then she'd wasted some time running Internet searches for family law attorneys and scrolling through her law school friends' Facebook and LinkedIn profiles trying to find someone she could trust but who wasn't in her social circle.

Only when she was sure her floor was deserted, had she blown her nose, steeled herself, and raced across the public space to the elevator bank.

Across the table, Martine was trying to get her attention.

"Clarissa? You okay?"

"Yeah, sorry. I was just thinking."

Martine nodded, sympathetic and understanding. "What are you going to do?"

"I'm going to leave him."

"Well, sure. Do you have your ducks in a row?"

"I think so. I have the same divorce attorney El-len was using. He said to just act normally until he serves Nick with the papers."

"When's that going to happen?"

Clarissa checked her watch then sipped her juice. "Right about now."

Nick was at his weekly card game at his Greek social club. Andy was going to send someone to the windowless concrete block building on the South Side with the divorce complaint. She'd had a lock-smith come over and re-key the door as soon as Nick had left. With any luck, the next time she'd see his smarmy face would be in court.

Martine's eyes widened. "Oh, wow. Okay. Tell me about this attorney. Is he good?"

"He's got a reputation for being a bulldog. I guess he's good."

"He's at WC&C?"

"Oh, God, no."

Clarissa hadn't even considered hiring a divorce attorney from one of Prescott's peer firms. The thought of sharing the details of Nick's infidelity with someone she might later run into at a benefit or on a bar committee turned her stomach almost as much as the adultery itself.

She'd left the office that Friday night planning to spend her Labor Day weekend getting referrals to family law firms. And, then, in a stroke of luck, she'd literally run into a guy who worked for Andy Pulaski.

She'd barreled off the elevator and charged through the lobby, her head down, in a hurry to get to the elevators that led to the parking garage. And had banged into a chest.

"Oh, pardon me." She'd managed to get the words out without crying, which had felt like an accomplishment.

A young guy—in his early twenties, maybe—had given her a slow, easy grin. He was dressed like a bike messenger: cargo pants, long-sleeved t-shirt layered under a short-sleeved t-shirt, ratty canvas bag.

"In a hurry to get your party started?" he'd asked, as he pressed the call button for the elevator.

"Excuse me?" Clarissa had squeaked. Then, she'd remembered: it was the start of a holiday weekend. "Oh, not exactly."

He'd looked at her closely from under his mop of floppy brown hair. "Are you okay?" he'd asked in a kind voice, full of concern.

Clarissa had felt the tears building behind her eyes and, to her horror, had been unable to stop them.

"Not really," she'd said, "I just found out my husband's cheating on me."

"Aw, that's beat. I'm sorry."

He'd dug into one of his pockets and pulled out a linty, crumpled tissue.

Clarissa had waved it off and wiped her eyes with back of her hand.

As the bell dinged to announce the arrival of the elevator, he'd said, "My boss is a really good divorce attorney. You should give him a call."

On their short trip to the second floor of the parking garage, the kid had produced, from yet another of his innumerable pockets, a bent business card that proclaimed Andy "Big Gun" Pulaski was the guy who'd see her through the war of divorce.

Now, she drained her drink, wishing it actually contained vodka, and told Martine, "His name is Andy Pulaski. His offices are out in Monroeville."

Martine wrinkled her nose at the idea of a strip mall attorney but said nothing.

She took a sip of her drink then said, "I'm so sorry, Clarissa."

"Thanks," Clarissa said.

There was really nothing else to say. She couldn't tell Martine about the baby, not when she hadn't even told Nick.

She wondered if Nick had the papers yet. She'd turned off her cell phone as soon he'd left for the club. She didn't want to talk to him—ever again, if she could arrange it.

17.

SASHA WAS NOT UNCOMFORTABLE WITH silence. She could sit companionably next to a friend, a relative, or a total stranger and be alone with her thoughts. Truth be told, she preferred it to incessant yammering on about nothing, just to have something to say. Usually.

Tonight, though, with Connelly sprawled across her couch, pretending to read some behavioral economics book, the quiet was making her edgy—the quiet, and the fact that Connelly hadn't turned a page in at least twenty minutes. He was just staring into the book.

Their dinner conversation had been strained and awkwardly polite, as they danced around the topics of her new murder case and his potential new job. It had felt like a bad first date.

She perched on the arm of the couch behind his head.

"How's the book?"

"Uh, good," he said, turning it over on his lap to hold his place and twisting his neck to look at her. "I think you'd like it."

"Really? How would you know?"

He wrinkled his brow at the question, then he laughed. "Yeah, I guess I'm pretty distracted tonight."

"Thinking about the job offer?" she asked

"Yeah."

It hung there between them for a while, then he pushed himself up on an elbow to turn to face her full on, and said, "You could come with me."

"I really can't. I have to spend the weekend getting my arms around the Lang case."

"Not this weekend. For good."

He looked at her for a long time.

"You *are* going to take it?" she asked, ignoring his question for the time being.

"Yes," he confirmed.

She'd figured that was the case—this visit was a formality. Hearing him *say* it felt like a hammer fist punch to the sternum.

She nodded. He reached up and put his hand over hers, waiting for her to respond to his offer.

He wanted her to give up her practice and move to D.C. with him.

"I ... need to think about it," she said, finally.

They sat like that, silent, for a moment, then she stood and crossed the room to get the criminal practice materials Larry had lent her. She had work to do.

Connelly watched her with sad eyes as she gathered her papers. Then he turned back to the book he wasn't reading, and silence filled the room again.

18.

Thursday

CAROLINE WORRIED ONE PEARL EAR-RING: she pinched her earlobe with her thumb and index finger, turning and rubbing the glossy white globe over and over. Where was Mr. Prescott?

She glanced down at her desk. It was still there.

She'd arrived, as always, at precisely ten minutes before eight and had unlocked the door to her office. When she'd crossed the threshold to turn on the light, she'd heard a rustling and had looked down to see a white, Tyvek envelope underfoot.

She could see the thick block letters spelling out "PERSONAL AND CONFIDENTIAL."

Her heart started to flutter in her chest, like a trapped bird. She bent to retrieve the envelope, then carried it as if it were glass and gently placed it in the center of her desk. Where it had now been sitting for forty minutes. Waiting for her to do something.

It's marked 'personal and confidential.' Mr. Prescott will be here soon. Just disregard it.

She repeated the three sentences in an effort to slow her heart and quell her imagination. It wasn't working.

Caroline turned her attention to her computer monitor and busied herself with completing an expense report. Her right hand, unbidden, returned to her earring. It was no use. She wheeled her chair back to the center of her desk and stared down at the envelope.

The door opened at eighty-thirty, and Mr. Prescott strode into the room.

"Good morning, Mrs. Masters," he said, raising his attaché case in greeting.

"Good morning," she said, as she snatched the envelope from her desk and hurried around to hand it to him. "This was on the floor when I arrived. Someone must have slid it under the door."

They had never discussed the first envelope, but she could tell from the way his face turned gray that he recognized that this one was its twin.

He took the envelope from her slowly, as if he really didn't want to, but only said, "Very good. Thank you."

He went into his office and shut the door behind him.

~ ~ ~ ~ ~

Cinco rubbed his mouth and stared at the envelope. He didn't want to open it. He had to, though. He cracked his knuckles and wished he'd gone to design school instead of law school. Then, he steeled himself and slid the edge of his letter opener under the seal.

He turned the envelope upside-down and shook out a five-by-seven photograph. It landed face-down on his standing desk. He flipped it over with the tip of the letter opener.

Ellen, Clarissa, and Martine smiled up at him in their party gowns. Ellen and Clarissa's grins were partially obscured by red Xs. "TWO DOWN" was written across the bottom of the picture.

Cinco closed his eyes and willed himself not to vomit. He took several breaths. When the nausea subsided, he pressed a button on his phone and buzzed Caroline.

"Mrs. Masters," he said, working to keep his voice even, "call down and tell Clarissa Costopolous to come up to see me. If she's not in yet, leave a message for her to come up as soon as she arrives."

"Right away, Mr. Prescott," she assured him in a voice that betrayed nothing.

He released the button and stared out the window. Despite her calm tone, he was pretty sure his secretary knew as well as he did that Clarissa wouldn't be coming to work today.

Cinco wasn't sure how long he stood like that, looking out the window without seeing the city skyline that unfolded in front of him. He thought about calling Greta. But he didn't know what help his wife could offer at the moment. Besides, what would he say? *Darling, someone's serially killing the female partners at the firm; what should I do?* He shook his head at himself. No, don't bring anyone else into this ... mess.

He was about to buzz Caroline again to tell her to round up the Management Committee, when she raced through the door with a stricken expression.

"Clarissa's in the parking garage. She's ... dead."

19.

INCO, FLANKED BY THE FOUR other
members of the Management Committee,
stepped off the elevator and scanned the
parking garage's third floor, where a shopper returning to her car with an armful of bags from the
clothing boutique in the building had found
Clarissa's body.

Cinco spotted the sobbing shopper sitting on
the trunk of a black-and-white police cruiser with
a blanket thrown over her shoulders and a sympathetic female patrol officer rubbing the woman's
arm. He headed in that direction.

As he neared, he nodded to Samantha Davis, the
firm's chief security officer, who was standing with
an older African-American man in a navy suit. They
were huddled close to Clarissa's Lexus.

"Mr. Prescott," Sam said, as they approached, "this is homicide detective Burton Gilbert. Detective Gilbert, Charles Prescott, V. He's the head of the firm."

The detective slipped a small notepad and pen into his breast pocket and extended a hand.

"Mr. Prescott," he said in a deep, gravelly voice.

"Detective," Cinco said.

He waved a hand behind him. "These men are my senior advisors."

Detective Gilbert nodded to the cluster of anxious faces over Cinco's shoulder. "I'll need to get names and contact information here from you gentlemen, but first Ms. Davis and I can walk you through what we know."

Sam smoothed back her wavy silver hair and looked down at her own small notepad.

"Okay, at oh-nine-ten, building security got a call that a female was screaming on the third floor of the garage."

She pointed to the uniformed officer and the shopper, and Cinco noticed for the first time the building's rent-a-cop standing alongside the patrol car.

The building provided security for its tenants, but Cinco had not found it particularly impressive. In fact, it appeared to be principally decorative. After a Christmas season in which sixteen firm-issued laptops had walked out of the building, four secretaries' pocketbooks had been stolen from their desks, and innumerable young associates had complained of missing electronic devices that Cinco had never heard of nor cared about, he'd hired Sam Davis.

Sam was a former FBI agent and a member of his wife's book club. She had retired from the Bureau and moved to Pittsburgh when her husband had been offered a position as the chief financial officer at some technology company in the Strip District. She was well credentialed, bored senseless, and didn't need the money. Cinco had made her a low-ball offer and she'd taken it.

Her eyes were shining now, and Cinco could see she was hopped up on the excitement that had been in short supply as the chief security officer of a staid law firm.

She gestured at the green Buick LaCrosse parked to the left of Clarissa's car and continued, "Mrs. Woolson, the woman who found the body, had hit some VIP early-morning sale at Creations Boutique. She was coming around to the passenger side of her car here to put her packages on the front seat—"

Porter interrupted her, asking "Why not in the trunk? Or the back seat?"

Cinco turned to frown at him. "What difference does it make?"

Sam shook her head and said, "No, it's a good question. She has some kind of long-haired dogs and the backseat is full of dog hair. Their crates are in the trunk because she dropped them off at the groomer this morning. So she walked around to open the front passenger side door and noticed the blood."

She stepped in front of Cinco and pointed with her pen to the front driver's side window of Clarissa's car. Five sets of eyes followed her hand.

Red blood splattered the driver's side window in a spray pattern that reminded Cinco of spin art.

When he was a child, his father had insisted the entire family attend the firm's annual Kennywood picnic. Even then, Cinco had found the amusement park to be sticky, dirty, and inexplicable. He couldn't fathom why people would wait in line to be scared, jerked around on a rickety wooden roller coaster, or spun in circles until they were queasy.

He had, however, loved the spin art booth. You paid your money and chose your colors. Then you would squeeze the paint from plastic condiment bottles onto your canvas, while it spun around like a record album.

The firm still held an annual Kennywood picnic, and Cinco still went to it each year. It had been at least ten years since he'd last looked for the spin art booth. At the time, the high school student manning the recording studio, where the talentless and hapless recorded abysmal covers of popular songs, had looked at him blankly.

He stared at the window. Clarissa's vibrant blood and clotty gray matter clung to it and obscured his view, but he could see her body slumped across the center console.

The detective said, "I took a look inside when I got here, but I can't let you do so. We need to wait for the coroner and the forensics team to get here and do their thing. Can't risk disturbing the scene. But the doors were unlocked. She appears to have been beaten with a blunt object. My guess is a claw hammer."

Marco spoke up. "You can tell that by looking at her?"

Sam swallowed a laugh, and Detective Gilbert twisted his mouth into a smile.

"No," he said, "there's a blood-covered claw hammer on the floor of the passenger side, so I have deduced as much."

Cinco watched as Marco reddened.

Then he turned back to the homicide detective and said, "The firm will cooperate with your investigation, of course, limited only by our obligations to our clients to preserve their confidentiality. Let Ms. Davis know if you need anything."

"I'll be in touch," Detective Gilbert promised.

Cinco nodded his goodbyes and turned to head back toward the elevators, stepping over the yellow crime scene tape. The others trailed behind him, whispering. He stifled a sigh. He saw more meetings in his future.

20.

SASHA, NAYA, LARRY, AND GREG squeezed around the small round conference table in Sasha's office. A takeout container of coffee and pastries from the coffee shop below sat, untouched, in the center of the table.

Greg squirmed under the weight of the unimpressed stares he faced. He'd been there for twenty minutes and, so far, he'd done a lot of tap dancing instead of answering Sasha's questions. Naya rapped her pen against the table and bit her lip.

Sasha wondered if Naya would continue to hold her peace in the face of Greg's apparent refusal to help himself. She hadn't asked Naya to join her practice because of Naya's diplomacy: she was outspoken, and her instincts about people were sound.

If Greg continued to feed them a line, Naya would eventually lose her patience.

"Let's try this again," Sasha said to Greg, holding up the picture of him with the earliest date. It showed him at a poker table at 10:30 a.m. on the third Tuesday in June. "Do you remember how you came to be at the casino instead of at work this day?"

Greg exhaled through his nose. "I told you, I don't know. I guess I just got the idea to stop by on my way to work. I drive right by the North Shore, you know."

"Okay, sure, but why that day?" Sasha probed.

"I. Don't. Know." Greg cut off each word, making his irritation clear.

Finally, Naya made hers clear, too.

"Listen, Mr. Lang," she began, pushing back from the table, "we're trying to help you. Do you think someone who knew your gambling would set off your wife *just happened* to be at the casino, with a camera, on the same Tuesday morning that you got an urge to pull off the exit from 279 instead of taking your sorry ass to work?"

Greg stared at her, slack-jawed, then said, "I guess I never thought about it."

"You never thought about it," Sasha repeated.

She arched a brow and looked at Larry, who shrugged, like he'd heard it all and didn't consider this to be outside the realm of possibility.

Greg went on, haltingly, "I mean, I guess, if I had thought about it, I might have wondered if she was having me followed, maybe?"

"Was she?" Sasha asked.

"She said no. I thought we were on pretty solid ground, until she found out about the gambling. We did a bike trip through the French countryside last spring. We were getting along fine—no, better than fine. I don't think she had any reason to be suspicious." He spread his hands wide and said, "But I don't know."

Naya shook her head but said nothing.

"It's true. We were in love once, you know," Greg insisted. "And, it's not like we'd ever had a big falling out. It's just that life, work—her work—got in the way, buried us. But in the Loire Valley, we spent our days riding through rolling hills dotted with heather and sunflowers turning their faces to the sun and our nights drinking wine under the stars in the courtyards of ancient chateaus. There was nothing in the way. Just us. It gave us a chance to uncover what had been there all along. I don't care if you believe me or not, things were the best they'd been in years," Greg finished, choking back tears and staring down at the table.

"Let's get back to that morning in June," Larry suggested in a neutral voice.

Larry had asked Sasha if he could sit in on the meeting to get a sense of Greg's personality and demeanor, but he planned to play a behind-the-scenes role. Sasha couldn't wait to hear what Larry thought of their client: Greg had been agitated and short-tempered ever since he'd arrived ten minutes late for their nine o'clock meeting. Now he'd finally shown a flash of humanity.

"Okay," Greg said, wiping his eyes with the back of his hand. "Fine."

"Try to remember why you chose that particular day to go to the casino."

Greg rolled his eyes to make sure they understood how put upon he felt and repeated, "Fine."

He fell silent for a moment, searching his memory—or at least pretending to do so. Then, he said, "My comp was about to expire."

"Your comp?"

He sighed. "Yes. Around Memorial Day, I guess it was, I got an introductory certificate in the mail, inviting me to try out the table games at The Rivers. There was a coupon I could exchange for fifty dollars in chips, but it expired at the end of June."

"Hold on," Naya interrupted. "Aren't you a recovering gambling addict?"

Anger flashed across Greg's face. "No. Look, I got in a jam with some guys on sport betting ages ago. Before Ellen and I were even married. It was stupid, and they were ... unsavory people. Ellen helped me out. My going to Gamblers Anonymous was *her* requirement. I wasn't then—and I'm not now—*addicted* to gambling."

Naya opened her mouth to respond, but Sasha beat her to it.

"Nonetheless, you had given up gambling completely, correct?"

Greg answered right away. "Yeah. I hadn't set foot in a casino or placed a bet of any kind in fourteen years. Until that day. And, you know, to be clear, I wasn't gambling. I was playing poker. It's a game of *skill*."

From the way he said it, at once defensive and aggressive, Sasha knew he'd tried that argument on Ellen. She imagined Ellen hadn't found it any more persuasive than she did.

"Let's leave that aside for the moment. Do you believe the marketing department of a casino randomly sent a certificate for chips to someone who could be considered a recovering gambler? They're pretty heavily regulated; I don't think they can just send out that sort of thing unsolicited."

Greg reddened. "The brochure had a cover letter that claimed it was sent in response to my inquiry, but I swear, I didn't sign up for anything. Besides, I was in France most of May, biking seventy-five miles a day. How could I have? I figured it was a mistake, but, it was fifty dollars. I didn't see the harm. I'd cash it in, play a little bit of poker, and then head to work."

Sasha could see in both Larry's and Naya's eyes that they thought the same thing she did: Greg Lang was, quite possibly, the perfect patsy.

The phone rang; its electronic beep cut off Greg's efforts at self-justification.

Naya stepped over to Sasha's desk and picked it up.

"The Law Offices of Sasha McCandless."

After a pause, Naya continued, "I'm sorry, Ms. McCandless is in a client meeting. May I take a message?"

Naya started to scribble a note on the pad beside the phone, then she stopped.

"Please hold, and I'll see if she can be interrupted," she said, pressing the hold button.

Sasha gave her a quizzical look. She couldn't stop and take a call in the middle of this.

Naya held out the receiver toward Sasha and said, "It's the crime beat reporter for the *Post-Gazette*. He got your name from Greg's former counsel. He wants to know if you have any comment."

"On what?" Sasha asked.

"On the fact that Clarissa Costopolous was found dead in her car in the P & T garage this morning," Naya said, her face unreadable.

Sasha blinked and processed the news. Then she said, "Okay, have him hold." She felt light-headed.

Sasha and Larry huddled together to craft a sound bite for the reporter. After she'd provided the quote and gotten the reporter's contact information, Sasha turned to Greg, who had been silent since Naya had broken the news of Clarissa's murder.

"I guess this is helpful news for our defense," she said, ignoring the self-loathing that came with those words.

Greg, his head down, mumbled something at the table.

"I'm sorry," Sasha said, "I didn't catch that."

He raised his head and repeated, "I said I have to go."

"Why?"

He cleared his throat and hesitated, then said, "Because Nick Costopolous is asleep in my guest room. I need to break the news to him that his wife is dead."

Sasha didn't want to—knew she shouldn't—but heard herself ask, "Why is Nick at your house?"

Greg looked her straight in the eye and said, "Last night, Clarissa had divorce papers served on him while he was at his club. He tried to call her but she didn't answer her phone. When he left the club to go home, his key didn't fit in the lock. Apparently, that sneaky little bitch had gotten the locks changed."

"And how'd he end up at your house?" Naya asked.

"We're friends. I mean, the girls were friends, so we sort of just ended up pals. Me, Nick, Tanner Landry."

"Nick called you?"

Greg nodded. "Right. He was crying and slurring. He'd been drinking. I told him to call a cab and come over. He didn't. That big idiot drove his truck, but he came over and passed out on my couch. Around two a.m., I woke him up and set him up in the guest room. When I left this morning, I could hear him snoring in there. Anyway, I have to go. He's going to lose it when he hears about this."

Greg pushed back his chair and stood with his feet planted hip-distance apart, as if he expected someone to try to stop him. No one did.

"Call Naya to reschedule, though, Greg. We need to get a cohesive story in place," Sasha said as he started for the door. She added, "And please give Mr. Costopolous my condolences."

He nodded and walked out.

As soon as the door banged shut behind him, Sasha turned to Larry and Naya.

"Clarissa's death could give credence to Prescott & Talbott's idiotic theory that someone is killing female partners to make the firm look bad. But if Greg and Nick are buddies, that also could lend itself to a theory that they had some kind of pact or something to kill their wives. Especially since Nick was just served with divorce papers, too," Sasha said, working through this new development, trying to decide if it was a net positive or negative for her case.

Naya jabbed a finger in Sasha's direction. "What makes you so sure they *didn't* have a pact?"

21.

CAROLINE SCRAPED HER TEETH ACROSS her bottom lip even though she knew she was leaving tooth marks in her lipstick. She was trying to decide how to get Mr. Prescott to stop poking around in the filing cabinets and tell her what he needed. She realized many of the attorneys whispered about her boss's personal quirks and lack of legal acumen, but she had always enjoyed working for him. He was a boss who understood his place.

Unlike so many of the younger attorneys, he didn't insist on doing his own word processing, entering his own time entries into the electronic system, or drafting his correspondence on his own. No, he dictated all of his documents—mainly, she thought to show off the fact that *his* assistant knew shorthand.

Equally important, he didn't burden her with endless personal errands. She selected his wife's birthday, Christmas, and anniversary gifts and had the jeweler wrap them. That was the extent of it.

Some of the other senior partners were, in her view, far out of bounds in the requests they made of their secretaries. Marco DeAngeles, for instance, not only had his secretary fire his children's nanny, but required her to interview and select the replacement. And Lettie Conrad had recently told her that Kevin Marcus asked her to log into his personal bank account and take care of paying his mortgage and utility bills each month.

By comparison, Mr. Prescott was an excellent boss. Usually.

She had to put a stop to this business of him rifling through the floor-to-ceiling filing cabinets across from her desk. He'd been there ever since he'd returned from the grim scene in the parking garage.

Whatever he was looking for, it was clear he wasn't going to find it. First, of course, because she did all the filing. And, second, because he had insisted she not label the drawers, explaining that labels detract from the minimalist aesthetic he strove to achieve in his surroundings. So he was doing nothing more than opening and closing unlabeled drawers at random.

When he had first hurried into the office after seeing Clarissa's body, she'd asked if she could help him find something. He'd said that the documents he was looking for were "sensitive" and he would handle it personally.

That had stung. Caroline prided herself on her discretion. As the personal assistant to the chair of the firm, she'd seen more sensitive documents than most of Prescott & Talbott's attorneys combined.

She knew who earned how much, which partner had amassed—and submitted for reimbursement— an enormous hotel bill watching pornographic movies, and which staff members were on performance improvement plans. And she had never breathed so much as a word of it.

In fact, her refusal to gossip had left her a social pariah. Once the other secretaries had realized she intended to maintain Mr. Prescott's confidences, the lunch invitations and suggestions that she join a group of girls for happy hour had evaporated.

Not that she'd minded. Caroline took her position seriously and had always believed that Mr. Prescott valued her loyalty. Yet, here he was, rooting around in her filing cabinets for some documents that were too "sensitive" for her eyes.

She told herself to give him some leeway; after all, the poor man had lost two attorneys in the space of a week. Two murders. Two creepy hand-delivered envelopes. Caroline shuddered.

He pulled open another drawer, flicked through the folders, and slammed it shut in apparent frustration.

She saved and closed the memo she'd been typing and walked around to join him in front of the cabinet.

"Mr. Prescott," she said in an even tone to his back, "if you would just tell me, in general terms, what you are looking for, I could at least direct you to the correct set of drawers."

He straightened and stood still for a minute, trying to decide, then turned to her and said, "Okay. That would be a help. Where are the personnel files from 1996 through 2001?"

Caroline arched a brow despite herself. Here he was digging around in the locked confidential files in search of personnel records that had been archived off-site years ago. The man had no earthly idea how she ran his office.

"I'll have to order those files up from off-site storage," she told him with a gentle smile. "Are you interested in all of the files or just those of certain employees?"

She watched as he calculated the mess and clutter all those boxes would create. A prudent lawyer would have said to order up all the files, but she was not surprised when his love for order won out, and he said, "Let's begin with all associate attorneys who joined the firm in 1996 and 1997. Tell the vendor to expedite the order, please."

"Very good." She graced him with another smile.

He dropped the keys to the filing cabinet into her open palm and retreated to his inner office, back where he belonged.

22.

ARRY HAD LEFT TO MEET Bertie and some friends for a late lunch and their standing canasta game. Naya was on her way to The Rivers with Greg's pictures to see if she could convince the security staff to locate tapes that showed either the photographer or the subject. The casino had discouraged Naya from coming when she'd set up the appointment, but she'd persisted. Without a subpoena and depending, as it did, on Naya's charm and the goodwill of strangers, they both knew the trip was a long shot. But it was something tangible they could do to move forward.

Sasha sat behind her desk and worked her way through the piles of documents that seemed to multiply overnight. Every morning, she sorted and purged the mound of papers on her desk; she scanned those she wanted to keep, as part of her Sisyphean effort to run a paperless office, and tossed the hard copies along with the pure junk. Despite her paperless goal, each morning, the document mountain seemed, if anything, taller.

She was feeding correspondence into the scanner function of the printer/copier/scanner beside her desk, when she heard footsteps in the hall. She swiveled her chair around to face the door, half-expecting to see Connelly's face in the doorway.

Instead, she saw Greg's. Behind him, Nick Costopolous. She recognized Nick at once, despite his rumpled clothes, mussed hair, and aviator shades. Greg had obviously dragged him out of bed.

Whenever she'd seen Nick at Prescott & Talbott functions, his hair had been gelled and carefully arranged to appear casual. He wore tasteful, expensive clothes and hipster shoes. He had olive skin, jet-black hair and eyes to match, and a blindingly white smile. He was tall and fit. She had a vague memory that his job involved a lot of physical activity.

Sasha usually gave him wide berth. He was overtly flirtatious and borderline creepy, as far as she was concerned. She had never really understood what Clarissa had seen in him, beyond his looks, but one of the secretaries had once mentioned that the two had been high school sweethearts, and their families were partners in some sort of business. A restaurant, maybe.

Greg rapped his fist on the doorframe and gave her a weak smile. "Knock, knock."

"Come on in," she said, waving them inside.

Greg stepped through the doorway, followed by Nick, who pulled the door shut behind him and stood just inside, shifting his weight from one foot to the other.

Sasha walked around to the front of the desk to greet them. Front and center in her mind was the thought that she was alone in her office with two men whose estranged wives had been brutally murdered within the last week.

"I'm sorry about Clarissa," she said to Nick, careful not to stand between him and Greg. She didn't feel that she was in any immediate danger, but she saw no point in being careless.

Nick pushed the glasses up through his unruly hair and perched them atop his head.

"Thank you," he said. He looked straight at her. Dark circles ringed his eyes, and a five o'clock shadow completed the picture.

She could smell liquor and stale cigars on his clothes. She glanced at Greg, who seemed to have pulled himself together and taken charge of the situation.

"We need to talk to you," Greg said.

"Go ahead and sit down," she said, gesturing to the pair of Queen Anne guest chairs in front of her desk.

Nick collapsed into the closer of the chairs and slumped forward. Greg clapped him on the shoulder as he walked past him to the farther chair.

"How about a cup of coffee?" Sasha suggested.

Greg shook his head. At the same time, Nick nodded.

"Please," Nick said. "Cream and sugar."

Greg shrugged. "Okay, sure. Just Sweet'N Low for me. Thanks."

Sasha started toward the door.

"Wait. Where are you going?" Greg snapped to attention.

"I'm going to run downstairs and get us coffee. I'll be back in three minutes, tops. Hang tight."

She pulled the door shut and hurried down the stairs to the coffee shop.

The shop was empty. Through the pass-through, she could see Kathryn in the back, flirting with Jake.

"I'm grabbing some coffees," Sasha yelled.

"You're going to drive me out of business!" Jake yelled back.

Sasha scooped up a handful of stirrers, creams, and sugar packets and tossed them into her cardigan pocket, making sure she grabbed the artificial sweetener for Greg.

She poured coffee into three of the glossy black mugs from the stack near the thermos on the counter. She threaded the thumb and fingers of her left hand through two of the handles and picked up the third with her right.

As she walked gingerly toward the door, maintaining posture that would have made her late Nana Alexandrov proud, Kathryn came around the corner, still giggling over something Jake had said.

"Whoa, do you need a hand?" she asked.

"Thanks, but I think I've got them."

A hand would have been nice, but Sasha thought Nick might jump out of his skin if Kathryn walked through the door. He was keeping it together by a thread.

"Okay, then. See you later."

"See you," Sasha called over her shoulder as she started her careful trip up the stairs, focusing on keeping the mugs level.

When she neared her closed door, she could hear Greg and Nick talking in low, serious voices. She tapped on the door with the toe of her pump. She waited a few seconds and was about to tap again, when the door swung in.

"Thanks," she said to Greg. "Here." She nodded toward the mug in her right hand, and he closed the door behind her and took the coffee from her. He returned to his seat.

She transferred one mug from her left hand to her right. She stopped at Nick's chair, and he took the mug from her right hand with shaking hands. She reached into her pocket, doled out the creamers, sweeteners, and stirrers, and then took the seat behind her desk.

She sipped her coffee and watched Nick struggle to tear open a sugar packet with trembling fingers. He dumped the sugar and creamer, then stirred the coffee in a hurry.

Beside him, Greg had neatly torn open the corner of his pink Sweet'N Low packet and was shaking just a bit into his mug. Then he carefully folded over the top of the open packet and placed it on the corner of Sasha's desk while he stirred his coffee with a slow, precise motion.

Sasha let them both take a drink before she spoke again.

"Listen, before you guys tell me what's going on, we need to get some things straight."

Greg continued to sip his coffee, unperturbed, but Nick immediately put his down on the small table between the two guest chairs, sloshing coffee over the side of the mug with his unsteady hands. Nick leaned forward.

"I don't know what this is about, but I represent Greg in his criminal matter. Anything he tells me related to that matter is a privileged attorney-client communication." Sasha looked directly at Greg and said, "There's a question whether anything you say about the case in front of Nick would be deemed privileged, so we're not going to discuss your case right now. Is that clear?"

"Yes," Greg said immediately. "This isn't about me."

"That's fine," Sasha said, "as long as we're clear."

She turned to Nick. "And, Nick, I *don't* represent you. So anything you tell me here, especially in front of Greg, is not going to be privileged."

Nick nodded, his eyes confused, and then turned to Greg.

Greg paused, the mug halfway to his mouth, then placed it on the table beside Nick's. He gave Nick a meaningful look and then said, "If you'll excuse me, I need to use the restroom."

"Down the hall to your right. It's the last door on the right," Sasha directed him.

He held Nick's gaze for a moment then walked out of the room, pulling the door shut behind him.

"I need a lawyer. I need you to be my lawyer," Nick said; the words tumbled out fast and desperate as soon as the door closed. He lifted the coffee mug again with shaky hands.

Sasha pursed her lips, considering her response.

"Let's not get ahead of ourselves," she said. "This is a prospective client meeting, okay? You go ahead and tell me your situation so I can evaluate whether I can or will represent you."

Nick nodded, fast, and fixed his red-rimmed eyes on her.

"The police think I killed Clarissa. I didn't, I swear."

She knew it had been too much to hope he just wanted to know how to get back into his house.

"Why do you say that? Have you spoken to the police?"

"No. But they've called my cell phone, asking me to come in and identify her body and talk about the divorce. How do they even know about the divorce? I only found out last night!" His voice rose, panicked and angry.

"Nick, I need you to calm down," she said in the tone she used when she babysat her nephews. "Start by telling me what happened last night."

He swallowed hard and said, "Thursday nights I go to the Greek social club over on East Carson Street. Play some cards, watch whatever game is on.

Drink some Ouzo, eat some mezethes. Just hang out."

"Okay, did you see Clarissa before you left?"

"Yeah, she came home from work about an hour before I headed out. She was bitchin—er, complaining—about being tired. She went to bed, said she needed to rest. I figured she was, you know, still upset about Ellen."

The coffee was back on the table, and Nick was drumming the rim of the mug with his fingers while he spoke. Nervous, but not obviously lying, as far as Sasha could tell.

He continued, "Before I left, I yelled up the stairs to let her know I was going. She didn't answer, so I figured she was sleeping. I tried not to make too much noise on my way out."

"Had you two been having problems?"

He shook his head. "No." He sounded lost, like a small boy.

"Okay, when did you get the divorce papers?"

He thought for a moment. "The playoff game was on, but I wasn't really paying attention. If the Pirates are out of the running, the season's over as far as I'm concerned. I guess it must have been the bottom of the seventh, maybe. Around ten o'clock or a little after. Anyway, there was a commotion at the door. It's a private club, but you know, there's no security or anything. We all have keys. Usually, though, we leave the door unlocked, 'cause guys come and go all night long."

"What kind of commotion?"

"Some young guy pushed through the door and walked in like he owned the place. George and Demetri grabbed the guy, told him the club wasn't open to the public, and tried to steer him back outside, down the street to a bar. He got real loud, yelling that he needed to see me, had something important to tell me about Clarissa."

Nick stopped and looked down at his shoes.

"What?" Sasha prompted him.

"I thought maybe she'd been in an accident or something."

He was lying. Whatever he'd thought, that wasn't it.

"Okay, go on."

"They brought him over to me and he shoved this envelope at me with a big shitty smirk on his face. He said I'd been served, and my marriage was over." Nick's face darkened at the memory.

Greg rapped on the door. He eased it open and poked his head into the room.

"Is it okay to come back?"

"Actually, would you mind waiting downstairs in the coffee shop? If you take your mug down and tell them you're a client, they'll give you a warm up for free," Sasha said.

She didn't dare suggest he wait in Naya's office. If Naya returned and found Greg Lang in her space, she would not be shy about making her displeasure known.

"Sure, I guess," Greg said. He trotted over to the table and grabbed his mug. Before he hurried out of the room again, he gave Nick a concerned look. Nick nodded at him, as if to say he was doing okay.

The door swung shut and Nick resumed his story. "Things got kind of crazy after that. Some of the fellas tossed the guy out onto the street, and I tried to read the complaint. But the words were swimming on the page and I—" His voice broke and his eyes filled with tears.

Despite her gut reaction to the man, Sasha felt a twinge of sympathy. Just as Will had asked her to do for Greg, she put herself in Nick's shoes for a moment and thought about how his life had been upended. She held out the box of tissues she kept on her desk, but he wiped his eyes on his shirt-sleeve and went on. "I didn't understand what was happening. It didn't make sense. I tried to call Clarissa, but her phone went straight to voicemail. I guess, after that, I had too much to drink."

"Do you have the complaint?"

"Um, yeah. Here." He half-rose from the seat and pulled an envelope, folded length-wise, from his back jeans pocket and handed it to her.

"Thanks. I'll look at it in a bit; let's get through the rest of your night."

"Okay. I drank ... a lot. I kept calling Clarissa's cell phone and the house phone, but the cell rolled to voicemail and the answering machine kept picking up at home. Finally, I just left. I don't know exactly what time it was."

"That's okay, Nick."

Sasha wanted to pull out her notepad and jot down some notes, but she restrained herself: It would be counterproductive to break Nick's rhythm; and, if she were being honest, she didn't want to have a record of their conversation in case she decided not to represent him. If she did decide to take him on as a client, she'd memorialize their discussion, along with her impressions, as soon as he left.

"Um, so I shouldn't have done this, but I drove home." He looked up at her, sheepish and contrite.

"I see."

"Yeah, so I got home. I was drunk and confused, maybe a little bit angry. I went to the front door and I couldn't get my key to work."

"So what did you do?"

"I pounded on the door. Hollered for her to let me in or at least come talk to me. Nothing. She didn't yell back or turn on a light or anything. I was getting ready to go around and try the back and then I guess I noticed the lock. It was really shiny. I realized the key didn't work because the lock was new. She'd changed the locks."

Sasha didn't react to the anger in his voice.

"Go on."

"Well, at that point, I knew she wasn't going to let me in. I called Greg. Asked if I could crash at his place."

"Then you didn't actually see Clarissa last night?"

"Uh, no. Not after I left for the club."

"You don't even know for a fact that she was home when you returned, do you?"

Nick stared at her, uncomprehending. "Where else would she have been?"

"I don't know. But neither do you, right? You know she had the locks changed, but after that, she could have gone out, met up with someone and ... decided to spend the night elsewhere, couldn't she?"

Nick curled both hands into tight fists. "You saying she had a boyfriend?"

"No, Nick. I'm saying maybe you have an alibi."

"An alibi? Why the hell would I need an alibi?"

It was Sasha's turn to stare. She searched his face for understanding, but it was empty. He really didn't understand just how bad his situation was.

"Because it's always the husband. When the police learn that Clarissa served divorce papers on you, and you later came home, by your own admission, blind drunk and yelling in the street within hours of her being found murdered, do you think they're going to look any further?"

"But ... I didn't kill her. Greg said her body was found at the office building this morning. I was at Greg's all morning." Nick was stammering.

He resisted following the logical train of his own sentence, so she helped him aboard. "Right. You couldn't have killed your wife because you were having a sleepover with a man who was just charged with killing *his* wife. See any problems with that story?"

Nick hung his head and sobbed. He made no effort to control his anguish, as his shoulders heaved and comprehension sunk in.

Sasha handed him the tissue box from her desk and went off in search of Greg. Nick was going to need a friend with him as he moved from denial into reality. And it looked like she was going to be representing two accused murderers, just as soon as someone got around to accusing Nick.

23.

EO STARED DOWN AT THE box in the palm of his hand. *Now what?*

He'd been on his way to Sasha's office to see if she wanted to grab a late lunch at the crepe place around the corner. And then, of their own volition, his legs detoured and pushed through the front door of Henne Jewelers—a Pittsburgh institution, from what he'd been told.

As soon as he'd walked into the space, he'd regretted it. His throat had tightened and his face had grown hot and flushed. He'd felt like a stupid, lumbering giant. And he'd been certain everyone was staring at him.

A smiling saleswoman had glided over to him, placed a cool hand on his arm, and guided him to a seating area off to the side of the brightly lit room.

"You look a bit uncomfortable," she'd said in a tone somewhere between a mother comforting a toddler and a psychiatrist encouraging her patient to unburden himself.

Leo had laughed in relief, and a jumble of information about Sasha, his job offer, and the move had cascaded from his mouth in a rush.

Two hours and forty minutes later, he found himself standing on the corner of Walnut Street and South Highland Avenue, balancing a small, velvet box in the palm of his hand.

What the hell had he just done?

He pried the lid open and stared down at the ring. A large, square (the saleswoman had called it emerald-cut) ruby flanked by two small diamonds stared back at him.

When she had led him to the first ring display, after talking with him about Sasha and her taste, he'd spied the ring at once. The fiery red stone had jumped out at him from among the rows of glistening diamonds and the occasional sapphire. Different. Fierce. Sasha.

He'd looked up at the saleswoman and said, "It is it an engagement ring?"

"It is if you want it to be," she'd answered with a hint of a smile.

Leo jammed the box into his pocket and checked his watch. It was almost five, so he headed toward Sasha's condo, still edgy and out of sorts. It wasn't in his nature to be so impulsive.

24.

ASHA HAD SENT GREG AND Nick back to Greg's with strict instructions: Nick was to keep his cell phone turned off and they were to stay put. The fact that Nick had dropped off the face of the earth after his wife's dead body was found wasn't going to win him any popular support, she knew, but right now she just needed to buy some time before she let him talk to the police.

She sat with her chair turned away from her desk, facing the window. The last bits of sun streaked the sky. She chewed on a pen and read Clarissa's divorce complaint against Nick. Odd. Just like Ellen, Clarissa had sought a fault divorce, alleging she'd suffered indignities that rendered her condition intolerable and her life burdensome.

And, again like Ellen, she hadn't set forth any specific factual allegations to support that claim.

She flipped to the end of the complaint to check the signature block. Clarissa was represented by none other than Andy "Big Gun" Pulaski. It couldn't be a coincidence. Could it?

Naya rapped on the door and stuck her head in. "I'm going to take off."

"Okay," Sasha said absently, her mind still on the odds that Ellen and Clarissa would share the same misogynistic divorce attorney.

"Mac? You okay?"

Sasha turned her chair around and looked up to see Naya wrinkling her forehead in concern.

"Yeah, sorry. I was thinking. Have a good night."

"Why don't you come downstairs? We'll go over to Mad Mex. Margaritas are on me."

Sasha smiled. "Your winnings burning a hole in your pocket?"

Naya had returned from the casino to report that The Rivers had been a bust as far as the Lang case was concerned. The marketing team couldn't—or wouldn't—tell her how it had gotten Greg Lang's name, and security had offered no comment on the use of still photography by any patrons. They'd actually laughed at her request to review the security camera data. Naya had, however, managed to win sixty dollars playing Paigow poker, so she had been in an unusually mellow frame of mind when Sasha had broken the news of their newest client.

"C'mon. You could use a drink."

A margarita and a bowl of salty chips with Mad Mex's house-made salsa sounded about perfect. But there was no way. Not tonight. Not with Leo leaving in the morning.

"Sorry, Naya. I wish I could. I have too much to do. Maybe tomorrow? We could do a proper happy hour."

"Sure, okay. Especially with fly boy gone. We're going to need to keep you busy."

Sasha spread her hands wide and gestured at the papers covering her desk.

"I think I'm plenty busy, Naya."

Naya laughed and pulled the door shut before heading down the stairs.

Sasha thought for a moment and then punched Andy Pulaski's telephone number into her phone.

The Big Gun himself answered on the third ring. She'd been banking on the fact that he probably sent his receptionist home at five and then stuck around to do paperwork.

"Pulaski," he said in an abrupt growl.

"Mr. Pulaski, my name's Sasha McCandless. I represent Nick Costopolous," she said.

"That was quick," he commented.

From his tone, Sasha thought he might not have heard about Clarissa.

"You do know Clarissa's been murdered, Mr. Pulaski?"

"What? When?" he said.

Sasha pulled the phone away from her ear while he bellowed.

"Early this morning. A shopper found her in the parking garage attached to her law firm."

"Aww, shit. Another one."

"I'm sorry to be the one to tell you. I'm surprised you hadn't heard. It's been all over the news, apparently."

"I was in a deposition all day. Some broad's accused my client of hiding all his money. Doesn't want to believe she bled the poor sap dry, I guess. Who the hell has twenty-eight thousand dollars' worth of couture shoes? Anyway, what do you want? If Clarissa's dead, she's dead. Just don't answer the complaint."

"Actually, I'm not representing Mr. Costopolous with regard to the divorce."

"Oh. So, again, what do you want?" His voice was edgier, more demanding now.

"I'd like to come talk to you in person. Please."

Sasha wasn't about to get into it over the phone.

"Listen, lady, I don't have time for this. If you aren't Costopolous's divorce attorney, then we don't have anything to talk about. Give your dirtbag client my condolences."

Pulaski slammed the phone down in her ear.

25.

ANDY SLAMMED THE PHONE DOWN in frustration, knocking a stack of exhibits to the floor in the process. They fell out of the redweld and scattered.

"Son of a—" He stopped and reminded himself that he needed to make his anger work for him, not against him. Manage it. Harness it.

It was not what his most recent ex-girlfriend had meant when she'd said he had anger management problems. But it was what he'd decided to do. Andy was angry most of the time. He figured he might as well channel his rage into his work.

He snatched the stupid, squishy stress ball from his desk and squeezed it. Squeezed it like it was opposing counsel's neck and savored the image.

Then he dropped it back on the desk and yelled for Rich.

"Rich! Get in here!"

He heard the kid's heavy hiking boots shuffling along the carpet as he scurried down the hallway.

"Yeah, boss?" Rich stood in the doorway, not meeting Andy's eye.

The kid was like an abused dog. Always skulking around, meek and apologetic. But Andy had to admit he was handy. Having a dedicated runner to drive into the city and hand deliver documents, serve defendants, and file papers in court had made Andy's life a ton easier. Before Rich had shown up looking for a job, Andy had been forced to either stop what he was doing and burn a few hours sitting in traffic or pay the obscene fees of a messenger service. Now, he just handed the documents to Rich and sent him out the door. And, to give the kid his due, he'd even scored a few clients. Of course, they were all dying.

"I was just told that the Costopolous chick got murdered. Is that true?"

Rich stared down at his feet while he answered. "I guess."

"You *guess*? What do you mean, you *guess*? She's either dead or she isn't."

The kid's face flushed pink, and he stammered, "She is. Dead, I mean. That's what they said on the noon news. I saw it while I was eating lunch."

Andy grabbed the remote control from his desk and aimed it at the television sitting on the cart against his wall. He rarely watched it; every once in a while he turned it on to try to catch one of his commercials. But it was just after six o'clock. A dead chick lawyer—the second in a week—would probably be the lead story.

An attractive black woman wearing a bright purple suit filled the screen. She stood at the entrance to a parking garage.

"... savagely beaten to death with a hammer," she said, her eyes wide and her expression serious.

She went on, "Earlier today, Detective Burton Gilbert of the homicide squad told us the dead woman's husband, Nick Costopolous, is a person of interest."

The camera cut away to a shot of a guy in a gray trench coat walking into the garage. Andy could tell he was the detective by the cop walk: his head bent, his body pitched forward. The guy raised a hand in greeting to the camera but didn't slow his pace.

A picture of a smiling Nick Costopolous came on the screen; Andy judged it to be several years old, based on the more recent still shots he'd seen of Nick sucking face with the hottie.

The reporter prattled on, "Police have been unable to locate Mr. Costopolous, a master carpenter. His employer, Woodcrafters, had no comment. Anyone having information regarding Ms. Costopolous's death or the whereabouts of Nick Costopolous is asked to contact the Homicide Squad."

The camera returned to the reporter, who somehow managed to smile and come across as somber at the same time.

"Charlie, Linda," she said, addressing the off-screen anchors, "this is, of course, a tragic situation. It's made even more so by the fact that this is the second murder to rock the venerable Prescott & Talbott law firm in just a matter of days. Over the weekend, another lawyer at the firm, Ellen Mortenson, was brutally murdered in her home. Police have charged her estranged husband, Greg Lang, with the crime."

"Shocking," murmured Linda as the picture switched to her and Charlie, sitting shoulder to shoulder in the studio.

Charlie nodded his agreement and shuffled his papers on the desk in front of him. Then he added, "We've reached out to Prescott & Talbott, but the firm did not agree to an interview. It issued a statement this afternoon saying 'We ask for privacy for our employees during this difficult time. Please keep them in your thoughts as they mourn the loss of their colleagues and friends.'"

Andy jabbed the off button and turned to Rich.

"Some lawyer named Sasha McCandless called. Said she represents Costopolous, but not on the divorce. She must be his criminal lawyer. Track her down and give her a copy of the pictures. And take one to the homicide squad, too."

"Why?" Rich asked in a soft voice.

"Why what?" Andy said.

He didn't have time for Rich's endless questions today. The kid was eager to learn—a trait Andy appreciated—but it was like employing a four-year-old child with all the incessant freaking questions. He needed to get a hold of this homicide detective and tell him the pictures were coming.

"Why are you giving them the pictures?"

Andy looked at Rich for a long moment, then he said, "I'm giving them to the police because they could be considered evidence of a motive. If I sit on them, and then the police find out about them, they're going to want to know why I withheld them."

"Okay. So why are you giving them to the criminal attorney?"

"Because," Andy explained, working hard to muster his patience, "the district attorney will probably dick her around for a while before he turns over any evidence. It doesn't matter to me if Costopolous goes down for killing his wife or not, but I don't like the DA's little games. As a result, Ms. McCandless gets a freebie."

Andy had dabbled in criminal law before his divorce practice had really taken off. And, the assistant district attorneys had all seemed to share a nasty habit of dragging their feet about handing over evidence, especially if it was exculpatory. Since the pictures pretty much signed Costopolous's fate, they probably wouldn't hold them back from his lawyer, but Andy saw no harm in giving her a preview.

"You heard the reporter. He's a carpenter. She was killed with a hammer. Of course, he did it," Rich said.

"Kid, in this country, you're presumed innocent until you're proven guilty. If he did it, then the cops will make their case. Just get copies made of the pictures and deliver them. If it makes you feel better, take a set over to the cops tonight, but you can hold on to the lawyer's until tomorrow. She's probably left for the day anyway."

Rich opened his mouth like he wanted to argue about it. Andy glared at him, and he snapped his mouth shut fast and nodded.

"Got it," he said on his way out.

26.

WHEN MR. PRESCOTT RETURNED FROM his lunch appointment at the Rivers Club, Caroline tilted her head toward a tower of bankers' boxes stacked neatly in the corner.

"The files you requested are here."

He blinked. "Already?"

Caroline thought he sometimes failed to realize his power. When she'd invoked his name with the off-site archivist, the man had practically hung up on her in his hurry to pull Mr. Prescott's files.

She nodded and said, "Shall I bring them into your office?"

He wrinkled his nose, and she knew he was picturing all that paper cluttering up his pristine private space.

"No. I'll work through them one by one. Please hold my calls," he said, as he hefted the top box from the pile and disappeared into his office.

Caroline fielded his phone calls all afternoon. He emerged periodically only to return a box to the pile and take the next one.

She couldn't recall the last time he'd worked so long without interruption. Most days, she would receive multiple calls from people who urgently needed Mr. Prescott to authorize a decision or resolve some dispute, but the afternoon was oddly quiet—particularly given the news about Clarissa.

There had been a handful of calls from people outside the firm, but Mr. Prescott's internal line was silent. Caroline wondered who was dealing with the attorneys and their inevitable questions. She presumed Mr. Porter, since Clarissa had been in his practice group.

Right at five o'clock, Mr. Prescott dropped a pile of redwelds on her desk, and she jumped. She hadn't heard his office door open.

She blinked and looked down at the stack.

"Filing?"

"No," he said. "Shredding."

"Very good," Caroline said, reaching for the intraoffice mail pouch under her desk. She would put the documents to be shredded in her outgoing bin for delivery to the document center, where the contract employees who made the firm's copies, delivered the faxes, and ran the industrial shredders would handle the actual shredding.

Mr. Prescott put a hand on her shoulder to stop her. "Actually, Mrs. Masters, I'd like you to shred these documents personally. Don't send them to the document center."

She looked up. He had never, not once in twenty-odd years, asked her to shred anything herself. Not his income tax returns, not the drafts of the settlement agreement the firm had entered into with Noah Peterson's widow, not anything.

He met her eyes. "These documents are highly confidential. Please handle the shredding yourself."

"Of course," she said automatically.

"Please don't mention this to anyone."

"Of course not."

"Thank you. Why don't you take care of that and then call it a day? Today has been so ... trying. I'm going to be leaving shortly myself," he said and returned to his office.

She watched him go and tried to recall the last time either of them had left the office before six-thirty. He'd long ago decided that six-thirty was the appropriate time for the chair of the firm and his personal secretary to end their day. It was late enough to show that he was a serious business person, but early enough to allow him to sit down to dinner at a civilized hour. The schedule meshed nicely with her husband's work hours, so it had suited Caroline just fine. Leaving at five? It seemed decadent.

She looked down at the redwelds, all filled with documents that Mr. Prescott had instructed her to destroy.

She tapped her fingernails on the tower of folders, then she lay her palm flat on the top folder, hesitating.

Finally, she reached inside and pulled out the first item: a familiar white Tyvek mailing envelope with a border of green triangles. She slid her hand into the envelope and took out the photograph she knew she would find: Ellen, Clarissa, and Martine. Two red Xs over the dead women's faces. And the threat—or was it a warning?—across the bottom. She shoved it back into the envelope. Beneath the envelope was a second, identical envelope, which presumably contained the first picture.

Her pulse jumped. Weren't these photographs possible evidence of a crime? It didn't seem right to shred them. The police would want to see them.

Caroline cut her eyes toward Mr. Prescott's closed door and then flipped through the rest of the papers in the top redweld: a folder containing

Ellen's performance evaluations dating back to her first year with the firm; similar folders for Clarissa and Martine; and, lastly, all three women's partnership candidacy packets. All of the remaining redwelds contained the case files from a 1996 pro bono representation. Caroline paged through them and saw pleadings, internal memoranda, and client correspondence.

She restacked the files and thought, twisting a pearl earring between her finger and her thumb. Mr. Prescott was the chair of the firm. It was his prerogative to shred firm materials. But those photographs were a different story. She shook her head. And, truth be told, destroying the dead women's personnel files before their bodies were even in the ground seemed disrespectful and callous. She didn't feel good about this. Not at all.

Before she had a chance to second-guess herself, she slid open her bottom desk drawer and removed an oversized green, pebbled leather tote bag. She swept the documents inside, tossed her wallet on top of them, and buzzed Mr. Prescott.

"Yes?"

"Are you sure it's okay for me to leave for the day? And do you need anything before I go?"

"Yes, go ahead. And I don't need anything. Thank you. Good night, Mrs. Masters."

"Good night," she said in reply.

"You'll take care of those files before you go?"

"I'll take care of them."

"Thank you." He hung up.

Caroline zippered the tote bag closed, switched off her desk lamp, and shut down her computer. She grabbed the bag and hurried out of the office.

27.

CINCO SHOOK HIS ROCKS GLASS, tinkling the ice against the sides of the glass.

"Stop that," Marco said.

Cinco looked at him and jiggled the glass again. He didn't work for DeAngeles.

"Please," Marco added. "I meant, please stop that."

Cinco put down the glass and looked around the table. The most powerful members of the firm were gathered around an elegant table in a private room in the most powerful club in town. Behind the Duquesne Club's staid facade, titans of industry had been gathering to conduct their business in private since 1873. The Club's founders, clients of the firm, had invited Cinco's great-great grandfather to join, and the Prescotts had belonged ever since. With the exception of Fred, who was frugal in the extreme, the others at the table were all members of the Club as well.

The Club was known for its delicious cuisine, its state-of-the-art fitness center, and, most of all, its discretion. And, tonight, the five members of Prescott & Talbott's Management Committee were interested principally in the discretion. And the alcohol.

They'd sent their menus away with the tuxedoed waiter and instructed him to keep the drinks fresh, but the interruptions minimal. It would be a delicate balance, given the speed with which their beverages were disappearing, but the Club's wait staff was up to the task.

John took a long swallow of his vodka gimlet, then said, "So? We're here, Cinco. Do you want to fill us in on all the cloak and dagger?"

Cinco took a moment to gather his thoughts and run through the talking points he'd crafted on his walk to the club.

"Of course. And, John, as an initial matter, I take issue with the characterization of this meeting as 'cloak and dagger.' I think we all recognize the delicacy of the current situation."

Cinco caught Fred rolling his eyes but elected to ignore it. He went on, "That said, we have a serious problem."

John snorted. "Do you think, Cinco? Two dead attorneys in the space of a week? Killed by a maniac who's blackmailing the firm? Is that a serious problem?"

Kevin, who was seated next to John, put a hand on his arm.

"Calm down. We know you're upset about Clarissa, but getting hysterical isn't going to accomplish anything."

Kevin's tone was neutral, devoid of emotion or any hint of his personal views. It was his specialty; he was the dispassionate business litigator.

John swallowed hard. "You're right. I'm sorry."

Cinco said, "Let me address John's statement. For one thing, I don't think it's accurate to say we're being blackmailed. The messages written on those pictures could be construed as threats, but there has been no other communication. No suggestion that if we do X or pay Y, he will stop. For another thing, whoever the killer is, it's not Malcolm Vickers."

That caught their attention. Even Fred sat up a little straighter.

"What do you mean, it's not Vickers? Who else could it be?" Marco demanded.

Cinco spread his hands apart and said, "I don't know who it is, but Vickers died in 2008. It's not him."

"Are you sure?" Kevin pressed him.

"Positive. I asked Samantha to run some discreet inquiries. I thought if we could locate Vickers, we could find out what was driving him and work something out," Cinco said.

"Who the devil is Samantha?" Fred asked.

"Sam Davis, Fred. She's the firm's security officer," Kevin explained.

"Since when?" Fred asked.

Cinco ignored him. "In any event, Malcolm Vickers was active in the fatherhood rights movement during the late '90s and early 2000s and died in a hospice of lung and bone cancer in June of 2008."

Silence fell over the table.

"Well, gentlemen, anyone have any thoughts?"

"If it's not Vickers," Marco said, slowly, thinking it through, "who could it possibly be?"

"I don't know," Cinco admitted. "I pulled the case file and read through it. No other names jumped out at me."

Kevin frowned. "There will be a record of your assistant calling up the file from the archives. You realize that, don't you?"

"Of course, I do," Cinco lied.

He decided not to mention that he instructed Caroline to destroy it, among other things.

Fred raised his glass of bourbon. "Let's toast Clarissa and Ellen, shall we? Two fine lawyers, taken from us too young."

He drained his glass as the others lifted theirs.

John followed suit, then added, "She was pregnant, you know."

"Who?" Marco asked, tossing back his martini.

"Clarissa. The medical examiner told her mother."

Another blanket of silence covered the room.

Cinco thought of Clarissa's last moments; he wondered if she knew there was a life inside her and realized she was unable to protect it. He shivered.

Then Fred asked, "They're looking at her husband, too?"

"Yes," Kevin said. "He's a carpenter. She was killed with a hammer. Not too many dots to connect there."

"What's this going to mean for the Lang case?" Marco asked. "Shouldn't the fact that there have been two killings so close together work in both Lang's and Costopolous's favor? It seems to indicate one killer, doesn't it?"

Cinco watched them preen and posture, feeling removed and detached, as if the scene were playing out in a movie. No one in the room had one whit of criminal law experience. But they weren't about to let such a minor detail as that interfere with their speculating and expounding.

John shook his head. "No. The methods of killing were very different—Ellen's throat was slashed, and Clarissa was bludgeoned to death with a hammer. The acts themselves have nothing in common."

Kevin chimed in. "Not exactly. While the modus operandi differed, both killings were personal, even intimate. That doesn't point to one killer, necessarily, so much as it points to each of them being killed by someone she knew intimately, such as a husband."

Fred leaned forward. "Who gives a good goddamn? We all know these women weren't killed by their husbands. Now, we thought they were killed by Vickers, but Cinco here tells us that's not so, not unless he's some sort of zombie. Thus, we face the following issues: Who killed them? What does the killer want from us? Do we warn Martine? And, how much, if anything, do we need to tell Sasha? We can't let another woman go to the slaughter, gentlemen. And we can't let Nick and Greg go to prison."

He sat back, looking satisfied with himself, folded his hands over his belly, and waited for them to agree with him.

There was a soft knock on the door, and then it swung inward. The waiter entered, carrying a buffed and polished silver tray, heavy with a third round of fresh drinks. The talk turned to golf handicaps and college football while he quickly switched out their empty glasses for full ones.

"Thank you, Jason," Cinco said to his back as he departed.

"You're quite welcome, sir," he answered with a small head bob.

After the door closed, John looked at Cinco and said, "His name is Carson, not Jason, you self-involved ass."

Marco and Fred roared with laughter.

Kevin frowned. "Gentlemen, we need to stay united and focused on the problem at hand. Sniping at Cinco over a mistake isn't going to accomplish anything."

Cinco stared at the closed door for another moment, then said, "It's Carson? Really? I've been calling him Jason for at least a decade."

John shook his head. "Forget it. Kevin's right. It doesn't matter. Fred raised the issues, so let's figure out what to do."

Marco took charge. "Let's start with Martine. If those pictures aren't a demand, they're certainly a threat or, at the very least, a warning. Does the firm have a duty to advise a former partner that her life may be in danger?"

"Yes," John said.

At the same time, Kevin said, "No."

Cinco sipped his scotch and waited for someone else to jump in.

"Why do you say no, Kevin?" Marco asked.

"Mainly because right now we don't have anything to tell her. What're we going to say? 'Perhaps you've noticed your former colleagues are dropping like flies? We don't think their husbands are offing them. We thought it might be that guy, Vickers, who you three screwed over back when you were just pups, but it turns out he's dead himself. You might wanna check your doors at night and make sure they're locked.' What good is warning her when we don't know who the killer is?"

Marco nodded. "Good point."

John stiffened.

Fred piped up again. "On the other hand, what harm would it do to tell her about the pictures and allow her to decide for herself what steps, if any, she thinks it prudent to take for her own protection?"

"I agree," John said, immediately.

Cinco rubbed his eyes. *It figured.* He was going to have to break the tie. The others watched him and waited to hear what he would say.

So much responsibility. Always. He gulped his drink and thought.

Finally, he said, "We do nothing. Our duty is to the firm and its current members. Martine is a bright woman. Surely, she'll realize it's a bit odd that her two closest friends at the firm were murdered within days of each other. With regard to Sasha, she's purportedly competent, and, I'll remind you, she told us in no uncertain terms not to micromanage her case."

He was pleased to hear the firmness in his own voice. He didn't want to engage in endless debate that would require him to reveal that he'd destroyed the photographs. As much as he knew they would all secretly agree that had been the best course of action, he also knew they would feel compelled to posture and wring their hands over whether it had been the *right* thing to do.

He drained his glass and set it on the table with a thud. No one spoke for a moment, and then Fred cleared his throat.

"Now, let me see if I have this straight," Fred began, and Cinco recognized his *I'm just a regular guy trying to make sense of all this mumbo jumbo* routine. Fred spread his hands wide and continued, "We're *not* gonna tell Martine someone wants to kill her. We're *not* gonna tell Sasha that someone has been in touch with us, and, given that he seems to have killed *both* Clarissa and Ellen, it sure as shootin' isn't her client. In short, we're gonna close our eyes and hope this just goes away?"

Marco leaned forward and looked hard at Fred. "Not at all. I think what Cinco's saying—and he can correct me, if I'm wrong—is that it would be irresponsible for us to share the limited information we do have with Martine or, for that matter, Sasha. The only purpose that would serve would be to frighten Martine and, unless we're willing to share those photographs, frustrate Sasha."

"Correct," Cinco said. Before Fred could open his mouth again, he went on. "Of course, the firm will continue to investigate. If we can determine with some degree of certainty who's behind this, then, yes, we'll speak to Martine and Sasha."

"And the authorities, I should hope," John chimed in.

Kevin held up a hand. "Let's not get ahead of ourselves. We do have a duty to the firm not to embroil it in a murder investigation."

"That's quite right," Marco said. "If you recall, that's why we reached out to Sasha in the first place. We can't directly *do* anything; we need an outsider we can have do things for us." He paused and glared around the table. "Of course, as it turns out, you were all wrong about our ability to turn her head with a few hundred thousand dollars, so we have no way to control her anyway. But for better or for worse, we do nothing."

"Unless doing nothing rises to the level of interfering with justice," John interjected.

Fred and John shared a look.

Cinco could tell they were about to start up again with their argument about concealing evidence of a crime. A nice buzz from the scotch was starting to kick in. Cinco wanted to savor that warm feeling—ideally, in the arms of his wife; he did not want to engage in another round of strategizing with the brain trust.

"I think we've reached an agreement for now. I'll have Sam Davis dig a little deeper into Vickers's past and we can reconvene if and when something else changes."

He pushed back his chair and stood up quickly before anyone could object; he wobbled a little but righted himself. The others downed their drinks and followed suit.

28.

ICH SAT IN HIS CAR and stared up at the massive stone building. It stared back at him with its thick glass eyes, two blocks of light peering out from the dark facade. He'd never been to the Pittsburgh Bureau of Police Headquarters before. It looked like a Transformer, with the two slanted pieces jutting up from the roof. It looked like a place you wouldn't want to walk into under any circumstances. Especially not these circumstances.

He swallowed. There was no way around it. Andy had called the detective and told him Rich was coming. They were expecting him.

In books and movies, killers got a twisted, delicious thrill out of interacting with the authorities who were investigating their crimes. Not him. Bile burned his throat, and his hands shook. He exhaled, slow and long. Then he picked up the manila envelope addressed to Detective Gilbert from the seat beside him and pushed open the driver's door.

As he closed it, his eyes fell on the other envelope, the one addressed to that lawyer lady, and his stomach tightened.

He'd checked her out on Google to get her office address and had skimmed the page of hits. She was a former Prescott & Talbott attorney. As if that weren't bad enough, according to some profile piece in the newspaper, she had singlehandedly prevented a plane crash and solved the murder of a judge—all within the past year. She was the *last* person he wanted to see with a copy of the pictures. He imagined someone like her could screw up his plans for Martine if she stuck her nose into things. He didn't want that to happen, especially not after the Clarissa disaster.

He shook his head. That wasn't his fault. He hadn't known she was pregnant. It had all worked out, though. Just not according to his plan. The final act, Martine, had to proceed flawlessly, though.

He leaned in, grabbed the second envelope, and then pulled the door shut.

As Rich walked through the parking lot and neared the building, his entire body flushed; he was hot, dizzy, and lightheaded. He mumbled his name and Gilbert's to the uniformed woman at the front desk, struggling to stay on his feet and appear normal. His heart thudded in his chest as she called ahead to Gilbert to announce him.

She returned the phone to its base and pointed Rich to an elevator bank, rattling off directions in a rapid monotone. He couldn't make out what she said; his ears felt like they were full of water and his pounding pulse drowned out her words.

He squinted at the bright overhead lights and tried to remember which floor she'd told him to go to. He couldn't think through the ringing in his ears. He leaned against the wall and slowed his breathing. He could feel the woman at the desk watching him.

The elevator bell dinged and the doors opened. A distinguished-looking black man stepped off the car and nodded toward him. Rich recognized him from the news footage.

"You from Andy Pulaski's office?" Detective Gilbert asked. His voice rumbled in his chest, serious and intense.

"Yes," Rich managed to squeak.

The detective walked over. He had a long, fast stride.

Before Rich had worked out what to say next, the detective was standing beside him.

"We appreciate Mr. Pulaski's assistance," Gilbert said, staring at Rich's forehead.

Rich felt the droplets of sweat gathering in his hairline.

"Warm in here, huh?" he said. He gave the detective a weak smile.

Gilbert raised a silver eyebrow. "I hadn't noticed. Are those the pictures?" He jerked his head toward the envelopes.

Rich looked down at his hands and immediately regretted it, as the sweat started to trickle down toward his nose. He wondered if the detective could hear the roar of his heartbeat.

"Uh, yeah. Here."

Rich thrust both envelopes into the other man's large hands.

"Thanks."

Gilbert flipped to the second envelope. "Hang on, I don't think this one is mine. Says 'Sasha McCandless' on it."

"Oh, oops," Rich said, "that's a copy for Mr. Costopolous's attorney. Boy, would Andy be mad if I'd left that with you." He held out his hand and considered adding a nervous laugh. Given how jangly his nerves were, he knew it would sound genuine, but he didn't want to overdo it. Better to let the detective come to the idea on his own.

"His attorney?" The eyebrow arched up again. "Mr. Costopolous has retained counsel?"

Rich winced. "Oh boy, now I've done it. I don't know the details, Detective. Ms. McCandless called Andy this evening and said she represented Mr. Costopolous." He shrugged.

Gilbert looked down at the envelope and then at Rich's outstretched hand. He was quiet for a moment, then he said, "Tell you what, son. I'll see that Ms. McCandless gets this envelope."

Rich bit the inside of his cheek to stop the smile he felt starting. "Well, if you're sure ..."

"I'm positive. Thanks again for your assistance." Burton tucked both envelopes under his left armpit and stuck out his right hand.

Rich wiped his own clammy hand on his pants before taking the detective's outstretched paw. He turned to leave, forcing himself not to run toward the door on his shaky legs.

29.

SASHA AND CONNELLY STOOD SHOUL-
DER to shoulder in her kitchen. Even though
it had been almost eight o'clock by the time
she'd gotten home, Leo had insisted on teaching
her how to make her favorite dish.

All the ingredients for his slow-cooked short
ribs had been lined up on the island when she'd
walked through the door. She hadn't had the heart
to tell him that once he left for the weekend, she'd
go back to her standard dinner of a Greek yogurt,
with a square of dark chocolate and a beer for des-
sert. Instead, she'd dropped her briefcase by the
stairs and tied on her striped apron.

"You want to cut the vegetables uniformly, so
they'll cook evenly," he explained, trying to guide
her hand.

She jerked the chef's knife away. "I can cut a carrot, Connelly."

He looked at her pile of unevenly sized carrot chunks but said nothing. He went back to trimming the short ribs.

Sasha sighed and put down the knife. "I'm sorry. I just ... I'm stressed out about these murder cases. And even though I didn't know Ellen or Clarissa that well, I worked with them, you know? It's just all I can think about. But I shouldn't have snapped at you."

Leo put down his knife, too, and searched her face. "Maybe you're also stressed out because your boyfriend is probably going to take a job out of state and has invited you to move there with him, but you haven't answered? Do you think that might be part of it, too, Sasha?"

She stared down at her pathetic carrots.

"Maybe."

He tilted her chin up. "Come with me."

"Connelly—" she started, but he stopped her.

"Wait. Let me do this right."

He reached into his pocket. At the same time, her cell phone rang.

She grabbed it from the island and checked the display. She didn't recognize the number.

"Don't take it," Connelly said.

Sasha had already reflexively picked up the call.

As she said her name, she glanced over and saw a small black box in Connelly's palm. Her mind began to spin.

"Ms. McCandless," said the voice on the other end, "this is Detective Burton Gilbert with the Pittsburgh Police Homicide Squad."

Sasha processed that fact while trying to determine if the box in Connelly's hand was what she thought it was.

The detective continued, "I apologize for calling so late, but it's come to my attention that you represent Nicholas Costopolous."

He paused. Sasha knew he was waiting for her to confirm that information. Was that a *ring box* in Connelly's hand?

"Ms. McCandless?"

"Sorry. Yes, I represent Mr. Costopolous."

The detective's voice grew serious. "Does he know the police have been trying to contact him?"

"I can't discuss anything he and I have talked about, Detective, as I'm sure you're well aware."

Connelly placed the box on the counter and pantomimed hanging up. Sasha turned away from him and listened to Gilbert's measured words.

"As I understand it, Counselor, you're not an experienced criminal defense attorney, so I'm going to give you the benefit of the doubt here. Your client was a person of interest, but now, thanks at least in part to his own behavior, he's the prime suspect in the murder of his wife. The district attorney tells me we have sufficient evidence to arrest him. You choose: he can turn himself in at headquarters within the next hour or we'll get a warrant and issue an all-points bulletin on him. If you choose option B, I'll also be seeking a warrant to charge *you* as an accomplice after the fact," the detective said in a deep, serious voice.

Her stomach dropped, but she told herself he was bluffing. She hoped. She cleared her mind and tried to think like Larry, like a criminal defense attorney: pragmatic, realistic. It was hard to think at all with that little velvet box staring at her and Connelly playing charades.

"Give us ninety minutes. And I'm coming in with him," she said.

She hung up before he could respond.

Connelly stared at her, then he said, "Tell me you're not going out."

She untied the apron and folded it into a neat square.

"I'm sorry, Connelly. Nick Costopolous has to turn himself in. I'm his lawyer."

"Can't it wait until morning?"

"No, it really can't." She decided not to mention the detective's threat to charge her if she didn't produce Nick. It would only serve to get Connelly in a lather.

She headed up the stairs to the bathroom to wash her face and put on some fresh lipstick. Connelly followed.

He stood in the doorway to the bathroom and watched her. After she'd made the necessary repairs and checked her reflection, he opened the ring box.

"This isn't how I wanted to do this, Sasha. But I guess I don't have a choice. You know I love you. I want you to come to D.C. with me."

He took out a ring and pinched it between two fingers. The center stone shone brilliant red.

"Is that an engagement ring?" she asked.

"It is if you want it to be."

Sasha waited a beat before she answered.

"Connelly, I can't think about this now. I have a client accused of murdering his wife. Please tell me you understand." She searched his eyes.

Connelly nodded. "Sure. No problem." His face was blank.

"Connelly, please." She reached out and took the ring, turning it between her fingers. "It's stunning."

"Try it on," he urged.

"Let's wait until we can talk, okay? We need to figure out what we're doing first, don't you think?"

She handed the ring back to him, and he returned it to the box.

He nodded again. "You're right." He snapped the box shut.

"You know I love you, too, right?" she said.

"I know."

She stretched on to her tiptoes and kissed him. He accepted the kiss, but Sasha could tell by the rigid way he stood that she'd hurt him. She felt a pang of guilt, but she couldn't ignore her obligation to Nick.

"I'll be back as soon as I can," she promised.

They walked hand-in-hand down the stairs to the foyer. At the bottom of the stairs, he peeled off and headed for the kitchen.

"What are you doing?" she asked, as she wound a fringed scarf around her neck.

Connelly looked up from the cutting board. "I'm going to finish making these short ribs. All you'll have to do this weekend is reheat them. That way I won't have to worry that you're eating peanut butter straight from the jar."

"*Once.* I did that *one time.*"

She'd returned from a double sparring session and a six-mile run and had felt woozy and faint. A quick hit of protein had perked her up, but, of course, she'd timed it to coincide with Connelly's unannounced arrival.

Even on her way out the door to tell Nick that he was likely going to spend the night in jail, and even with the ring and Connelly's new job buzzing around in her brain, she laughed at the memory of the look of pure horror on Connelly's face when he'd caught her with a jar of peanut butter in one hand and a spoon in her mouth.

30.

A S SHE RUSHED TO HER car, Sasha tried Greg's cell phone first. Five rings. No answer. Then, she tried Nick's, even though she'd insisted that he keep it turned off. She was relieved when her call went straight to voicemail. She left no message.

On the short drive to Greg's house, she tried to reach Larry but wasn't surprised when no one answered there, either. Larry and Bertie were up before the sun rose, but they retired not long after it set. It was well past their bedtime.

She pulled up in front of the house and was pleased to see lights on in the living room but no sign of Nick's truck. He must've had the sense to put it in the garage. She parked in the dead center of the driveway, effectively blocking the road, just in case her client got any ideas about fleeing.

Sasha killed the engine and scrolled through her phone's address book. She cleared her mind of everything not related to Nick Costopolous. She'd deal with her exploding personal life later. Right now, she needed to talk to someone who could explain the process of surrendering to the police. And fast.

Will picked up on the first ring.

"Hello, Sasha."

"Hi, Will. I'm sorry to bother you so late," she said, even though she wasn't sorry at all and they both knew it. Taking a business call at home late at night might not be fun, but it was part of being an attorney.

"It's no bother at all," Will lied. "What can I do for you?"

Sasha skipped the niceties. "I'm representing Nick Costopolous."

"Clarissa's husband?"

"Right."

"For what?" Will asked.

"He's about to be charged with her murder, Will." Sasha tried hard to keep her impatience out of her voice.

"I see."

"Will the firm post his bond?"

"Oh. I don't know ... I mean, I presume so. I'll have to check with Cinco, though."

Sasha exhaled loud enough for him to hear. "Is Cinco the head of the criminal defense practice or are you?"

"Now, you know that's not how it works."

She did know. And she felt momentarily chastised for trying to goad him.

"Can you find out, please? I have—" she paused to check the time, "—about an hour to show up at police headquarters with Nick. It'd be nice to know before we walk in."

"He's turning himself in?" Will's view of the wisdom of this decision was evident.

"He doesn't really have a choice. He pulled a disappearing act. They've been looking for him all day and *someone* told them I was his attorney."

"It wasn't me, if that's what you're insinuating, as I had no earthly idea that you were representing him. And, as a friend, Sasha, I'm not sure it's a good idea. I don't mean to denigrate your ability in any way, but you've never handled a criminal matter before, and now you've taken on two high-profile murder defenses?"

"I not only appreciate your concern, Will, I share it; that's why I've asked Larry Steinfeld to assist me."

The relief in Will's voice was palpable. "That's an excellent idea. Larry's a seasoned veteran and a very sharp man. Please give him my regards."

"I will. Will you call me on this number after you talk to Cinco?"

"Of course."

"Please point out to him that this second gruesome murder actually supports his theory that someone is out to get Prescott."

The brief silence that followed made clear that Will understood Cinco's strengths as a manager were balanced by some fairly significant shortcomings as a legal strategist. After a moment, he said, "Certainly."

"Thanks."

She depressed the button to end the call and stepped out of the car. The night air was cool, and gauzy clouds hung across the moon. She tossed the phone in her bag and hurried up the walkway to the porch.

She pressed the doorbell and heard the long chimes echo through the house. She waited but didn't hear footsteps approaching the door. She jabbed the bell again. Waited again. Still nothing.

She rapped hard on the door. Another moment passed.

She had her fist raised to pound again, when she heard shuffling and murmuring on the other side.

Greg's pale face filled the glass in the top of the door. Sasha waved and smiled up at him. He didn't smile back, but the deadbolt slid out of place, and the door swung inward.

He stopped the door mid-swing. He didn't invite her in, but stood in the doorway with his left arm braced against the doorframe, and a foot jammed against the door. In his right hand, he held one of his dirty tumblers, mostly full of what looked to be scotch. Over his shoulder, Sasha could see Nick leaning against the wall, his fingers wrapped loosely around the stem of a martini glass; he swayed, and the liquid inside sloshed from side to side as if he were on a boat.

"Sasha," Greg said, over-enunciating in his effort not to slur. "What are you doing here?"

Great. They were drunk.

Her first instinct was to push her way in and chew them out for getting plastered. But that course of action, as satisfying as it would be, was unlikely to result in her showing up at the police station in less than an hour with a reasonably cooperative Nick in tow. Instead, she pasted a concerned look on her face.

"I just wanted to check on you guys," she said, ducking under Greg's arm and slipping into the house before he could object.

He pushed the door closed behind her and rested his forehead against the heavy wood. Sasha walked over to Nick and swept the martini glass out of his hand.

"Hey!" he protested, swinging his arms after her.

She continued straight to the back of the house and surveyed the open kitchen. She poured the drink down the drain and set the glass in the sink.

Greg and Nick trailed in, grumbling in loud boozy whispers. She ignored them and turned her attention to a single-serve Keurig coffee maker beside the sink. She selected two packets of the strongest option from the cloth-lined basket of various coffees that sat on the counter and popped one into the machine. As the liquid started to stream into a pastel blue mug, she dug through the silverware drawer and found a spoon.

Uncomfortable in her own kitchen, Sasha was surprised to find herself bustling around an unfamiliar space, but she knew her best chance at ensuring compliance from her drunk clients was to keep moving. They would be slow to process what was happening. With any luck, she'd have Nick halfway out the door before he could object.

Sasha pointed to the square oak table. "Have a seat," she directed.

Nick hurried over, tripped, and landed sprawled in a chair.

Greg narrowed his eyes and stayed where he was.

She put the first mug of coffee, along with the cream and sugar, on the table in front of Nick, who dutifully started to fix his coffee. She got the second mug started on the coffee machine and then walked over and stood close to Greg.

"Nick's going to need your support in a few minutes. And I'm going to need your assistance. It'd be nice if you were in a position to be helpful," she said in a low voice, looking up at him and holding out the mug of coffee.

Greg sighed but traded her his tumbler for the coffee.

"Thank you."

He nodded. "You're welcome."

He joined Nick at the table, and his drink joined Nick's down the drain. Sasha rinsed both glasses and then made a final mug of coffee for herself. The only sound was the hissing coffee machine.

She joined the men at the table, carrying a cheerful red mug. Not until she'd taken a seat did she notice the words *I Got Lei-ed in Hawaii!* printed across the front. Judging by Greg's snicker, it was printed on the other side as well.

"Nick, the police want you to come in and talk to them," she said.

Anger sparked in his eyes, but he said, "Fine. I told you before, I don't have anything to hide. Let's go. The sooner they rule me out, the sooner they can catch the bastard who killed Clarissa."

She put a hand on his arm to keep him in his chair and said, "They think *you're* the bastard, Nick."

He crumpled into himself. "They think I killed her?"

"Of course, they think you killed her. You're the husband—the *estranged* husband, no less," Greg said.

Sasha shot him a look that said *you're providing the support, remember?*

Greg dropped his eyes to the table, and when he spoke again the tightness and bitterness in his voice were gone. "Just tell them the truth, Nick. It's all you can do."

Nick nodded slowly and looked at Sasha with large, sad eyes. Like a puppy.

"They just want to talk to me?" he asked, his voice betraying that he had not a shred of hope that was true.

"They're probably going to arrest you and process you. I've reached out to Prescott to see if they want to post your bond, provided we can get a bond."

Nick's face turned gray.

"Before we go anywhere, though, you're going to have a cup of coffee and a hot shower," Sasha told him.

"Why?"

"Because you look and smell like you've been on a bender," she explained.

Nick shrugged, a concession that it was true, and picked up the coffee.

Sasha turned back to Greg. "Have you two eaten anything?"

Greg squinted and bit his lip while he thought about it. "Not since lunch," he said finally.

Just as she resigned herself to making them sandwiches or something, Greg pushed back his chair. "I'll make some pasta. It'll be done by the time Nick's out of the shower."

"Are you sure you're up to it?" Sasha asked. She didn't want to add dealing with a house fire to her evening's activities.

Greg didn't answer but walked with exaggerated care to the cabinet and pulled out a shiny, new-looking pot then filled it with water and set it on the cooktop. Sasha watched for a minute to satisfy herself he could stay on his feet, and then she turned her attention back to Nick.

"Go take a shower and shave. See if Greg has any clothes that will fit you. Nothing flashy. Just clean and unwrinkled."

"Okay," Nick said, gulping his coffee.

"While you're in the shower, I want you to think hard about your life with Clarissa. Is there anything you need to tell me? Anything at all that the police could view as giving you a reason to kill Clarissa?"

Nick nodded. "I will," he promised.

"Also, think about anyone who Clarissa might have talked to about her plans to divorce you. Family, maybe? Or close friends?"

Nick shook his head. "Not her family. I would have heard about it. Our parents are old friends, from back in Greece. There's no way she could have told her sisters or her mother that she was leaving me without my mom hearing about it. No way."

He sounded sure, so Sasha accepted it. "Okay, then, friends?"

Greg was cutting up a sausage at the kitchen counter. Over his shoulder, he said, "Martine, Nick. If she told anyone, it was Ellen and Martine."

"Martine Landry?" Sasha asked.

"Yes," Nick confirmed, "Clarissa, Ellen, and Martine were really tight. They started at Prescott together."

"The Terrific Trio, right?" Sasha said.

"Exactly," Greg confirmed, as he passed by the table on his way to refrigerator. He selected a hunk of cheese and headed back to check on his pasta water.

"That'll boil faster if you salt it," Sasha offered, happy to share one of the few cooking tips she'd retained from Connelly's lessons.

Greg didn't acknowledge the comment, but he tossed a pinch of salt into the pot.

Sasha returned to the subject of Clarissa's friends.

"Do you think she told Ellen or Martine?" she asked Nick.

He gave her a helpless look and spread his hands wide, "I honestly don't know. She saw Ellen every day, practically. And it wouldn't surprise me if she had confided in her. I mean, I know they talked about Ellen and Greg's ..." he trailed off and nodded toward Greg's back, then looked back at Sasha. "But the thing is, she really wasn't unhappy. This divorce stuff came out of nowhere. We weren't fighting. Everything was fine."

Obviously not, Sasha thought.

What she said was, "Nick, there had to be *something*. Clarissa didn't file for divorce because she was perfectly content in your marriage. That didn't happen. When you're getting cleaned up, I need you to really think about what could have precipitated that."

Nick started to object, but she fixed him with the look she reserved for small children and idiots. She assumed he'd realize he wasn't a small child.

"Okay," he said, "I'll think about it, but we were happy. At least, I thought we were."

"So you think she may have told Ellen," Sasha prompted him. "What about Martine?"

Nick shrugged.

Greg pushed the sausage around in a pan until it sizzled, then rested the spatula on a trivet, and joined them at the table.

"I doubt it," he said, gesturing with his coffee cup like it was a conductor's wand.

"Why?" Sasha asked.

"Well, I know Ellen didn't tell Martine about our, uh, problems," he explained.

"She didn't?"

"No. I ran into Tanner, maybe two weeks ago, at the squash club, and he was talking about having us over for dinner. So either Ellen didn't tell Martine, or she did and Martine didn't mention it to Tanner. Unlikely."

"That's the sort of news a person would generally share with her husband," Sasha agreed.

The water on the stove bubbled over the edge of its pot, shooting white foam down the side and causing the flame to rise.

Greg hustled back to his dinner preparations and covered the pot with a lid. He lowered the flame.

"Why wouldn't Ellen tell Martine?" she asked. "I thought they were tight."

Greg dumped some ziti into the boiling water and stirred it.

Then he turned back to her and said, "The girls were close, but after Martine left Prescott & Talbott, there was a bit of a divide. Ellen and Clarissa were still in the belly of the beast, you know. And Martine's focus was different. She had all those kids, and she dabbled in teaching and consulting, but she wasn't the hard-charging ballbuster that she'd once been. The three of them would get together for drinks or a spa day pretty regularly, but it was just … different."

At the table, Nick nodded his agreement.

"Okay. How long until that's done?" Sasha asked.

Greg checked the timer. "Twelve minutes."

Sasha turned to Nick. "Go make yourself presentable. Can you do it in twelve minutes?"

A hint of the old, creepy Nick broke through his morose drunken fog, and he winked at her. "I'll be looking good in no time."

He stood, steadied himself, and headed for the stairs.

Sasha watched him leave and then told Greg, "Clarissa had retained Ellen's divorce attorney."

"That cretin Pulaski?"

"One and the same."

Greg shook his head. "That guy. I truly believe Ellen and I could have worked things out if he hadn't been whispering in her ear. He was so vicious."

The description squared with what Greg's attorney had said.

"How so?"

"He just had this scorched earth approach. For instance, Erika suggested the four of us meet, informally and off the record, to at least discuss the possibility of a collaborative divorce. Ellen and Pulaski agreed to the meeting, but then they walked into the conference room, and he literally threw a set of the pictures of me at the casino at Erika. He tossed them right in her face and started screaming, red-faced. He was ranting about how, when he was through with me, I'd be a shell of a man."

"What did Ellen do while this was going on?" she asked.

Greg's entire face drooped and he said, "She just stood behind him and looked at me with this satisfied little smile."

"Do you know how Ellen found him? Erika said he typically didn't represent women."

Sasha didn't expect him to know; but she hoped the question would distract him from the memory.

"I don't know," he said in vague voice, "I assume one of the bloodsuckers at the firm referred her to him." He turned his attention back to his pasta.

Sasha listened to confirm that the water was running upstairs and then tackled the next delicate subject.

"There's something else we need to talk about," she said to Greg's back.

"What is it?" he asked without looking at her.

There was no point in sugarcoating it.

"Nick's going to be arrested for Clarissa's murder."

"I know," he said.

"You're his alibi, to the extent he has one," she told him.

Greg turned away from his dinner preparations.

"I know that, too," he said, a hint of irritation in his voice.

"Do you also know that having your name dragged into yet another murder investigation isn't exactly going to help your own case?" Sasha said.

Greg exhaled, blowing his hair off his forehead. Then he said, "Yes, I do."

"I'm in a delicate spot here," Sasha said. "As your attorney, I must advise you not to get involved."

"And as Nick's attorney?"

"As Nick's attorney, I'm inclined to think he needs all the help he can get. And being alibied by another accused wife killer is perhaps marginally better than having no alibi at all." Sasha kept her tone neutral and added, "But that has to be your decision."

Greg was silent for a long moment.

Finally he said, "Can't the guys at Nick's club alibi him?"

Sasha shook her head. "That won't work. What can they say? A stranger came into the club, served Nick with divorce papers, and Nick proceeded to get hammered. They don't know where he went after he left the club. And then it gets worse. I'm sure the police will beat the bushes, if they haven't already, until they find some neighbor who either saw Nick go to the house last night or heard him shouting for Clarissa to let him in."

Greg rubbed his temples. "I could say he called me and told me she locked him out and I invited him to come here. And he was here all night and all morning."

"Yes, you could. But if you do that, the police will view it as an invitation to look at your life even more closely than they already have. They'll be all over you," Sasha said.

"So will the press," Greg added, "don't forget those vultures."

"That's true."

She couldn't lead him to a decision. She was maintaining a precarious balance as it was.

He stirred the ziti with a wooden spoon. He tapped the spoon against the side of the pot and watched the water drip off it, then looked back at Sasha and said, "I want to do it. I know I didn't kill Ellen. And I know Nick didn't kill Clarissa. I want to help him prove it if I can."

"Are you sure?"

"I'm sure," he said, setting his mouth in a firm, grim slash.

Upstairs, the water shut off. Greg went back to the pasta.

31.

CAROLINE STOOD AT THE KITCHEN window and stared out in to the backyard; she was looking toward her garden, although she couldn't see it in the darkness. She knew the wild roses were making their last display of the year and the earliest mums were just budding.

But she wasn't thinking about her flowers. She was thinking about the files she'd shoved under the passenger seat of her car. When she'd pulled into the driveway after work and lifted her bag from the seat next to her, she'd balked at bringing those gruesome pictures into her home. She knew she was being silly, but she had arranged the house according to feng shui principles, and the thought of bringing such negative energy into her sanctuary bothered her. So under the seat the files went.

She fetched a teacup from the cabinet beside the stove and packed the teaball with chamomile leaves and dried lavender from her garden. While she waited for the kettle to whistle, she moved back to the window and peered out at the car. She'd parked in the driveway, because the detached garage was filled with her gardening equipment and Ken's fishing gear.

She stared out the window, lost in thought, until the tea kettle chirped its shrill, steamy whistle.

Caroline turned away from the window again and fixed her cup of herbal tea. She focused on the ritual of making the tea and letting it steep. Then she took her teacup into the sunroom and sat in the quiet darkness, sipping it slowly, while she considered the files she'd taken.

She returned to the kitchen and retrieved her purse from the window bench. She rifled through it and unearthed the pocket-sized directory of home phone numbers for the various members of firm administration and management.

She punched Samantha Davis's number into her phone.

As the phone rang, Caroline tried to form the words she wanted to say to the chief security officer. *I stole some photographs that Mr. Prescott wanted me to shred. I think Ellen and Clarissa's murderer sent them.*

"Hello. Davis residence," Samantha's silvery voice said on the other end of the line.

Caroline stared at the receiver in her hand.

"Hello?" Samantha said, more sharply this time.

Caroline clicked off and slammed the cordless phone down hard on the base.

She picked up her teacup, and her trembling hands sent the hot liquid splashing over the side. With tears of frustration pricking at her eyes, she ran to the sink and dumped the tea down the drain.

32.

ICH POUNDED THE GROUND WITH a gloved fist. His legs were cramping, his stomach was rumbling, and his entire body was chilled through. He'd been crouching in the bushes outside the Landrys' house for over an hour, squinting into the brightly lit den.

And what did he have to show for it?

A fat lot of nothing, that's what, he thought.

The two older kids, whom he judged to be in their early teens, had been busy working on one of those giant jigsaw puzzles—from his vantage point it looked like a picture of a mountain range. The youngest, who looked to be about nine or ten, was sprawled on his stomach on the floor creating a complicated Legos structure.

Honey, the family's idiotic golden retriever, who lacked the sense to even sniff out Rich's presence, was curled into a blob of fur in front of the couch. Every so often, it would whimper and its legs would twitch, like it was dreaming of chasing a rabbit.

Martine had curled herself into a similar whimpering ball, with a soft-looking little brown blanket over her shoulders, snuggled into Tanner's side. She was crying softly, and Tanner was stroking her hair and murmuring into her ear words that Rich couldn't hear but assumed were comforting.

Rich did derive some satisfaction from the thought that she was sobbing over her dead friends, but it didn't outweigh his frustration.

He been tailing Tanner for weeks now and hadn't gotten so much of a glimpse of a vice. The worst Rich could say about the man was that he was sometimes absent-minded. But for the most part, Tanner seemed like a decent man, a good father, and a loving husband.

He hadn't expected it to be this hard. The other two had been a breeze.

Rich had been keeping tabs on the three chick lawyers for a while—just casually, not with any real purpose. But when Ellen and Greg had jetted off on their European vacation, their empty mansion had proved irresistible. He'd broken in easily, just slipped a credit card through the side door leading from the garden. Poking around, he noted with interest Greg's straight razor and the assorted Gamblers Anonymous pamphlets in his sock drawer.

Once the idea had taken root in his mind, figuring out a way to get at Costopolous hadn't been difficult either. Rich had known, just from watching Nick's comings and goings and the way he stopped to check himself out at every reflective surface, that he was a ladies' man. His second stepfather had had the same weakness for women and his own reflection.

But Tanner was different, steady and responsible. In fact, he reminded Rich of his old man. He allowed his kids do their own thing but stuck nearby in case they needed a hand.

Take this puzzle they were working on. Every so often, one of the kids would look up and ask for help, and he'd pat Martine on the head, then unfold his long legs and stride over to the table. He'd point out a few pieces they might want to focus on, watch for a few seconds to be sure they got it right, and then return to comforting his weepy wife.

And when the little one had said he wanted a snack, Tanner had popped to his feet and hurried to the kitchen. He'd returned several minutes later and handed individual bowls of popcorn to all three children. All the while Martine had sat on the couch like a stupid, crying statue.

Watching the Landrys at home made Rich feel like someone was squeezing his head in a vise. He didn't want to sit through any more family nights in the bushes. He wanted to find Tanner's weakness, exploit it, and then mail some incriminating pictures to Martine and get the ball rolling.

But Tanner didn't gamble. He didn't drink. Or chase skirts. He didn't even seem to golf or have any hobbies or interests that Rich could see outside of his wife and kids.

The thing that really made Rich's head ache was that he did know how to get at them, but he didn't want to have to do it. He'd told himself at the beginning of his plan that he wouldn't involve any children. He'd promised himself in his father's name that he wouldn't.

But if he didn't come up with something else soon, he wasn't going to have a choice; he'd have to get to them through one of their kids. It had been one thing to let the Landry piece of the plan proceed at a slower pace; it had lacked the elegance that all three women receiving their pictures on the same day would have delivered, but the plan had still be doable. Now, though, time was running out. Especially because Nick had gotten that attorney involved.

Martine let out a shrill wail and started to sob harder. All three kids rushed to her and huddled around, trying to help Tanner comfort her. He could hear them, through the windows, telling her how much they loved her.

33.

ASHA AND NICK WALKED INTO police headquarters ten minutes after Detective Gilbert's deadline had passed. Nick was, if not sober, at least faking it well.

He'd been subdued during the drive to the North Side. Sasha had suggested that he call his parents, who hadn't heard from their son at all since the news of Clarissa's death had broken, but he'd shaken his head no and then leaned back on the headrest and closed his eyes.

When they entered the building, blinking at the harsh overhead lighting, a pleasant-looking middle-aged man with a silver buzz cut greeted them heartily, like they were regulars at a neighborhood bar. She figured they looked like a respectable young couple who'd wandered in for directions.

"Hello, you two!" he beamed. "What can I do for you?"

"Hi," Sasha said with considerably less enthusiasm. "We're looking for Detective Gilbert."

"Then you're in the right place," he said, picking up the telephone. "Who should I tell him is here?"

"Attorney Sasha McCandless and Nick Costopolous."

The grin faded and he punched a number with his finger. "Burt, the Costopolous perp's here. With his lawyer," he said in a clipped tone.

He nodded at whatever the detective said and then hung up.

"Suspect," Sasha said in her sweetest voice.

"What's that?" the desk sergeant demanded.

"I said, Mr. Costopolous is a suspect—a person of interest, more accurately. Bereaved husband is also acceptable, if you prefer." She smiled.

The man rolled his eyes and waved them away from the desk.

"Detective Gilbert will be down from Homicide in a minute. Make yourselves comfortable."

Sasha turned and looked. He was pointing to a cinder block wall. The height of comfort.

She and Nick walked over and leaned against it.

"Are you okay?" she asked in a low voice.

"I guess."

He didn't look okay. She hoped Gilbert was hurrying, because her client was jittery, like he was getting ready to sprint out of the building.

"Take a breath. You need to stay calm, okay? Remember what we talked about in the car."

"I remember. I still don't understand why you told Greg not to come," Nick mumbled.

Sasha had firmly dissuaded Greg from tagging along to provide moral support. She didn't care to imagine the reception they would have received if she'd walked into police headquarters with two men accused of murdering their wives. One was plenty.

She'd explained to her skeptical clients that she would inform the detective that Nick had an alibi and offer to arrange a time for him to speak to Greg. In light of Greg's own pending murder trial, the contours of that discussion would need to be agreed to in advance by Sasha and whichever assistant district attorney had been assigned to Nick's case.

"Here," Nick said, handing her his watch and a soft leather wallet, "take these."

The gesture seemed unnecessarily final and dramatic, but maybe Nick knew something she didn't. For all she knew, personal property routinely disappeared from the police station.

She turned the understated titanium watch over in her hand. On the back, a worn inscription read *All my love. For all time. C.*

Nick watched her read the love note from his dead wife. His eyes flashed with pain.

Sasha tucked the watch and wallet into her bag and was about to offer some additional words of meaningless encouragement when the elevator bell chimed and the doors opened with a slow whoosh.

A fit-looking African-American man in a conservative suit stepped off.

"Ms. McCandless?" he said, striding over to them.

"Detective Gilbert," she answered, extending her hand.

He pumped it in a fast, firm handshake and then turned to Nick.

"Mr. Costopolous, thank you so much for coming in. I'm Detective Burton Gilbert, with the Homicide Squad. On behalf of the entire department, my condolences on the loss of your wife."

Nick looked at Sasha, momentarily confused, then offered the detective a weak handshake. "Uh, thanks," he said.

Sasha shook her head slightly, trying to warn him. Nick could not make the mistake of thinking the detective was his friend. She had been very clear with him in the car: don't volunteer anything;

answer only the questions asked; and don't answer anything immediately, so she'd have time to object. She didn't know much about police interviews, but she'd defended enough depositions to know nothing was more disastrous than an eager-to-please client who believed he had a rapport with his interrogator.

"Well," Gilbert said, still playing the genial host, "let's get set up in an interview room. Can I get you two anything? Coffee? Water?" he asked as he led them toward the stairway. "Okay if we take the stairs? I have to get my exercise somehow."

"No problem," Sasha said, following him into the stairwell. "And no thank you on the beverages. Mr. Costopolous would, however, like to use the facilities before we begin."

Behind her, Nick whispered, "I don't need ..."

She turned and gave him a look. "Just go. Take a minute to yourself before we get started."

She wanted to interrupt Gilbert's efforts to bond with Nick, break his rhythm. In addition, she'd watched enough television shows to suspect that Gilbert planned to ply Nick with coffee and water until he needed to use the facilities and then make him wait.

Gilbert led them up one flight of stairs and held the metal door for them. Once they were in the antiseptic-looking hallway, he pointed Nick toward the restroom.

Sasha took in the white tile floor and mint green walls.

"Nice place," she said, needling him to see if he'd drop the friendly facade when Nick wasn't around.

The detective just shrugged and said, "Your tax dollars at work." He turned one corner of his mouth up in a brief smile and said, "You shouldn't believe everything you see on cop shows, you know."

"Pardon me?"

"It's unconstitutional to coerce a confession."

Sasha bristled. "I'm well aware of that, Detective. I'm glad to know you are, too."

"Right," he continued, "and the Supreme Court has ruled that depriving a suspect of access to the bathroom is unconstitutional coercion."

Sasha felt her cheeks burn but willed herself to ignore her embarrassment. He was trying to throw her off-balance.

She took a centering breath before she answered. "Thanks for the information. I realize you think I'm inexperienced, but I do know some criminal law. As I'm sure *you* know, on occasion, your brethren have been known to break the rules in their zeal to secure a confession. I'm certain you'd never do such a thing, but let's not pretend it doesn't happen."

He raised a brow but said nothing.

"Listen," Sasha said, "I produced my client as a show of good faith. I know you think he's guilty for some reason. Just do yourself a favor and hear what he has to say."

"Do *myself* a favor?"

"Yes. Because you're wrong. He didn't kill Clarissa."

Detective Gilbert gave her a knowing smile. "Of course, Counselor. If Nick convinces me he's not our man, I'm not going to arrest him. I want the dirtbag who did this. I just happen to think I already have him."

The restroom door swung open and Nick emerged, drying his hands on his pants.

As he approached, Gilbert said, "I understand you've decided to bring counsel with you today, Mr. Costopolous, and that's your right, of course. Just so we're clear, this is simply an initial interview. At this point, you are not being detained and are free to leave."

Hope bloomed in Nick's eyes.

Gilbert went on, "If, however, you don't consent to speak to us voluntarily, I do have sufficient evidence to arrest you."

The hope wilted, and Nick said, "Let's get this over with, then."

Gilbert clasped Nick on the shoulder and pointed toward a steel door to their right.

"Right through that door."

Nick hung back, so Sasha entered first.

The room was a small square with three gray-green walls, one floor-to-ceiling observation mirror directly across from the door, and dark blue carpet. A long, particleboard desk was shoehorned into the room, with just enough space for a cheap plastic chair behind it. Its mate was in the middle of the room, about a foot from the end of the desk. Three feet in front of that, was a metal folding chair, perpendicular to the desk. No clock. Strong overhead light.

The walls began to close in on Sasha before Gilbert had even closed the door behind them. She checked on Nick, whose fear was evident.

A quick calculation made it clear that Nick was supposed to sit in the metal chair facing Gilbert while Sasha was stuffed away in the corner, out of Nick's line of vision.

Oh no, you don't, she thought.

"Here." She took Nick's arm and directed him to the seat behind the desk; then she hurried over to claim the other plastic chair before Gilbert could take it.

Nick looked around the room, his eyes a bit unfocused, then sat behind the desk.

Gilbert scowled at Sasha and then cut his eyes over to the one-way mirror. Now he had to decide if he should make everyone switch seats so he could maintain his psychological upper hand over Nick or if the act of calling attention to the seating arrangement would further weaken his position.

Sasha watched him, her face impassive, while he worked through it.

After another second, he picked up the metal chair one-handed and turned it ninety degrees, so that he was facing Nick. He banged it down and then took a seat.

Perfect. Nick had a clear line of sight over the detective's shoulder.

She smiled at him. She could communicate with Nick, and Gilbert would be able to see her only peripherally, if at all.

Gilbert's stiff shoulders and clenched left fist told her his displeasure with this set up matched her delight.

Her cell phone vibrated in her bag. She opened her purse and peeked at the phone's display. Will was calling. She let it roll to voicemail.

Gilbert rolled his shoulders, relaxed his hand, and smiled at Nick; determined not to let his irritation stand in the way of his interrogation.

"Okay, Nick—can I call you Nick?"

Nick nodded his head, but Sasha caught his eye and gave a short shake of her head. Nick stared at her. Gilbert turned to see what he was looking at.

"Mr. Costopolous is fine," Sasha told the detective.

Gilbert turned back to Nick with a look that said *can you believe this lady?* Nick shrugged.

"Mr. Costopolous," Gilbert said, giving the formal name heavy emphasis, "we've spent the better part of today trying to find you. Any reason you went missing after your wife's brutal beating death?"

Nick waited a beat, like Sasha had told him to do, before he answered.

"I can't really answer that."

"Because your lawyer told you not to?" Gilbert said, jerking a thumb toward Sasha without looking her direction.

"No, because I don't know when Clarissa was killed."

He looked at the detective with no expression.

Gilbert snapped his fingers. "Oh that's right. You and your wife were estranged, right? Now, when did she kick you out?"

Nick's nostrils flared. Sasha shook her head in warning. She didn't know how Gilbert had learned about Nick's recent marital troubles, but he had. Nick needed to stay cool.

He didn't.

"That's a damned lie!" Nick half-rose from the chair. "We weren't having problems, and she didn't throw me out."

"Oh, no? So Clarissa hadn't filed for divorce?"

Nick's anger deflated as quickly as it had bloomed, and he sank back into the chair.

He answered in a soft voice, "Okay, that's true, she did; but, as God is my witness, I don't know why. We hadn't been fighting or anything. All I know is I went to my social club last night—"

Gilbert cut him off. "What time was that?"

"I don't know. Maybe six-thirty or seven?"

"Go on," Gilbert said, nodding his approval of the time estimate.

"I went to the club—"

Gilbert cut in again. "Did you see your wife before you left your home?"

"Yes. She went upstairs to rest, and I yelled a goodbye up the stairs."

"Go on, please."

Sasha needed to cut in herself, just to break up the volleying.

"Nick, isn't it true that this is a standing date? You go to your social club every Wednesday evening, isn't that right?"

"That's right," Nick agreed. "I meet the guys for dinner and drinks. We play some cards and watch whatever game's on."

Gilbert was looking at Sasha out of the corner of his eyes. He was irritated, she felt sure, but unwilling to address her or even acknowledge that she'd spoken.

Good.

She added, "Did Clarissa have standing Wednesday night plans—that you know of?"

Nick considered the question.

"Not really. She usually did go out. Sometimes she went over to her folks' place; sometimes she met up with her girlfriends; sometimes she went shopping or whatever. For a while, she took a Wednesday night pottery class, but she missed too many of them. You know, work emergencies."

Gilbert spoke up. "So you went to your club. Anything unusual happen?"

Nick had been looking over Gilbert's shoulder at Sasha. Now he narrowed his eyes and met the detective's gaze.

"You obviously know that something unusual happened, Detective. Yeah, some asshole barged in and served me with divorce papers."

Sasha raised her hand level with her shoulder, palm toward the floor, and motioned for him to calm down.

He exhaled loudly and continued, "I'd never seen the guy before. He shoved the papers at me and then ... was escorted off the premises, I guess you could say. I tried to read the divorce papers, but I was kind of in shock."

Gilbert put on an understanding expression and nodded, "Of course you were, son."

Nick smiled, lapping up the feigned sympathy.

"Did you try to reach your wife then?"

"Of course. I called several times, but she didn't answer her cell phone or the home phone."

"And what time was this, roughly?"

Nick gave him the same answer he'd given Sasha. "It was the seventh inning or so of the baseball game, so maybe ten-thirty."

Gilbert nodded his head rapidly, like that was the right answer.

"Clarissa didn't answer. I guess you went home then? To try to talk to her, right?"

Nick flicked his eyes away from the detective and met Sasha's gaze. His temporary relief leaked away and he widened his eyes, asking what he should say.

Sasha looked at him, expressionless. He had to tell the truth. They'd been over this in the car: there were witnesses who had watched him get drunk. Their shared brotherhood in the Greek social club wasn't going to override the fact that a woman—a Greek woman whose father and brothers were also members of the club, no less—had been murdered.

He cleared his throat and returned his attention to Gilbert. "Uh, no. Actually, I didn't."

"You didn't?" Gilbert echoed, his surprise so exaggerated that Sasha could tell he wanted Nick to know he already knew the truth. "Well, what did you do then?"

Nick plowed ahead, as if saying the words faster would make it better. "I had some more to drink. I tried to call her a few more times, and she still didn't answer. Eventually, I did go home."

"Would you say you were inebriated when you left?"

"He's not an expert, Detective," Sasha interjected. "Mr. Costopolous can't know if he was over the legal limit."

Gilbert finally turned to look at her.

He raised an eyebrow and said, "I'm not looking to charge your client with a DUI, Ms. McCandless. I just want to know if, in his subjective opinion, he felt as though he were intoxicated. He's an expert on how he feels, isn't he?"

Nick waited for Sasha to give him permission to answer.

Sasha shrugged. "Go ahead and answer," she told him.

"Yeah, I guess I was probably drunk," Nick said.

"You probably were," Gilbert agreed. "As I understand it, you had no fewer than eight shots of ouzo after you received the divorce papers. Does that sound about right?"

Someone from the Greek club had talked.

"Maybe. I lost count," Nick mumbled.

"So, after drinking heavily for several hours, you went home to confront your wife."

Gilbert phrased it as a statement, not a question, but Nick answered it anyway.

"I didn't go home to confront her. I went home, because I live there and I was tired. I mean, sure, I figured we could talk about whatever was going on with her, but I didn't go home to pick a fight. I just went home."

"Did you?"

"Did I what?"

"Talk about why she filed for divorce?"

"No."

"And why's that?"

Nick dropped his eyes down to the desk and mumbled, "She'd had the locks changed while I was out. I couldn't get in."

"Now, I want to make sure I have this straight," Gilbert said, giving Nick a friendly grin. "You hadn't been having any marital problems, but you went out like you do every Wednesday night, and your wife proceeded to serve you with divorce papers and have the locks to your home rekeyed?"

"That's correct," Nick said, staring at the detective.

"Son, do those sound to you like the actions of a woman who is happy in her marriage?"

Nick didn't respond.

"Do they?" the detective pressed him.

"Of course not," Nick snapped. "I don't know why she did it. I have no idea."

"No idea, huh?" Gilbert said.

"None."

Gilbert's smile sharpened.

Sasha's pulse hammered. Gilbert was moving in for the kill. She didn't know what he had, but he had something. Judging by the ugliness in his smile, it was something big.

Nick looked back at Gilbert with wide, guileless eyes, unprepared for whatever hit was coming.

Gilbert reached inside his jacket and produced a set of photographs from his breast pocket. He tossed the top picture on the desk in front of Nick. Sasha couldn't see the image from where she sat, but Nick's expression told her it wasn't good. She hoped they weren't crime scene photos.

"Maybe she didn't like knowing you had a girl-friend?" Gilbert said in a casual tone.

Nick snatched the photograph and held it up to his face.

"It's not what it looks like," he said.

"It's not?" Gilbert asked. "What is it, then, Mr. Costopolous?   Because what it looks like is you kissing a very attractive, very young—possibly even underage—female."

Gilbert slapped the next photograph down.

"In addition, it looks, in this embrace, as though you've got one hand on her breast and one hand on her buttocks while you're kissing her."

Nick stared down at the photo and gulped for air like a fish.

Sasha gritted her teeth to keep from yelling at him. Clients and their lies. If Nick had simply told her about the girl, she could have prepared him for this line of questioning. Instead, he had insisted there was nothing to tell; now, there was little, if anything, she could do to help him.

Gilbert continued, almost gleeful now. "That photograph makes it seem like you and she had a sexual relationship, but this picture here, this one's my favorite. The way you're cupping the girl's face in your hands and staring soulfully into her eyes, it's very loving. Tender, even."

He tossed the last photo toward Nick and said, "In fact, knowing women, I'll bet that last one upset your wife more than the others. Especially given how emotional they become when they're pregnant."

Nick had been staring at the pictures as if he were in a trance. Once Gilbert's words registered, he jerked his head up, a look of anguish seared on his face.

"Clarissa was pregnant?"

Sasha's stomach sank. She forced herself not to rub her temples.

Unbelievable.

Nick began to sob.

"Mr. Costopolous needs to take a break," she said.

"Of course," Gilbert replied, not bothering to hide the triumph in his voice. "I'll give you a few moments of privacy."

He stood as though he were going to leave, and Sasha stood, too.

"We'd like some actual privacy, Detective Gilbert. Not to sit in this room and have our conversation recorded while you and your colleagues watch," she said with a nod toward the observation mirror. "We're going to take a walk outside, so Mr. Costopolous can get some fresh air."

Gilbert folded his arms across his chest, and she could see his muscles tensing even through his strained jacket sleeves. He was silent for a moment.

"Mr. Costopolous is not in custody, correct?" Sasha pressed him.

"Not yet," Gilbert conceded.

"We'll be back in five minutes," she said, as she started toward the door and gestured for Nick to follow her.

"Take the pictures," Gilbert offered. "I have copies."

She scooped them up from the desk and strode out the door. Nick stumbled along behind her.

~ ~ ~ ~ ~

Sasha turned on Nick as soon as the thick glass door shut behind them and they stepped out into the dark night.

"What's wrong with you? I asked you if there was anything I needed to know. Why didn't you tell me?" she demanded

He blinked at her through his tears.

She couldn't afford to feel sympathy for him now. Not if she was going extricate him from the trap he'd just walked into.

"I ... I didn't know she was pregnant," he said.

Sasha pulled him away from the building. They stood under a tall spotlight that illuminated the first several rows of the parking lot in a pool of yellow light.

"But you knew you were cheating on her," Sasha said, trying not to yell.

Nick shook his head, rejecting the words.

"I wasn't."

Sasha pushed the pictures in her hands toward him.

"What then, Nick? You were walking down the street and tripped? You stumbled into this girl and your tongue landed in her mouth?"

"It wasn't how it looks," he insisted, pouting.

"How was it, Nick? You need to start talking. Fast."

"Okay, a couple weeks ago, maybe a month, I don't know, this girl wandered into the club. I told you sometimes people come in looking for a bar or whatever, right?"

"Yes."

She forced her anger back and focused on his story, searching for some sliver of evidence she could use to save him.

"So she came in, real timid and shy, and looked around. She was trying to find My Sister's Place."

"What's that," Sasha asked, "a bar?"

He shook his head. "I'd never heard of it. She said it was a battered women's shelter."

"Wait. Was she speaking to you directly or just to the room in general?"

Nick thought.

"She scanned the place, nervous, when she came in. I smiled at her, you know, to put her at ease."

And to flirt with her, Sasha thought.

"Go on," she said.

"I guess she thought she could trust me or something, because she came straight over to me."

"Okay, she came over to you and asked if you knew where this shelter was?"

"Right. She said her boyfriend had a bad temper and had beaten her up pretty good. She was leaving him."

Sasha rolled her eyes. "Go on."

"Well, she was pretty scared. Jumpy like. So I told her I'd buy her a drink and then help her find the place."

"Just being chivalrous?"

"Yes. I wasn't putting the moves on her, I swear."

Sasha held up the photograph again.

"Just listen. I got her a glass of wine."

"I don't suppose anyone checked her identification?"

"No, it's a private club. I'm telling you, she wasn't a teenager. She was in her early twenties; I could just tell."

"Her age is the least of your problems right now."

He continued, "So we had a drink; she was pretty quiet. She didn't talk much. She was kind of in a hurry to find that shelter. So we left."

"You left with her, but you had no intention of getting together with her, right?" Sasha asked.

"I swear I didn't."

Sasha looked at the picture. The girl was beautiful in a California girl way. She was tall and athletic, with straight, long blond hair. A pert nose and huge blue eyes. She was right out of central casting. And a stark contrast to Clarissa Costopolous, who was a short, curvy olive-skinned woman, with curly black hair and a classically Greek nose.

"But she's an attractive girl, wouldn't you say?"

"Yeah, she's pretty hot," he admitted.

"So what happened?"

"The address she had was about two blocks away. I put a hand on her back while we walked, just because she was shaking like a leaf. Sasha, the girl was terrified her boyfriend was going to find her."

Sasha raised a brow but said nothing.

"When we got to the address, I asked if she was sure it was the right place. It looked like just a regular townhouse. She said that was it. There was no sign or anything, because it was a secret place."

"Sure."

Nick continued, "She kept thanking me. She asked if she could give me a hug. She said I might have saved her life."

Even now, Sasha could see him puff up at the notion of his nobility. She resisted the urge to shake him by the collar.

"She hugged you," Sasha prompted.

"Right and then she kissed me. I wasn't expecting it. It was so sudden. And she put my hands on her ... you know, like in the second picture."

Nick was staring out into the darkness now, not meeting her eyes.

"Are you telling me you resisted her, Nick?"

He didn't answer.

"Nick? We don't have time for this."

"Okay, maybe not at first. I was just, you know, stunned. I might have kissed her back, I guess."

"You guess."

"Yes, I kissed her. But then, I realized what I was doing. I couldn't do that to Clarissa again. That was when I took her face in my hands. I told her, as gently as I could, that I was married. That's all."

"What do mean, you couldn't do that to Clarissa *again*?"

Nick waved the question away. "Nothing. It doesn't matter. It was a long time ago."

Sasha stared at him until he started talking again.

"Fine. I cheated on Clarissa before we were married. Like I said, a long time ago."

"How long?"

Nick thought. "I guess she was in law school, or maybe it was her first year working at Prescott."

"Who was she?"

"Just a girl I knew."

"A Greek girl?"

Nick shook his head. "No. In fact, when Clarissa found out, she called her Malibu Barbie. Come to think of it, she kind of looked like this girl," he said, nodding toward the picture.

Sasha stared at him.

"What?" he asked.

"It was a honey trap," she said.

"A what?"

"Nevermind," Sasha said. "This first girl, Malibu Barbie, how'd Clarissa find out?"

"Her name was Kristy. She called Clarissa and told her. She wanted to break us up."

"What happened?"

Even in the shadows, Sasha could see a blush stain Nick's cheeks.

"Clarissa was devastated. I thought she was going to leave me. Ellen and Martine sure tried to get her to. But we worked it out. It made me realize how much I loved her. I didn't want to lose her. I broke things off with Kristy, and I swore to Clarissa that I'd never cheat on her again." He held Sasha's gaze for a long time. "And, I didn't. I wouldn't. I'll be the first to admit I have a wandering eye. And, yeah, maybe I flirt sometimes, but I have never broken my marriage vows."

"Well, until a month ago," Sasha reminded him.

He clenched his jaw. "Okay, fine."

It was time to move on before Gilbert came looking for them.

"So you were out on the street when this woman threw herself at you?"

"Right."

"I assume you didn't notice anyone with a camera?" Sasha asked.

Nick shook his head.

"Did this girl have a name?"

"She didn't tell me, and I didn't ask. She was going into hiding, remember?"

"Right. And you watched her go into this townhouse?"

"No."

"No?"

Nick shrugged and explained, "She said she felt safer already, she was going to sit on the porch and pull herself together before she went in."

"So you just left this allegedly terrified, impossibly hot woman sitting there?"

He shoved his hands into his pockets. "Look, I got her there. And it was kind of awkward. I had just rejected her. I wished her luck and headed back to the club."

"Did you see her go in? Or even go on the porch?"

"No, I didn't look back," Nick said.

Some white knight he was.

"I don't suppose you remember the address?"

"Of course, I do."

Sasha stared at her client. "You do? You're sure?"

"Yeah. I'm sure. I recognized the street name because I'd done some work around the corner about a year ago for a couple who wanted custom kitchen cabinets. The townhouse we went to was two in from the corner."

Sasha suppressed the hope that fluttered in her chest.

"Let's go. You can try to sell this to Gilbert."

Nick put out a hand to stop her.

"But you believe me, right?"

His warm brown eyes searched her face.

She sighed. "Actually, I do."

Apparently, she had not one, but two, gullible clients who'd been set up by an unknown photographer who knew their character weaknesses.

The trick would be to convince Gilbert.

34.

ETECTIVE GILBERT WAS NOT CON-
VINCED.

He threw back his head and laughed.
"So, let me get this straight, you weren't cheating
on your wife. You were just a good Samaritan
caught in a compromising position."

"That's right," Nick said, earnest and wide-eyed.

"And," Gilbert went on, "there just happened to
be a photographer handy to capture this mislead-
ing kiss."

Nick turned to Sasha, a silent plea for help.

They were back in the stuffy square of a room,
the three of them squeezed around the desk, shoulder to shoulder, looking down at the pictures,
which Nick had spread out like a fan.

"Don't you find it odd that there's photographic evidence of this ... encounter?" Sasha asked the detective. "Doubly so, considering that similar photos exist of the accused husband in another recent death of a Prescott & Talbott attorney?"

She hoped that by easing Greg Lang into the conversation, she could get Gilbert to consider the possibility that the two husbands had been framed without having to say it directly. If she suggested they'd been framed, she knew he would reject the notion outright. If he thought he'd come to it on his own, however, maybe they had a chance.

Gilbert was unimpressed. "Not really. I'd say it's likely that two women, who happened to be colleagues and close friends, both had their suspicions about their husbands. Either together or separately, they decided to have their husbands followed by a private investigator or, perhaps, the ladies followed them themselves. It happens quite a bit." He shrugged off the coincidence.

The way he put it, it sounded plausible, even likely, that the dead women had done just that.

"But Ellen Mortenson said she received the photographs anonymously in the mail," she countered.

Gilbert fixed her with a look. "First of all, we're not here about Mr. Lang—this is about Mr. Costopolous. Although I did investigate Ms. Mortenson's death, that was a separate homicide investigation. The Department sees no reason to link the two deaths simply because the two victims worked together. Second of all, as far as I know, the only support for the claim that Ms. Mortenson received photographs of her husband at the gaming tables in the mail from an anonymous sender is Mr. Lang's say-so. No offense, but I'm not going to take his word for it. Are you representing Lang, too?" he finished, his voice quizzical.

Sasha ignored the question. "At least check out Mr. Costopolous's story. He remembers the address. Go to the townhouse and see if it is, in fact, a shelter. See if anyone there remembers a woman matching this girl's description."

She picked up the middle photograph, the one with the best angle of the girl, and waved it at him. She'd kept her tone neutral, although she wanted to plead with him. If he didn't bite, her next move was going to have to be to use Greg to alibi Nick.

Gilbert looked at her for a long moment. Then he shrugged.

"Sure. I'll send a uniform out to run this down. You and Mr. Costopolous make yourselves comfortable."

He gathered the photographs into a pile and tapped the bottoms on the table to square them, then left the room.

Nick considered the metal chair. Then he walked over to the wall and slid down it to sit on the floor.

"Why didn't you tell him I was with Greg?" he asked, hugging his arms around his knees.

Sasha frowned and jerked her head toward the observation window to remind him they weren't actually alone. Their conversation was almost certainly being recorded.

She was glad for an excuse not to answer him, though. She still hadn't decided whether it was worth the risk to Greg to use him to alibi Nick, given how little weight that alibi would carry with Gilbert. Nick, understandably, would want her to use everything in her arsenal. Her stomach lurched as she considered the ethics.

Nick twisted his mouth into a knot.

"Trust me, okay?" She patted his arm and then checked her phone.

It was nearly eleven o'clock. This was not how she had envisioned spending her night.

She thumbed out a text to Connelly: *Am running late. Not sure when I will be home. Sorry. Love, S.*

Then she played Will's voicemail. As expected, Cinco had agreed to post Nick's bail if he was, in fact, arraigned, which she had to admit seemed likely.

She figured the news would cheer her client, so she powered off her phone and said, "Prescott & Talbott will cover your bail if it becomes necessary, the same as they did for Greg."

Nick raised his dark eyes. They were filled with anger, not the gratitude she'd expected to see.

"I would hope so. It's the least they could do."

Sasha considered this statement. She recalled the crushing hours, missed vacations, and broken plans that had littered her years at the firm.

"Nick, were Clarissa's hours causing a problem between you two?" she asked in a soft voice.

"Not like you think," he said. "The stress was preventing us from conceiving." His face drained to white as he realized they had, in fact, conceived.

He swallowed hard and continued, "I mean, it had been. We'd been trying for a while. Finally, we saw a fertility doctor. She told Clarissa her body wasn't going to allow her to get pregnant while she was working eighty-hour weeks and not taking care of herself. I tried to get her to go to part-time status, but she refused. I finally convinced her to at least take a vacation. We went to Greece in July to visit the fishing village where our parents were born. We snorkeled, met about a million distant relatives, ate too much, and kicked back in the sun." Nick smiled at the memory, but the smile faded into a frown.

"What happened?" Sasha asked.

"John Porter called. We had scheduled the trip for two weeks, but ten days in, he called and asked her to come back. He had some big filing that couldn't wait four flipping days and he claimed no one else could possibly handle it in her absence. I told her to tell him to go pound sand, but, of course, she changed her flight and rushed back," Nick said in a clipped voice.

"But you stayed?"

That wasn't a great fact if they were going to paint a picture of harmony in the Costopolous home.

He gave her a sheepish look. "I did. I'll admit I was angry. Hurt, I guess. But when I got home, she sat me down and apologized. She said she realized it was shortsighted. She said ..." His voice broke, but he went on, "She said having a baby with me was more important. She promised to cut back some, just as soon as the fiscal year ended in August. Her plan was to get pregnant and have the baby next year. And, she did cut back ... a little. Enough, I guess."

He hung his head. When he looked up his eyes were wet. "Someone killed my wife. And our baby. You have to make them understand it wasn't me."

~ ~ ~ ~ ~

Just before midnight, the steel door banged open and hit the wall near the desk.

The air in the small room was suddenly charged. Sasha looked up from checking her e-mail messages on her phone to see Gilbert stride into the room, followed by a baby-faced uniformed officer. She rose from the cheap plastic chair, her legs stiff and slow to unfold.

Nick, who'd been sleeping fitfully on the floor under the observation window, bolted to his feet and looked around, confused.

Gilbert ignored Sasha and headed straight for Nick, stopping when he was about a foot away from him, and pulled a laminated card from his pocket. He nodded toward the uniformed officer, who circled around and stood behind Nick, with a pair of handcuffs dangling loosely in his hand.

"Nicholas Costopolous," Gilbert intoned, "you are under arrest for the murder of Clarissa Costopolous and Unborn Child Costopolous."

Nick wheeled around to look at Sasha; as he did so, the officer behind him clasped the bracelets around his wrists. Nick opened his mouth to protest.

Sasha put up her hand like a crossing guard to silence him. As she raced to his side, she said, "Nothing. Say *nothing*, Nick."

He clamped his mouth shut and nodded.

Gilbert extended his arm straight and held out the card, squinting at the tiny printed Miranda warning, which he surely had memorized at this point in his career. "You have the right to remain silent. Anything you say can and will be used against you in a court of law. You have the right to speak to an attorney, and to have an attorney present during any questioning. If you cannot afford a lawyer, one will be provided for you at government expense. Do you understand these rights?"

Nick looked at Sasha, then turned back to Gilbert. "Yes."

Sasha asked, "What about the townhouse?"

Gilbert returned his card to his pocket and said, "Dead end. The address your client gave us is a residence. An elderly husband and wife, Polish immigrants, live there. Despite their minimal English skills, the Milchecks made it clear that they'd never seen the girl and had never heard of the shelter. Officer Dickinson over there showed them a photograph of Mr. Costopolous, as well, and they didn't recognize him."

The officer nodded his agreement with this recitation.

Nick was wild-eyed. "That's impossible! She said she was going to My Sister's Place."

"Stop talking," Sasha said. She allowed a sharp edge to creep into her voice so Nick would understand she was serious.

"Here's an interesting fact about My Sister's Place," Gilbert went on. "There is an organization with that name, but it's not a women's shelter on the South Side. It's a group that provides housing and other services for single-parent families in the Mon Valley."

Sasha looked at Nick for a moment. He just raised his shoulders, confused.

She turned back to Gilbert. "So Mr. Costopolous was hoodwinked by some girl. That doesn't really seem to merit an arrest."

Gilbert gave her a tired smile. "Nice try. The assistant district attorney on call okayed a warrantless arrest. As I'm sure you know, we can hold Mr. Costopolous for up to twenty-four hours before we arraign him."

Sasha squared her shoulders and summoned her sense of outrage, but Gilbert held up a hand to stop her, just as she'd stopped Nick.

"We're not going to do that, okay?" he said before she could jump in. "Someone in the DA's office will write up the complaint in the morning and get your client in for his arraignment before lunchtime. I gave them your number and told them to call you and let you know what time. As a courtesy."

"Oh. Well, thank you," she said. "We can go then?"

Gilbert looked at her for a full thirty seconds before he spoke. When he did, his voice was almost gentle.

"Your client's going to lockup at the Allegheny County Jail, Counselor."

Nick's face stretched into a mask of fear and despair. Sasha had to look away.

Gilbert continued, "Mr. Costopolous will be processed and then placed in the custody of the sheriff at the jail. You should go to his place, get a change of clothes for him to wear for his arraignment, and then get some sleep."

She shook her head. "I can't get into his house. Clarissa changed the locks, remember?"

The detective nodded, a slow movement that revealed his fatigue. "That's right; I forgot. Officer Dickinson, I'll handle Mr. Costopolous's intake myself. You escort Ms. McCandless to the residence. Let her get her client a change of clothes."

"Yes, sir," the officer said.

Gilbert turned to Nick, "You take any medications? Wear glasses or contacts? Anything like that?"

Nick shook his head.

"What about a toothbrush? Toiletries?" Sasha asked.

"The taxpayers will provide those to Mr. Costopolous free of charge," Gilbert told her, slipping back into his jaded cop routine.

Sasha patted Nick on the arm. "I'll see you as soon as I can. Just remember, no talking to anybody. That includes your fellow ... inmates." She stumbled over the word.

Nick swallowed hard but nodded.

Officer Dickinson walked around to hold the door open, and she followed Gilbert and Nick out into the hall.

35.

Friday

SASHA STIFLED A YAWN AND checked the time. Three-thirty in the morning. She stretched; her back was tight, and the cold night air caused the muscles along her spine to cramp.

She wondered how much longer this could possibly take as she stood on Greg Lang's front porch and watched Officer Dickinson crawl around in the cab of Nick's truck.

And she'd been so close to making it home, she thought, as the door swung open and Greg stepped out onto the porch with fresh mugs of coffee for each of them.

"Here you go," he said, handing her the blasted *I Got Lei-ed* mug.

She wrapped her hands around it to suck up its warmth and took a long, greedy sip.

"Ah, thanks."

He nodded and raised his own mug to his lips, his eyes locked on Dickinson.

She'd been walking down the steep steps outside the Costopolous's house under Dickinson's watchful eye, when his radio had buzzed to life. She was taking her time because she didn't have a free hand; she had a suit, dress shirt and tie on a hanger in one hand and was carrying a reusable Trader Joe's grocery bag stuffed with Nick's dress shoes and clean boxers, socks, and a t-shirt in the other.

"Dickinson, are you still with Ms. McCandless?" Gilbert's voice had crackled over the air.

"Yes, sir," he'd said. "But we're wrapping up here. She's got a change of clothes and a pair of shoes in a cloth bag."

Sasha had been calculating how long it would take her to drive home and crawl into bed beside Connelly for a few short hours before the dawn broke and he headed to the airport, when she'd

heard Gilbert directing Officer Dickinson to proceed to a familiar address.

She'd turned her head and asked, "Why are you
going to Greg Lang's house?"

Dickinson had held up a hand to shush her
while Gilbert had continued, "Search Mr.
Costopolous's vehicle. He informs me he's been
staying with Mr. Lang. Search the guest room, too."

Two separate thoughts had taken off along par-
allel tracks in Sasha's brain, like racing trains. One
was that she was going to strangle Nick when she
saw him. What exactly did he think "Don't say anything" meant? Talk to Gilbert like he's your best
friend? The other train zipped through the recesses of her memory, pulling up every case she'd
briefed in Criminal Law as a first-year law student
twelve years earlier.

She had to decide whether to object to the
search of Nick's vehicle in Greg's garage. Greg had
a reasonable expectation of privacy in his garage
and its contents. The question was whether his
houseguest did. Remembering a case involving a
stack of boxes stored in a friend's garage, she decided she had a strong argument that Nick did have
such a privacy expectation, which would mean the
truck was off-limits.

"Detective," she'd said, before realizing that Gilbert couldn't hear her.

She'd slung the bag over her shoulder and gestured for Dickinson to depress the button so Gilbert could hear her.

"Detective," she'd begun again, "as Mr. Costopolous's counsel, I'm afraid I can't allow you to search his vehicle. Unless, of course, you've obtained a probable cause warrant, in which case, I'd like to see a copy."

Dickinson had rolled his eyes and thumbed off the radio so Gilbert could respond.

"Counselor," Gilbert had said, making no effort to hide the laughter in his voice, "your client volunteered the information that his vehicle was in the Lang garage and offered to let us search both it and the room he used at the Lang residence."

Sasha had gritted her teeth and said, "Press the radio call button, please."

Her frustration with Nick and Gilbert had been compounded by the logistics of conversation over a radio through an intermediary.

Before Dickinson could comply, however, Gilbert had rumbled on, "And don't bother chewing me out for questioning your client, Ms. McCandless. I repeatedly reminded him that he invoked his right to counsel and that you instructed him not to talk."

Gilbert had paused. Dickinson had shrugged and pressed the button, aiming the radio toward Sasha.

"What?" she'd demanded.

He'd clicked off.

"Oh, I just wanted to stop and give you a chance to thank me for looking out for your client. You're welcome, in any event. So, as I was saying, Mr. Costopolous, or Nick, as he asked me to call him, had a great deal to say. Fear will do that to people. And, I have to admit, he's a pretty-looking man. He has plenty to be afraid of at lockup."

Sasha had shaken her head at the way Gilbert was manipulating Nick by suggesting he was going to be raped.

"Is he there with you now?" she had asked, hoping to talk to Nick and get him to pull himself together before he was transported to the jail.

"Nope. He's off being fitted for his bright orange prom gown."

Sasha had closed her eyes and breathed through her nose. If Dickinson hadn't been standing there, she'd have gone into Tree Pose right there on the Costopolous's front steps. Instead, she just focused on inhaling and exhaling until she trusted herself to speak without shouting.

"No one touches the car until I arrive at the Lang residence. Are we clear?"

"Suit yourself," Gilbert had shot back through the radio. "If I had to be in court in the morning, I'd go home and get some shut-eye, but you're an adult. Do what you want. Dickinson can give you a ride, if you like."

"No thanks."

Sasha had felt foolish doing it, but she'd raced down the steps and sprinted to her car. She'd thrown the bag and the suit on the passenger seat and had fumbled with her Bluetooth. She'd decided to beat Dickinson to the house, so she'd at least have a chance to manage the scene.

As she'd started the ignition, she'd used her phone's voice-dialing function to call Greg before Dickinson had even reached his squad car. She'd pulled out and driven cautiously until she'd turned at the corner. Once she was out of Dickinson's sight, she'd gunned it.

Arriving a full three minutes before Dickinson, she'd prepared Greg to put up a fight. When the officer informed Greg he had Nick's permission to search his truck, Greg had refused to let the police officer into his garage. Instead, he had pulled the truck out and parked it in the driveway.

Officer Dickinson had hesitated, disappeared into his car, and reemerged, presumably after consulting with Gilbert. He'd shown no surprise when Sasha had further informed him that he was not welcome to search Nick's guest room and that Nick lacked standing to consent to such a search over the homeowner's objection. He'd merely shrugged and started combing through the pickup truck.

So now she and a keyed-up Greg stood ramrod straight on the porch and watched Dickinson inspect every square inch of cab of Nick's pickup.

"What is he looking for, I wonder?" Greg asked in a low voice, his eyes on Dickinson's boots, which were sticking out of the cab as he leaned across the steering wheel and dusted the dashboard.

"I have no idea. Blood?"

"Wouldn't they call a CSI unit out to do that kind of forensics work?"

Sasha didn't know and almost asked him who processed Ellen's crime scene, but she stopped herself.

"I suppose. Gilbert's probably just doing this to ensure I'm exhausted at Nick's preliminary arraignment tomorrow," she told him in an effort to change the subject.

As she said it, she realized it was more than likely true: the authorities were no different from any large law firm that used its almost limitless resources to bury some harassed, overextended sole practitioner in paper and motions practice. It seemed to her that anyone with sufficient weight had a corresponding, almost irresistible, urge to throw that weight around.

And that was fine by her. As someone light on weight, she'd honed her skills at using her opponent's weight against him. She figured it would work as well against Detective Gilbert and his friends at the district attorney's office as it had against everyone else she'd gone toe-to-toe with in the courtroom, in the sparring studio, or on the street.

She allowed herself a small smile.

Finally satisfied with his search of the interior of the car, Officer Dickinson backed himself out of cab, pushing with his elbows, and jumped to the ground. Then he closed the door with a gloved hand, walked around to the back, and, one-handed, vaulted into the bed of the truck.

His clear blue eyes met Sasha's and she realized he was showing off for her benefit. She filed that knowledge away for potential future use and drained her coffee.

She turned to Greg, intending to excuse herself so she could call Connelly. She hated to wake him, but, at Dickinson's current pace, he'd be gone by the time she made it home. Greg spoke first.

"I have to tell you something."

The way he said it left no question that whatever Greg wanted to say, it wasn't something she was going to enjoy hearing. Sasha felt herself droop, deflated.

"I'm listening."

"I haven't been completely honest with you," Greg said, staring into his coffee mug.

Greg's bombshell was hardly news, she thought. His timing, however, stunk. She waited for him to continue.

"I, well, I lied when I said I was just out walking around the night Ellen was killed."

He winced and raised his eyes to meet her gaze.

She nodded. "I assumed as much, Greg. Are you ready to tell me where you were?"

"Yes. I was with Nick."

Sasha didn't know what she'd expected him to say, but it wasn't that *his* alibi for his wife's murder was the same man for whom *he* was providing an alibi. She bit down hard on her lip and kept her face neutral.

"Nick Costopolous?" she asked, holding out hope that it was some other Nick.

"Yes. His social club has a weekly poker game, a big money game. The buy-in's five grand."

"Where'd you get five thousand dollars, Greg?"

He was silent.

"Greg?"

"I borrowed it from the safe in Ellen's home office," he finally mumbled.

"You stole it, you mean," Sasha said.

"Well, she didn't move the key. She knew I could access it …" he started, but trailed off in the face of Sasha's glare. "Fine, I took it without permission. I wasn't thinking clearly. I'd lost my job, I'd lost my wife. I didn't know how much longer Ellen was going to agree to let me stay at the house. And, Nick said it was a soft game. I figured I could make enough to get a place of my own. I planned to return Ellen's money to the safe. She would never have to know."

What a blazingly stupid plan, Sasha thought.

What she said was, "But you lost, didn't you?"

He nodded, a miserable, slow nod. "I did. And then I realized what a terrible thing I'd done and that Ellen was right, I do have a gambling problem."

He swallowed, a big lump visible in his throat, and sped up, with the words spilling out fast and jumbled.

"I knocked on her door when I got home to tell her she was right and that I was going to go back to Gamblers Anonymous. And to tell her about the money. I planned to come clean to her and beg her for another chance. Instead, I … found her."

Sasha really hoped he wouldn't cry. She didn't think she had it in her to comfort him.

"Why would you keep this a secret, Greg? It gives you an alibi."

"Two reasons. First, how would it look? I stole five grand from my estranged wife the same night she was murdered in our home? Come on, they'd just say we'd argued over the money when I got home and I'd killed her then."

She had to agree that was a distinct possibility. "Okay. What's the second reason?"

"I didn't want to involve Nick. Ellen and Clarissa were close friends. I knew if Clarissa heard about Nick taking me to a poker game it would cause huge problems for Nick."

"Do you think she did hear?"

Greg's alibi could be problematic for Nick if it gave him a motive to kill his wife. The Greg and Nick Show was growing tiresome.

Greg shook his head. "No. None of her relatives were at the game."

"This is great, though," Sasha said, suddenly energized. "We don't need Nick. The other players can alibi you."

Greg made a face.

"What?"

"Maybe. I mean, I didn't use my real name. Nick introduced me as Paul; he said I was an electrician he sometimes worked with. I was wearing a hat and sunglasses. It was dark in there. Yeah, maybe," he shrugged.

"You wore a disguise?"

"No, no, that's just my card-playing persona. You know, so no one can see my eyes."

"Why the alias?"

"That was Nick's idea. He doesn't play in that game; he says it's too rich for his blood, so he's not real tight with that group. But he wanted to make sure it didn't get back to Clarissa's father or any of her brothers that he'd brought me. I know it sounds stupid now. I know."

"Actually, Greg, it sounds unbelievable. As in, not credible," she said.

"It's the truth," he insisted.

"That doesn't really matter; it sounds like a lie."

He clenched his jaw and was about to respond when Dickinson raised his arm and waved.

"Ms. McCandless," he called, "I'm about to open Mr. Costopolous's toolbox. I'd like you to witness this, ma'am."

"Why's he want you to watch?" Greg asked, as he followed Sasha down the stairs and across the flagstone path to the driveway.

"Apparently, Officer Dickinson is smarter than he seems. He wants to head off any claim that he tampered with the contents by having me watch him open it."

They circled around to the pickup's truck bed, and Dickinson lowered the gate and hopped down. He reached forward into the truck and pulled a long, steel box toward the edge of the gate; then he hefted it and lowered it to the ground slowly.

"Heavy," he breathed.

He and Sasha crouched in the driveway, one on each side of the double-latched toolbox. Greg stood back.

Sasha could make out the contours of the box in the light cast by the recessed porch lights and the two lanterns mounted on the sides of the garage bays, but Dickinson switched on his heavy flashlight and aimed the beam onto the box.

"Wanna do the honors?" he asked.

She flipped open the latches and pulled back the lid. The top tray was divided into several small compartments that held nails, screws, bolts, screwdrivers, and a pair of wire cutters.

Dickinson reached over and removed the top tray. He shined the light down into the bottom of the box to reveal a level, a carpenter's square, and some stubby pencils. No hammer. Just an empty hammer-sized slot.

He looked up at her. Even in the shadows, his triumph was plain.

Sasha's stomach turned and she inhaled sharply.

Beside her, Greg whispered, "What's wrong?"

Sasha shook her head, but it was Dickinson who answered.

"It appears your pal, the master carpenter, doesn't have a hammer," he said, grinning up at them.

Sasha forced herself not to respond. Greg reared his head back, stunned.

Dickinson replaced the tray, and was closing the lid when Sasha put a hand on his forearm to stop him.

"What's that?" she said, leaning in to get a closer look at a square taped to the inside of the lid.

Dickinson bathed it in light.

It was a photograph of Clarissa, taken on her wedding day, judging by the veil that brushed her bare shoulders and the joy that filled her smile.

36.

CAROLINE ROLLED ONTO HER LEFT side and stared at the luminescent numbers on the alarm clock: 4:20. She sighed and flopped back to her right.

She closed her eyes again. It was no use. She glanced over at Ken. He breathed evenly and deeply—fully asleep. Careful not to disturb him, she eased herself from the bed and slipped her feet into the slippers lined up waiting for her. She picked up her soft cotton robe from the chair. Cinching it tight against the night chill, she tiptoed out of the bedroom and down the stairs, careful to avoid the squeaky board on the fourth step from the top.

She walked through dark rooms, confident in every step, with no need to turn on a light. When she reached the mudroom, she opened a drawer beside the utility sink and felt around until she located the slim orange flashlight. She flicked the switch forward with her thumb to test the light. Its beam was weak but adequate for the task.

She plucked her car keys from the pegboard hanging by the door and stepped out into the night, picking her way across the wet grass. The shortest path to the car was to cut across the lawn.

The flashlight illuminated about a foot of ground ahead. She kept her head down, looking for rocks or divots. The last thing she needed was to twist an ankle and have to explain to Ken why she was skulking around the backyard in her bathrobe in the middle of the night.

She hurried to the car and fumbled with the valet key, unwilling to press the electronic opener for fear that the beep would echo through the still night.

She reached into the passenger side and groped around under the seat to retrieve the files. After she'd locked the car door and closed it silently, she raced back to the house, suddenly feeling menaced by the darkness and the quiet.

Caroline pulled the door shut behind and engaged the lock. She hugged the files close to her chest and leaned against the door, the glass in its window cold against her back, and caught her breath.

Once her pulse slowed, she lowered the files and walked into the family room, where Ken had left a log in the fireplace, ready to burn if she'd joined him on the couch after dinner. But she hadn't, so the fire had gone unlit.

She picked up the box of long wooden matches from the hearth and waited until her hands were steady to strike the match. She sat and watched the fire spark to life, waiting for it to grow, with the pile of documents resting in her lap.

37.

ASHA CREPT INTO HER CONDO and eased the door shut with a soft click. She stepped out of her four-inch heels and padded up the stairs to the bedroom soundlessly.

Although part of her wished Connelly would hear her and wake up, she realized four-thirty in the morning was the very definition of an uncivilized hour, so she endeavored to make no noise.

She tiptoed through her darkened bedroom and into the bathroom. After closing the door, she patted the wall until she felt the light switch and turned it on. Harsh light flooded the bathroom, and she blinked.

She'd nearly finished brushing her teeth before her exhausted brain processed the fact that her

toothbrush had been the only one in the toothbrush holder. She pivoted to check the shower:
Connelly's shampoo and body wash were gone,
too. At that point, she knew, but she rolled open
the top vanity drawer, anyway: no razor, no shaving
cream. She let the drawer slam shut with a bang.

In the bedroom, her pulse twitching in her
throat, she flicked the wall switch and bathed the
empty room in light. No Connelly; no note; no sign
that he'd spent the better part of a year sharing her
bed.

She raced down the stairs and tore through the
kitchen, banging open drawers and cabinets. His
rice cooker, slow cooker, and mandolin were all
gone. The ramekins he used when he made mini-
soufflés for her birthday dinner—also gone.

She grabbed her phone from her bag and
punched the speed dial. Connelly answered on the
second ring, no sleep in his voice.

"Hello, Sasha."

"Hello yourself. Where are you?"

"When it became apparent you weren't coming
home, I decided to sleep at my place."

His place. His place was here, in her bed, not in
an antiseptic, long-term corporate rental apartment
in a business park near the airport.

"Why are you doing this?" she asked.

"What am I doing? I'm not the one who ran out on our last dinner. I'm not the one who's too emotionally stunted to discuss our relationship."

His words stung, but his tone was even.

"Emotionally stunted?" she repeated.

He sighed. "I don't want to get into this with you. Not like this. Not now. I need to be on a plane in less than three hours."

"You can't make an accusation like that and then shut down the conversation, Connelly. And, you aren't being fair. You're acting like I chose not to spend tonight with you."

"You did."

"We've been over this: I have responsibilities to my clients," Sasha bit off each word, trying to quell her frustration.

"Yes, you do. And to me. And to your family. But for some reason, your personal relationships are always expected to give in favor of your work. Why do you think that is?"

"Because the law is a jealous mistress. It's a saying for a reason, Connelly. It's part of the deal—"

He cut her off. "No, it's a convenient excuse. You hide behind your work to keep people at a distance. You keep *me* at a distance."

The adrenaline that had flooded her when she'd realized he'd left drained away, and her exhaustion returned.

"Are you saying this is it? Eight hours ago you were asking me to uproot my life for you and now it's over?"

She walked over to the window and pressed her forehead against the glass, looking down at the street below, while she waited for his answer.

"No. What I'm saying is, I'm moving. You're welcome to join me, but I'm not going to ask you again. When you're ready to talk about it, you know how to find me."

"This is an ultimatum, then?"

"No, Sasha, a decision. I've made mine; you need to make yours," he said in a gentle voice.

She just wanted to go to sleep.

"Can we table this discussion until next week, when you're back in town?"

"I'm not coming back."

"Of course you are. You can't just quit the Department of Homeland Security without giving notice. Now you're just overreacting."

"Listen, I wasn't going to tell you this—and I don't want you to jump to any conclusions—but my early retirement wasn't entirely by choice. I've been tagged as someone who is not a team player," he said in a raw, hurt voice.

"That's insane! Of course you're a team player! You're a top-notch investigator. You were instrumental in preventing Vivian and Irwin from crashing a second plane. And if you hadn't helped me in Clear Brook County ..." she trailed off, her stomach sinking. "They've asked you to leave because of me, haven't they? It's because you helped me."

"This is why I didn't want to tell you. It's not that simple, but, suffice it to say, my judgment has been called into question." He coughed out a bitter laugh. "And, considering your reaction to my gift tonight, I'd say my judgment *is* pretty questionable."

The ring. It had completely slipped her mind amidst all the criminal drama that had occupied her night.

She struggled for the right words and finally gave up, saying simply, "I'm sorry."

"I know."

"I love you."

"I know that, too. And I love you, Sasha, but I'm tired. I need to catch a nap."

"Okay. Well, goodbye then."

"Goodbye. And Sasha?"

"Yeah?"

"I left you some simple recipes. They're within your ability. Please feed yourself."

She smiled despite herself.

"Goodnight, Connelly. Safe travels."

She depressed the button, ending the call, and stared at the phone in her hand for a long moment. Then, she stumbled around her kitchen on autopilot, setting up coffee, charging her Blackberry, making preparations for a morning that was going to come all too soon.

She made her way back to the bedroom and collapsed face-down on top of her bedspread, still fully clothed. She was asleep within a minute.

~ ~ ~ ~ ~

Not quite two and a half hours later, she started awake, her heart hammering in her chest, convinced she'd overslept. She sprang up, pushed the hair out of her face, and blinked at the clock on her bedside table.

It wasn't yet seven o'clock.

She sighed in relief and stretched. Her arms and legs were sore, tight with tension and tiredness. Her head was thick, clouded with fatigue and sadness.

Coffee. A hot shower. More coffee.

She'd feel better, and maybe the heaviness in her chest would vanish in the steam.

38.

CAROLINE FOCUSED HARD ON MR. Prescott's billing sheet. Although he'd spearheaded the firm's purchase and installation of a cloud-based, computerized time entry system and made training in its use mandatory for all attorneys, he himself still recorded his own time in longhand on billing sheets that she had to special order from a stationery store.

His penmanship was thin, with a pronounced slant, and tended to degrade over the length of each line. She didn't mind the task of deciphering his scrawls and, today, she particularly welcomed the concentration it required. It distracted her from what she'd done and hadn't done.

She'd sat for nearly an hour, staring into the flames, but had been unable to burn the documents. They were back in her green bag. She had promised herself she'd shred them on her lunch break.

For now, she tried to decide if Mr. Prescott had "met with Management Committee re: public relations" or if he'd "met with mediation counsel re: political repercussions." Did the latter even make sense?

She looked up as a brisk, business-like knock sounded at the exterior door and it swung open to reveal Samantha Davis.

"Mrs. Masters," Samantha said, giving her a curt nod in greeting. No smile.

Caroline's hands began to tremble and she dropped them to her lap. She smiled widely to hide her fear.

"Is Mr. Prescott expecting you?" she asked.

"Not exactly. But he'll want to hear this," Samantha said. She waved her small notebook.

Caroline's stomach lurched. Samantha knew. But how? She resisted the urge to scan the ceiling for a hidden camera. Or perhaps Samantha had a tap on her home phone. The woman was former FBI, after all. How could she have been so stupid to have called her at home?

"Mrs. Masters, are you okay?"

Samantha's voice brought Caroline back from the edge of panic.

"I'm so sorry. I'm suddenly feeling quite ill, actually."

It was true enough, Caroline thought. She felt as though she could vomit.

Samantha appraised her. "You do look a little green around the gills. There's a stomach bug going around downstairs; I hope you didn't catch it."

Caroline smiled weakly and buzzed Mr. Prescott.

"Yes?"

"Ms. Davis is here to see you."

"Send her in," Mr. Prescott instructed.

"Right away. And, Mr. Prescott?"

"Yes?"

"I'm afraid I'm not feeling well. I may need to go home. I'll arrange for Lettie Conrad to cover your phones and otherwise assist you."

Caroline chewed on her lower lip while she waited for his response. She'd never before asked to go home sick.

"Oh, by all means," he said in a voice tinged with concern.

She knew the concern wasn't for her. Mr. Prescott was something of a germaphobe. She suspected Lettie would spend the better part of her day disinfecting every surface in sight, lest Mr. Prescott find himself the victim of a contagion.

"Thank you," she said.

She depressed the intercom button to end the conversation.

Samantha, who was on her way into Mr. Prescott's office, turned and said, "Take care of yourself, Mrs. Masters."

Caroline was sure the words carried a warning, or a threat, but she simply nodded. "I will."

She gathered her keys and wallet, trying to will her hands not to shake. She decided the sooner she put some distance between her and Samantha Davis's accusing gaze the better. She'd stop by Lettie's workstation on her way out of the building.

She stood and forced herself to walk rather than run to the hallway.

~ ~ ~ ~ ~

Cinco stood with his hands clasped behind his back and contemplated the skyline. The morning sky was a vibrant blue, crisp and full of promise, completely at odds with his mood.

He had a low-grade headache from the previous evening's drinking. Now he also had to worry about the invisible germs that lurked in his secretary's workspace, waiting for him to rest a hand on the edge of desk or lean against the door. A shiver of disgust ran up his spine.

The door opened inward and Samantha Davis strode into the room.

"Good morning," she said.

She stopped to blink at her surroundings and Cinco suppressed a smile. He'd forgotten she'd never been inside his space before. Most people needed a moment to absorb it.

He waited a beat and then motioned for her to have a seat on the snowy white leather couch.

"Please. Sit," he said, as he lowered himself into one of the matching captain's chairs that faced the couch.

"I'll just stand, if that's okay with you," she said.

She looked out of place, planted in the middle of the room in her tailored pants suit, clutching her small notebook with both hands, with her spine straight and her eyes darting around the room.

"Whichever you prefer," he told her, hoping to put her ease. He waved a hand, "Do you have something to report?"

"Two things," she said, flipping the notebook open to a page that she'd marked with a post-it note. "One, I received a call from Detective Gilbert. The police have arrested Clarissa's husband and charged him with her murder."

"I know," Cinco said. "He's apparently retained Sasha McCandless to represent him."

A silver eyebrow shot up Sam's unlined forehead.

He wondered, not for the first time, why she didn't color her hair. She was fit enough, and her skin smooth enough, that she could pass for a much younger woman if she chose.

"That's an interesting coincidence—particularly given that he claims Mr. Lang is his alibi for the time of the murder," Sam said.

Cinco tried to conceal his surprise.

"Greg Lang?"

"One and the same," Sam confirmed.

He suppressed a frown. Volmer hadn't mentioned that when he'd called to say Sasha was asking about Costopolous's bond.

"I presume that means the police are no longer interested in our files?"

"Not at the moment," Sam said. "The detective did ask that, for the time being, we suspend any document retention policy that would result in the destruction of files."

"Certainly," Cinco said, willing himself not to think about the files he'd instructed Caroline to shred. Sam had a tendency to make him nervous under the best of circumstances. Her piercing gaze always made him feel as though he had something to be ashamed of, even though he didn't know what it was. Now that he was guilty of something, he had to resist the urge to squirm in his chair like a schoolboy in trouble with a nun.

She looked at him a moment longer and then said, "The second thing is that I have a location on Malcolm Vickers's son."

Cinco leaned forward, interested. "You do?"

She glanced down at her notebook. "Yes, I had originally hit a brick wall, because I searched for him under Vickers and his mother's maiden name, but it turns out mom remarried—three times, actually—and moved to a different state with each new husband. All that moving around, plus the fact that the boy was adopted by stepdad number two, whose surname he kept, made him difficult to find. His legal name is Rich Moravian, and he lives here in town. Over on the South Side."

She was about to rattle off the address, but Cinco interrupted her. "That's quite good work, Sam."

"Thank you, sir. Do you want the address?"

He wasn't sure. If the others learned that he knew where Vickers's son was, he feared they'd want to go confront him, or offer him money, or some nonsense. Hell, knowing Marco, he might want to challenge the guy to a duel. No, for now, it was better to have reasonable deniability.

"Not just yet," he said.

She cocked her head and gave him a quizzical look. Then she said, "You know, I discovered something odd when I ran down the ex-Mrs. Vickers's full matrimonial history."

"Oh?" he said, trying to keep the fear out of his voice. "And what's that?"

She closed her notebook and looked hard at him. "When Marcus and Jessa Vickers divorced, she was matched through Neighborhood Legal Services' pro bono program with lawyers right here at this firm."

Cinco's tongue shot out of his mouth and wet his lips, as though of its own volition.

"Really?" he squeaked.

"Really. But not just any attorneys: Ellen Mortenson; Clarissa Costopolous; and a woman named Martine Landry," Sam said.

He looked at her inscrutable face, unable to read anything behind the words.

"That's quite a coincidence," he finally said.

She stared at him in silence for a moment that threatened to stretch on forever.

Cinco was on the edge of blurting out a confession—to what, he didn't know—when she finally gave a curt nod.

"That's what I thought," she agreed.

39.

ASHA GLARED UP AT THE bored-looking guard manning the metal detector as the line of irritated people who were queued up behind her, mainly tired-eyed women toting toddlers on their hips, mumbled curses and shuffled their feet on the tile floor.

He looked back at her with no expression.

"I said, are you wearing an underwire bra?" he repeated.

"Yes," she said evenly. She took a breath and exhaled slowly, "As I said, I'm Mr. Costopolous's attorney, and he needs these clothes for a court appearance later this morning ..."

"And, as I said, I don't care if you're Marcia Clark. You aren't on the attorney list, so you'll have to comply with all the policies that apply to the general public or you can't see your boy. There's a ladies' room around to the right or you can wriggle out of your bra right here. Your choice, but you lose your place in line if you go to the restroom." He smirked at her.

She stared at him and then shrugged. She unbuttoned her suit jacket and placed it across the metal table set up beside the x-ray belt. Then she snaked her right hand down through the neckline of the front of her sheath dress until she reached the clasp between her breasts. Grateful she had the good luck to have worn a bra that closed in the front, she opened the clasp. Then she lowered the straps, eased out her arms, and wormed the bra out of her dress through the right armhole. She flung it on the x-ray belt to scattered applause from the impatient line.

Without a word, she crossed the threshold of the metal detector a second time. Hearing no beep this time, she snatched her bra off the belt and retrieved her bag, jacket, and Nick's clothes.

The guard put an arm out to stop her.

"Not so fast, ma'am."

"Now what?"

He smiled. "Our visitor information clearly states no sleeveless dresses are permitted."

She knew he was baiting her. She knew he wanted her to lose her temper. And she knew she was about to explode anyway.

She gritted her teeth, but before she could respond, she heard a familiar laugh over her shoulder.

"Now, you tell Rosalie I asked after her," Larry Steinfeld said, clasping a white-haired, paunchy guard on the shoulder.

The two men skirted the line of visitors and made their way around the metal detector. The guard slowed his pace to match Larry's labored walk with the cane. As they approached, Sasha could hear the guard trying to convince Larry to take Bertie on an Alaskan cruise.

"We saw salmon jumping right out of the water!" the guard said, using his hands to mimic the motion.

He stopped short when they reached Sasha and her tormentor. The metal bar on his lapel read "Jagowski," but Sasha had begun to think of him as Officer Jag-off.

Larry spoke first. "Tom, I'd like you to meet my colleague, Sasha McCandless. She's not only a talented lawyer, she's one of Daniel's best students."

The man smiled and extended his right hand. "Tom Murtry. It's a pleasure."

"Pleased to meet you," Sasha managed, flushed with embarrassment over the lacy, black bra dangling from her left hand.

After releasing her hand, Tom fixed his younger colleague with a look.

"Captain, she's not on the attorney list," Officer Jag-off began.

Tom ignored him and spoke to Sasha.

"Officer Jagowski apologizes for his confusion. I'll show you to the female officers' locker room, so you can, uh, put yourself back together in private."

"I'd appreciate that," Sasha said.

He smiled. "If Larry's right, and you're one of Daniel's best students, I appreciate your not breaking Officer Jagowski's nose. It would have meant a lot of paperwork for me."

Jagowski reddened and returned to his metal detector duties without another word. He was greeted by a smattering of hoots from the waiting line.

"Thank you," Sasha whispered to Larry as they followed the captain along a narrow, brightly lit hallway.

Larry just patted her arm with his free hand.

They stopped in front of a door marked "Personnel Only." Tom knocked on the door and then ushered Sasha inside.

It looked like the locker room of every gym she'd ever seen. Rows of metal lockers lined the walls, and long scarred wooden benches ran along the middle of the room.

She made quick work of her sartorial repairs. After putting on her bra and zipping up her dress, she stood in front of a warped, smudged mirror and examined herself. She buttoned her jacket and smoothed her hair. She was as ready as she'd ever be.

~ ~ ~ ~ ~

Sasha and Larry sat side by side at the small metal table in the attorney visiting room and waited for the guards to bring Nick in. The county jail apparently shared an interior designer with the homicide squad. Same furniture, same carpet, same paint.

Larry was doodling a series of interlocking circles on his legal pad. They looked like chains. Not a good sign.

Sasha picked up her own pen and scribbled, "Can we talk freely in here?" She nudged Larry and pointed to it.

He shook his head no.

She figured. Despite the fact that attorney-client conversations were protected by privilege, she had heard that privilege was considered a joke by law enforcement. She took her pen and drew a series of loops across the words so they were no longer legible.

They heard boots striking tile, and then the door swung open. Two guards, one black and one white, entered the room with Nick sandwiched between them. His hands were cuffed together in front. He shuffled awkwardly because the cuffs were connected by a chain to leg manacles. He looked tired. Dazed.

The white guard pushed him into the empty seat.

The black guard addressed Sasha. "You have clothes for his court appearance?"

She handed over the bag and the suit.

"For future reference, court appearance clothes are accepted between seven and nine p.m. only and not more than three days before the scheduled appearance."

She opened her mouth to explain that Nick had only been booked hours earlier but decided it wasn't worth the effort, especially because Tom Murtry had probably pulled some strings to get them to accept the clothes.

"Got it. Thanks," she said.

He nodded.

Larry said, "The handcuffs aren't necessary, son. We aren't afraid of our client."

The white guard shrugged and unchained Nick's hands. "Suit yourselves. Heard he killed his pregnant wife. Don't expect him to have mercy on an old man and a chick. Just bang on the door when you're done or if he attacks you."

They left, banging the door closed and locking it behind them.

Nick rubbed his wrists and then ran his hands through his hair, making it stand on end. He stared at Sasha, unblinkingly.

"Well?" he said.

Sasha didn't see much point in asking how he was holding up. The answer was evident.

She introduced Larry. "Nick, this is Larry Steinfeld. He's retired now, but he served as an attorney for the Federal Public Defender and the ACLU for years. He's regarded as a scholar in the criminal procedure area."

Larry waved away the praise. He reached out to shake Nick's hand and said, "You have a fine lawyer, Mr. Costopolous, a fine lawyer. She's humoring me by letting me relieve my boredom by tagging along."

"Great. Good. Pleased to meet you," Nick said, shaking Larry's hand but staring at Sasha. "When are you getting me out of this hellhole?"

"I can only imagine how eager you are to get home, Nick. And today's court appearance is step one in that process, okay? I need you to keep it together. At eleven-thirty, we'll have a preliminary arraignment in front of a judge. In all likelihood, an assistant district attorney will show up to read the charges and ask for a bail amount. We won't present your defense. You'll just plead not guilty, and the judge will set bail. Short and sweet, okay?"

"And then?" Nick demanded.

"And then, we hope, you'll be transported back here while Ms. McCandless makes the necessary arrangements to pay the cashier," Larry explained.

"I'm not coming back here!" Nick banged his fist against the metal table for emphasis.

Larry flicked his eyes toward the door and frowned, letting Sasha know that Nick had to stay calm in case the guards were listening.

Sasha smiled at Nick and hoped it came across as reassuring.

"Let's not get ahead of ourselves, okay?" she said.

He curled his lips back into a snarl. "I mean it."

"It should only be for a few hours at most," Larry said.

Nick shook his head. "I won't come back here."

Larry glanced at Sasha and then met Nick's eyes. "If your concern is being returned to the general population, I'll arrange for you to be held in the processing area. You'll be in the holding cell. It's ... more public."

Suddenly, Sasha realized Nick's panic was about being attacked by a fellow inmate. She wondered what had happened the previous night.

"Can you do that? You're sure?" Nick asked, his anger bleeding away, replaced by desperation.

Larry's eyes were careful behind his glasses, "I should be able to make that happen, but, of course, there are no guarantees. There are no guarantees about any of this, but the preliminary arraignment is usually a formality. Often, the arresting officer attends instead of an assistant district attorney. Sometimes they even handle it through a videoconference."

Nick strained forward, agitated and anxious.

"So it should be a piece of cake?" he asked, his voice cracking.

Sasha looked at Larry.

Larry shrugged and said, "Ordinarily, yes, but you need to understand you have some bad facts."

"Right, the pictures. But I explained that to Sasha. You just have to find that girl," Nick said.

"It's not just the pictures," Sasha said.

"What else?" he asked.

She leaned in close to him. She supposed if the guards were listening, they'd hear her even if she whispered, but she lowered her voice anyway. "Why did you tell Gilbert he could search your truck?"

Nick shrugged. "I don't know. I don't have anything to hide. I know you told me not to talk to him, but I just thought maybe if I cooperated, he'd realize this was all a huge mistake and let me go home."

Unbelievable.

Sasha looked at him. He looked back at her.

"You don't know, do you?" she asked.

"Know what?" Nick asked, confusion clouding his face.

"Officer Dickinson searched your truck and then opened your toolbox."

"And?" Nick prompted.

"And," she said, staring hard at her client, "your hammer was missing."

He jerked back like she'd slapped him. Disbelief, chased by panic, flooded his eyes.

"What? No, that's not possible," he said in a loud, strained voice.

"Keep your voice down," Larry warned him.

Nick gave no indication that he'd heard. He grabbed Sasha's right arm. "That can't be right," he insisted.

Sasha placed her hand over his.

"Nick, I was there. I saw it for myself. There was no hammer in your toolbox," she said as gently as she could manage in the face of his idiocy.

He looked at her, puzzled. "It doesn't make sense. I didn't use ..." he stopped midsentence.

"You didn't use what, son?" Larry asked.

Nick bit his lip.

"Nick?" Sasha prompted him.

"Sorry," he said, slowly, "I'm trying to think. I haven't used my hammer in several days and I don't always lock my truck when it's in my driveway or the garage. Someone must have stolen my hammer."

Larry and Sasha exchanged a look.

"When's the last time you opened your tool box?" Sasha asked.

"Let's see. I did a walkthrough of a job site with the general contractor on Wednesday, so I didn't need it then. On Tuesday, I was waiting for a materials delivery," he said, chewing on the inside of his cheek while he thought back further. Finally, he said, "Last Friday. I was installing wainscoting in a dining room in Aspinwall."

"So your hammer could have gone missing at any point in the past seven days?" Sasha asked.

"It had to have," Nick said forcefully.

The three of them looked at one another wordlessly.

Nick broke the silence.

"I'm being framed."

40.

CAROLINE HESITATED ON THE SIDE-WALK, her hand on the door. She exhaled, pushed the door inward, and stepped inside as bells jangled overhead to announce her arrival.

To her right, sat a coffee shop. The heady scent of roasted coffee beans and the clatter of dishes drifted out through the entrance. Directly in front of her, at the end of a short hallway, a stairwell led to the second floor and, according to a discreet brass sign, The Law Offices of Sasha McCandless, P.C.

Caroline gripped the handrail and started up the stairs.

She'd fully planned to drive straight home and climb into her bed when she'd left the office. But after she'd exited the garage, she'd turned left instead of right and then had just flowed with the light, late-morning traffic until she'd reached Bigelow Boulevard. Almost without realizing it, she'd ended up, not in Upper St. Clair, but in Shadyside.

She'd pulled into a metered spot on Ellsworth Avenue and fed a handful of quarters into the parking meter. As she'd walked the block and a half, the autumn sun and the brilliant blue sky had barely registered through her trouble and worry. Not until she'd stood in front of the building that housed Sasha's legal office had she admitted to herself that it had been her destination all along.

The stairs dumped her out in the second-floor hallway, which was lined with three doors along each side. The first door on the right had a brass nameplate that matched the sign at the bottom of the stairs.

Caroline braced herself then rapped on the door. Her heart fluttered in her chest. No response.

She waited a moment. Then she knocked again, harder this time. Directly behind her, the first door on the left swung open.

Caroline turned to see a slim African-American woman standing in the doorway. She was not young, not old. She looked familiar, but Caroline couldn't place her.

"Sasha's not in, Mrs. Masters," the woman said, gesturing toward the other door.

Caroline searched her memory but found no name to attach to the woman.

"Please, call me Caroline," she said with a weak smile.

The woman arched a brow and waited. Finally, she said, "Naya Andrews."

Caroline nodded. Of course. The former litigation legal assistant with the take-no-prisoners attitude.

"Please forgive me, Naya. I have a great deal on my mind, and your name escaped me. How do you like it here—working for Sasha?"

Caroline realized she was prattling; her nerves were getting the better of her.

Naya blinked, then said, "It's great. Like I said, though, she's out of the office this morning."

Caroline tugged on the straps over her left shoulder, hugging the supple, green leather bag to her body.

"When do you expect her back?" she asked.

Naya shrugged. "She's in a client meeting. She's going straight to court from there, so not until lunchtime, at the earliest."

Caroline checked her watch. It was after eleven.

"I'll wait."

"Why don't you get a bite in the coffee shop downstairs?" Naya suggested. "They have great salads. I'll tell Sasha you're here when she gets in."

"I'd rather not," Caroline said.

Naya frowned at her but said nothing.

"Please," Caroline said, her eyes filling with tears, "I really don't have an appetite and ... I think I need a lawyer."

Naya looked hard at her for a few seconds, then she stepped to the side and ushered her into the office.

"In that case, come on in and we'll get a client intake started," she said, handing Caroline a box of tissues.

41.

ASHA AND LARRY WALKED ACROSS the lot from the county jail to the Municipal Court building.

Sasha had assumed the preliminary arraignment would be held in the imposing stone castle that housed the Allegheny County Court of Common Pleas, but Larry had set her straight. Not until the formal arraignment would a criminal defendant, even in a homicide, set foot in the big courthouse. Preliminary arraignments and preliminary hearings were handled by Municipal Court judges, just like traffic citations.

They proceeded without incident through the metal detectors at the entrance of the hulking brick and glass building. Sasha was pleased to see that the members of the bench apparently did not live in fear of her lingerie.

Up three flights, the courtroom of the Honorable Laurel Foster was a bazaar scene. They entered the room and were met by a din of wheedling, peddling, and bargaining, as lawyers tried to hammer out deals before the judge took the bench. It was like an island market after a cruise ship had pulled into port and unloaded a crowd of sunburned tourists. Of course, these vendors weren't hawking woven blankets, shot glasses, and tchotchkes, but reduced jail sentences, probation, and in-patient treatment programs. The mood struck Sasha as insufficiently somber, given the stakes involved. Larry seemed unperturbed.

She pulled him out into the hallway.

"Walk me through this one more time, please," she said.

Larry had insisted it would be an easy appearance to wing, but winging it was not her style. Sasha felt jittery. It was her practice to quell her jitters by preparing, preparing some more, and then over-preparing for her courtroom appearances. Unfortunately, she had had neither the time nor the knowledge necessary to adequately rehearse for her criminal court debut.

"It's like we told Nick. Either Detective Gilbert or some harried assistant district attorney will show up. Most likely, it'll be an ADA who was hit with a stack of files when he walked in this morning and hasn't had time to do anything more than glance through them—if that. Whoever it is will read the charges in a bored voice and ask for a high bail amount. There's not going to be anything dramatic," Larry assured her. "Municipal Court is all about efficiency; keeping the clogged wheel of justice turning. Stand up, poke Nick to get him to say not guilty, agree to the bail amount, get assigned a preliminary hearing date, and then sit down."

"Okay. Now, tell me again why the assistant district attorney isn't going to charge him with first-degree murder?" she asked.

She had reviewed Pennsylvania's criminal code after her morning run and had read that bail was not an option if the defendant faced charges that carried a life sentence or the death penalty. A first-degree murder conviction would result in a mandatory life sentence.

Larry said, "What's the upside? From what you've told me, they don't have anything. It's all conjecture—he was cheating and she asked for a divorce. So what? Half of all marriages end in divorce, not murder. They'll charge him with criminal homicide, like they did Mr. Lang, and get their ducks in a row. Later, at the formal arraignment, after they've had a month, two months to gather evidence, maybe they'll amend the charges. But now? It's not worth it."

He sounded certain. And the district attorney's office *had* agreed to bail for Greg.

Sasha could feel her jangled nerves begin to un-kink.

Then Larry continued, "What you *should* be worrying about is what you're going to say if the ADA comes charging off the elevator looking for you to make a deal before your case gets called."

Sasha shook her head. This again. Larry believed the district attorney would offer Nick a deal similar to the one Greg Lang had rejected: plead to voluntary manslaughter and serve a term of seven-and-a-half to ten years. And Larry believed Nick should jump on it.

"You were there, Larry. He has an explanation for everything: his hammer was stolen; he was rescuing that girl. He believes he can explain this away. And, frankly, I think he's right about being framed," Sasha said.

Larry shook his head. "So what if he is? If they offer him a deal like they offered Greg, he should take it."

The courtroom door swung open and a middle-aged man wearing his hair in a short ponytail poked his head out and shouted, "The bailiff said the bus is here."

"The bus?" Sasha asked, as he pulled his head back in and disappeared into the courtroom.

"The transport vehicle from the prison," Larry explained. "They drive the defendants across the parking lot. It would be quicker to walk them, but I suppose they have security concerns. Let's go in and find seats. The session will start soon."

They fell in with the mass of lawyers streaming into the courtroom. Nick's case was eighteenth on the list, so they found seats toward the middle of the gallery and settled in.

Larry passed the time receiving visitors. Every third lawyer who passed by stopped to ask about retirement, Bertie, or his canasta game. Sasha gave everyone who stopped a smile and a nod but kept her focus on her notes. Mere formality or not, she did not intend to embarrass herself at her first preliminary arraignment.

The bailiff stood up behind his cheap wood laminate desk and announced, "Okay, boys and girls, take your seats. Judge is on her way."

The chatter died instantly, and the stragglers hustled to find empty spaces on the rows of long benches, tripping over litigation bags and crawling over their colleagues, so they could sit down, only to pop back up when the judge appeared.

The door from chambers swung open, and several dozen heads turned in expectant unison. But it was just the judge's interns. One female, one male. Both impossibly young. They settled in two folding chairs set up alongside the bailiff's table and powered up their laptops, balancing them on their knees.

A moment later the door opened again. This time, it was not a drill.

"All rise. The Honorable Laurel Foster presiding," the bailiff intoned in a loud, clear voice.

As one, attorneys stood, shoulders brushing shoulders in the cramped room. Larry pushed himself up with his cane.

"Good morning, ladies and gentlemen," the judge said with a bright smile. "Have a seat, if you were lucky enough to find one."

As they lowered themselves to the benches, she continued, "Anyone who wants to introduce himself or herself to his or her client, feel free to go back to the holding pen. Attorneys only—no family. Just keep it brief, please."

A dozen or so lawyers stood and headed for the door. The back rows, packed with a mass of humanity in varying degrees of cleanliness and inappropriate dress, watched them go with naked jealousy. Sasha assumed these were the defendants' family members. She didn't see anyone who resembled Nick.

She leaned toward Larry. He shook his head before she had a chance to speak.

"Pfft," he stage whispered, "don't even think about it. There's no privacy. The real skells back there, the career criminals, all have ADAs on speed dial. They'll listen to your conversation and try to use it to barter their way to a better deal."

The judge adjusted her square-framed glasses and frowned down at her calendar.

"Well, as is always the case, we've got a jam-packed morning. I'm hopeful you fine people have spent your time wisely and we'll be able to dispose of some of these matters rapidly. All the same, I hope everyone had a hearty breakfast in anticipation of a late lunch."

The bailiff, who'd been muttering into his phone in a low rumble, slammed down the receiver and approached the bench. He waved a piece of notebook paper at the judge as he neared her.

She covered the microphone with her hand, and he whispered in her ear, showing her the paper. Sasha watched her short, curly hair bob wildly as she nodded her head. It was a quick, annoyed motion. She took the sheet of paper, scowled at it, and then swung the microphone back toward her.

"It appears we're going to have a special guest star today. The District Attorney herself is going to handle the preliminary arraignment for *The Commonwealth v. Nicholas Costopolous*." The judge paused and read from the paper the bailiff had handed her, "Attorney McCandless, come on down, you're our first contestant. Your client's on his way."

Sasha's mouth went dry. She whipped her head around and stared at Larry, whose eyes were wide and puzzled. He opened his palms and shrugged.

They stood and walked to the front of the room. Sasha could barely hear the buzzing crowd over the sound of her blood rushing in her ears. She steadied her hands and placed her legal pad on the table, then she pulled out a chair for Larry. While he lowered himself into it and arranged his cane and his papers, she concentrated on bringing down her heart rate.

"Welcome to Municipal Court, Ms. McCandless," the judge said. "Good to see you, Larry."

"Thank you, your honor," Sasha said.

Larry made a gesture as though he were tipping an invisible hat toward the bench.

The Judge smiled at him and then caught her female intern's eyes.

"I have to confess I find it refreshing," she continued, "as a woman and as a jurist, to be presiding over a matter where both sides are represented by women. It's surprisingly rare, even in this day and age."

Sasha was saved from responding by the arrival of two deputy sheriffs escorting Nick up the aisle.

She noted with approval that he had cleaned up nicely. In fact, having run a comb through his thick hair and dressed in an expensive Italian suit, he looked more presentable than most of the attorneys in the room, even with two days' growth on his face.

The handcuffs clamped around his wrists and the stubble were reminders that he'd spent the night in a cement block cell.

The officers deposited him in the empty seat between Sasha and Larry and retreated, leaning against the wall, bored but watchful.

Nick clenched his jaw and leaned in to whisper in Sasha's ear. His breath was hot and minty.

"What's going on? They called me out of order. This better not be about a deal. I told you, no deal," he said in a low growl.

Sasha started to whisper back that she doubted they'd have to worry about rejecting a deal, given the circumstances, but the door swung open again, and Nick turned his head.

Allegheny County District Attorney Diana Jeffries raced in, trailed by two ADAs, whose arms were loaded with accordion files. She dropped her handbag on the table with a thud. Her minions placed the files alongside it silently.

"Good morning, Ms. Jeffries," the judge said,

Sasha thought she detected a hint of steel behind the judge's smile.

"Good morning, your honor. The People appreciate your willingness to accommodate our scheduling request," the district attorney replied, smoothing her boucle skirt across her hips.

Sasha noted that the highest-ranking prosecutor in the county was wearing a sweater set and skirt to court. Sasha's late mentor, Noah Peterson, used to shake his head when a female attorney showed up for a court appearance having interpreted "suit" to mean any two pieces from her wardrobe. He believed jurors and male attorneys took women less seriously and that dressing down only compounded the problem. Sasha tended to agree and always wore a suit to a court appearance, client meeting, or deposition.

Despite the district attorney's appearance, Sasha had no intention of underestimating her. Diana Jeffries was a career prosecutor. She'd worked her way up through the U.S. Attorney's Office for the Western District of Pennsylvania during the 1990s. When she'd resigned to run for District Attorney in 2002, she'd been the chief of the organized crime division. But she'd seen her opening.

Much-revered District Attorney Jack Adamson had announced he wasn't seeking reelection, and his top deputies had slung so much mud at one another in their efforts to get the spot, that the voters had elected an outsider instead. The straight shooter from the U.S. Attorney's Office was popular with women, minorities, and Catholics.

After a decade in office, she'd shown herself to be tough as nails and committed to juvenile diversion programs. The scuttlebutt among the bar was that she was essentially unbeatable, and the liberal, avowed atheist law school professor who was challenging her in the upcoming election didn't stand a chance. Sasha couldn't think of a single good reason why she was handling Nick's preliminary arraignment personally.

The district attorney shrugged out of her cardigan and hung it over the back of her chair. Her pale arms were covered with constellations of freckles.

"Are we all ready?" the judge asked.

"Yes, your honor," Sasha and Diana said in unison. Larry and Nick nodded. They all stood.

The two ADAs sat motionless until their boss glared at them. Then they got to their feet with palpable reluctance. They were sulking, probably put out at having the district attorney swoop in and take over at the last minute. If they'd worked at private firms, Sasha thought, they'd be used to that sort of limelight hogging by this point in their careers.

"Then let's get down to business. This is the preliminary arraignment in the matter of *The Commonwealth of Pennsylvania v. Nicholas Costopolous*," Judge Foster said in a crisp voice.

Diana reached for a file, and the assistant district attorney to her left pushed it toward her. She opened the folder and ran her finger down the top sheet of paper, stopping about a third of the way down the page. She held her finger there and said, "Your honor, the Commonwealth is charging the defendant with first-degree murder in the heinous killing of Clarissa Costopolous and with first-degree murder of an unborn child in the death of her fetus."

Sasha's stomach sank and bile rose in her throat as a wave of understanding washed over her. The fetus. The District Attorney was going to cement her stranglehold over the election next month by making Nick's case big news. The law professor challenger for her office had gone on record as calling the criminal statute governing crimes against unborn children a back-door attempt by fundamentalists to disenfranchise women and undermine *Roe v. Wade*. His argument, though legally sound, had not been well received. And now, Nick was going to be cannon fodder.

Sasha looked at Larry. His eyes were closed, and he slowly shook his head. He looked how she felt. They were screwed.

Judge Foster's face clouded as she, too, realized what had just happened. The District Attorney had just hijacked the preliminary arraignment for her own purposes.

Diana pressed on. "Of course, because the maximum penalty for these charges is the death penalty, bail is out of the question."

A murmur rose from the gallery. Sasha shot to her feet. Nick tugged on her sleeve, but she kept her eyes on the judge.

"Your honor? Is the District Attorney saying she's going to seek the death penalty in this case?" Sasha heard her voice say the words, but it sounded far away.

"Good question. Ms. Jeffries?" the judge asked, turning to the district attorney.

The district attorney hesitated, then said, "It would be premature to make that decision at this time. It's not off the table, however."

"Understood," the judge said. She stared down at her hands for a moment and then raised her head and looked straight at Nick, although she addressed Sasha. "Ms. McCandless, regardless of the death penalty issue, murder in the first degree and murder in the first degree of an unborn child both carry a mandatory life sentence if the defendant is convicted. Accordingly, bail is not an option. That's mandated by statute. The defendant is remanded to custody until his preliminary hearing."

Sasha heard Nick swallow a moan.

Larry stood, leaning awkwardly on the table, and said, "Your honor, the defendant requests the earliest possible preliminary hearing date, given the circumstances."

"I think that's fair," the judge said. She looked at the bailiff. "Can we give them a time on Monday?"

The bailiff flipped through some papers, and said, "Nine-thirty works."

"With all due respect," Diana began.

The judge cut her off. "Mr. Costopolous is entitled to a speedy determination. If the Commonwealth wants to play this game, it should be prepared to play. Nine-thirty on Monday it is."

"Yes, your honor," Diana said.

Nick was pale and shaking.

"I can't do this," he whispered to Sasha.

"You have to," she said. She squeezed his hand, in equal parts to comfort him and to steady herself.

"Sasha. I didn't kill her. You have to get me out of jail, please," he begged her.

"Okay," the judge said, "next up, *The People v. Hector Allonde.*"

In a daze, Sasha gathered her papers while the deputies came to take Nick back to prison. As they marched him down the hall, he twisted his neck and stared back at Sasha, his dark eyes pained and frightened.

She waited for Larry, and they walked together down the aisle under the curious, sympathetic gaze of the assembled attorneys. Sasha pushed open the heavy doors that led into the hallway and held them for Larry. She felt hot and suddenly tired. Nick was already gone, whisked away to be caged—for the weekend, if he was lucky; for the rest of his life, if he wasn't.

As soon as the doors had closed behind her, one of the assistant district attorneys who'd been at the table with Diana trotted over to Sasha and shoved some papers at her wordlessly.

"What's this?"

He fixed his eyes on the floor and said, "Complaint in *The Commonwealth versus Greg Lang.* The preliminary hearing is set for Monday afternoon."

Sasha blinked at the papers in her hand and then looked at Diana Jeffries, who stood with her other assistant, smiling and laughing, by the elevator bank.

"Are you kidding?" Larry asked.

The assistant didn't bother to answer; he just scurried over to wait for elevator with his boss. Diana glanced over and smiled a cold smile at Sasha and Larry.

"Ms. McCandless, call my office if you'd like to discuss a deal. I'll be in until five today," she called across the hall.

"Don't respond to that," Larry said, banging his cane on the floor for emphasis. "Come on, we're taking the stairs."

"Larry, you can't manage the stairs," Sasha said. She'd love to take the stairs, but the man relied on a cane to get around.

"I'd sooner crawl down the stairwell than share an elevator with that dirty bird," Larry said.

Sasha had no intention of standing in the hallway and arguing with an irate, cane-wielding man. "Okay, let's go," she agreed.

They took the stairs slowly and silently, both still reeling from the district attorney's surprise attack.

When they stepped out into the parking lot, they walked headlong into a crowd of jostling, shouting camera people and reporters. In the center, sporting freshly reapplied lipstick, stood Diana Jeffries. She'd assumed a solemn face and was gesturing with her hands. Based on the downward chopping motion she was making, she was either explaining how to split a log or describing how Clarissa Costopolous had been pummeled until the life drained out of her ... and the baby she was carrying.

"Don't run," Larry said without moving his lips, "but don't engage them either."

They walked toward their cars, both careful not to make eye contact with any of the press, but several of the teams peeled off from Diana's press conference and headed toward Sasha and Larry.

"No comment?" Sasha asked as they stopped beside Larry's car. Her Passat was parked six rows away.

"If they catch you, you have to say something," Larry responded, as he shoved his key into the lock on his boxy, ancient Volvo wagon. He eased himself behind the wheel and locked the door, waving goodbye as he started the engine.

Sasha waved back and headed for her car. A reporter for WTAE trotted up alongside her, shadowed by a cameraman. She quickened her pace, but the reporter ran around in front of her and blocked her path.

"Are we rolling?" the reporter asked his cameraman over his shoulder.

"Yeah, you're good," the cameraman replied, aiming the bulky equipment at Sasha.

"Ms. McCandless, Seth Champerton, WTAE news. Can you confirm that you represent both of the Lady Lawyer Killers?" He shoved the microphone at her.

She suppressed a groan at the name. Of course, the journalists had come up with a name, they couldn't resist. She still remembered the rapist who had terrorized Shadyside in the mid-1980s. Back then, the reporters had named him Sneaky. Sasha had been in elementary school and hadn't understood the concept of rape, but she'd imagined Sneaky dressed like the Hamburglar from the McDonald's ads, tiptoeing around with a mask and a bag. The Lady Lawyer Killers was easily as bad.

"I represent Greg Lang and Nick Costopolous, both of whom have been wrongfully accused in their wives' deaths, if that's what you mean," Sasha said in a neutral voice.

"What do you think about the District Attorney's decision to charge Mr. Costopolous under the Unborn Child Statute?" he asked, making his eyes wide.

"Mr. Costopolous didn't kill his wife. And, he didn't kill his unborn child. In fact, he had no idea that his wife was pregnant until the police told him last night. His grief at the loss of his wife is now compounded by a sorrow you and I can only imagine," Sasha said, staring straight at Champerton instead of the camera. "In any event, I'm confident that once the district attorney has had an opportunity to gather and analyze the evidence in this case, she'll conclude that the facts don't support a first-degree murder count under any statute."

"Mr. Costopolous claims it was a crime of passion?"

"No, Mr. Costopolous maintains his innocence." She looked directly at the camera.

Champerton switched gears. "Do you have any comment about District Attorney Jeffries's motion to revoke Mr. Lang's bond and remand him to custody until trial?"

Sasha ignored the question. Instead, she said, "Both Mr. Lang and Mr. Costopolous are victims here, Seth. These men lost their wives. They didn't just lose them; they had them torn violently from their lives. What they want and deserve is the opportunity to grieve in private. As you likely know, Ellen Mortenson and Clarissa Costopolous were my former colleagues. I mourn their passing, too. But I think they'd both appreciate knowing their husbands' rights are being protected."

Champerton hesitated, chastened and unsure what to say. Sasha saw her opening. She nodded at the camera and hustled into her car. She had the

keys in the ignition and was driving off before the
reporter had formulated a response.

42.

SASHA HEADED STRAIGHT FOR NAYA'S office. She pushed through the door without bothering to knock first.

"Why didn't you answer your phone? I've been trying to call you since ..." Sasha trailed off when she realized Naya wasn't alone.

Caroline Masters, impeccably dressed in an ivory silk blouse and a black skirt, sat in Naya's guest chair, dabbing at her red-rimmed eyes with a tissue.

Naya inclined her head toward Caroline to let Sasha know she'd been busy.

"Caroline, could you excuse us for a moment? I need to speak to Naya in private," Sasha said.

"Of course," Caroline answered in a ragged voice that left no question she'd been crying.

Naya followed Sasha across the hall into her office. Sasha stopped just inside the door and turned to Naya.

"What's she doing here?"

"She needs a lawyer, Mac. Thank God you're back; I've been holding her hand all morning," Naya said.

"Whatever her issue is, make her an appointment for next week and then get rid of her. Please," Sasha added.

"I think you should listen to what she has to say. What's got your panties in a knot, anyway? Did Prescott & Talbott back out on the bail?"

"I wish. No. The District Attorney showed up personally and read the charges: murder in the first degree and murder of an unborn child in the first degree."

"Ouch. No bail, then," Naya said.

"Yeah, no bail. He's spending the weekend in custody. We got the judge to set the preliminary hearing for Monday morning, though. So maybe we can get him out then."

"That's good," Naya said.

"You'd think so. But after the arraignment, the DA served us with a motion to revoke Greg's bail. That hearing is set for Monday afternoon," Sasha said.

"I guess I know how we're spending our weekend."

Sasha nodded. "Right. Can you get rid of Caroline?"

"Trust me. You want to hear her out," Naya answered in a firm voice.

Sasha lacked the energy to argue with her.

"Fine," Sasha said, "let's talk to her. But when Larry gets here, you're going to have to peel off and help him. He can only stay for a few hours. He's got to get out of here before sundown."

Larry and Bertie observed Shabbat, the Jewish sabbath. He would be unavailable beginning at sunset and lasting until three stars were visible in the night sky on Saturday. Given Larry and Bertie's regular bedtime, she didn't expect him to be back at work again until Sunday morning, at the earliest. Naya, similarly, would be unavailable most of Sunday, because her weekly Baptist church service stretched on for hours and was followed by a potluck meal with the congregation.

Unlike Prescott & Talbott, Sasha didn't pay Naya enough to justify a seven-day grind. And Larry had refused to accept any payment for his assistance. She'd be glad for whatever help they were willing to give her over the weekend.

Naya headed for her office.

Over her shoulder, she said, "Let me grab a notepad and a pen. I'll bring Caroline right over."

Before Sasha, Caroline, and Naya had arranged themselves around the conference table where just one day earlier Nick had evaded Sasha's questions, Larry arrived.

Sasha made the introductions.

"Caroline, this is Larry Steinfeld, a lion of the criminal defense bar. Caroline Masters is the secretary to the chair of Prescott & Talbott, Larry. As I understand it, she has a somewhat urgent legal matter to discuss."

"It's very nice to meet you," Larry said as he shook Caroline's hand and gave her a grandfatherly smile. Over her head, he frowned at Sasha and shook his head.

"Naya will help you with the research for our other matters while Caroline and I chat," Sasha said, in an effort to forestall his objection.

Caroline cleared her throat and spoke in a soft voice, "If the other matters are your criminal cases for Ellen and Clarissa's husbands, you may want to stay, too. Mr. Prescott instructed me to destroy some documents that I think may be related to the murders." She kept her eyes glued on her hands, which were busy shredding a tissue into tiny scraps of lint.

Larry wasted no time dragging the last chair over to the table. Naya got him his own pad and pen, then shut the door. They arranged themselves and sat silently, with pens poised over paper.

"Just start at the beginning," Naya encouraged her.

"Wait," Sasha said, "did Naya explain that this conversation is privileged?"

"She did," Caroline confirmed.

Sasha would have to stop her if it sounded as though she'd destroyed any documents that might have exculpated either Nick or Greg. In that situation, she'd be conflicted out of representing Caroline with regard to any charges that might stem from the destruction of evidence. She would deal with that eventuality if and when it arose. For now, she wanted to hear Caroline's story.

Caroline swallowed visibly. Then she wet her lips and began.

"On Monday, Mr. Prescott was very busy dealing with the news of Ellen's murder. He had several long meetings; first, with the management committee, then with the partners, and finally with the administrative department heads, who met with staff. As you can imagine, the entire office was abuzz. It was a trying situation."

Sasha could imagine. She also noted that, in typical Prescott & Talbott fashion, no one had bothered to meet with the associates. Gossip and misinformation had no doubt flown through the associate ranks as they gathered what news they could from their secretaries and any income partners who were willing to share a stray nugget or two of information. The firm's management seemed to believe its associate ranks functioned best when treated like mushrooms: kept in the dark and fed a lot of manure.

"Of course. Please go on," Sasha prompted.

"In addition to all the internal meetings, he had all the outsiders to deal with. Ellen's clients, Prescott & Talbott alumni, other lawyers, and, of course, the press and the police. His phones rang non-stop. It was very stressful for him."

Naya rolled her eyes at the concern for poor Cinco. Sasha was inclined to agree, but she reminded herself that Caroline's sole professional purpose seemed to be to insulate Cinco from unpleasantness. Of course, she would worry about the effect of Ellen's murder on her boss.

Caroline paused to gather her thoughts and then continued her linear, straightforward recitation of the facts.

"Mr. Prescott was swamped. Then, late in the afternoon, a messenger arrived with a hand delivery."

"Wait," Naya said, holding up a hand to interrupt the narrative. "The messenger brought it up to your office? He or she didn't leave it with the mailroom?"

"Right," Caroline confirmed.

A look passed between Sasha and Naya.

Larry caught it. "What?" he asked.

"That's unusual. Typically, all deliveries, including hand deliveries, go to the central mailroom for distribution," Sasha explained.

Larry scribbled a note on his legal pad.

"It is unusual," Caroline said, "but it's not unheard of. In any event, I signed for the envelope and sent the courier on his way."

"Then what did you do?" Sasha said.

"I wasn't sure what to do," Caroline explained. "The envelope was marked 'Personal and Confidential' and there was no return address. Ordinarily, I give Mr. Prescott his personal correspondence unopened. But he was so busy, and the phone messages were piling up. So I decided to just open it and sort it along with all the other mail."

She shook her head with a slow, sad motion and added, "I certainly wish I hadn't."

"What was it?" Sasha said.

Caroline reached into her bag and removed a large white envelope. She handed it across the table to Sasha.

"See for yourself," Caroline said.

Sasha tore open the flap, which had managed to retain some stickiness, and shook out a photograph. She recognized it instantly. It was The Terrific Trio, resplendent in their formal gowns—the same picture that Ellen had displayed in her home office. In this copy, however, Ellen's face had been obliterated with a heavy red X. Along the bottom of the photograph, someone had written "ONE DOWN" in thick block letters.

Sasha's pulse sped up. She passed the picture to Naya, who stared down at it.

"That's sick," Naya said and handed it to Larry.

"That's Ellen Mortenson," Sasha explained to Larry, "the woman whose face has been crossed out."

"And next to her?" Larry asked without looking up from the photograph.

"Clarissa Costopolous," Sasha said.

Larry dropped the picture on the table as if it were hot. He peered down at it again, then he said, "Who's the third woman?"

"That's Martine Landry," Naya said. "She used to be a lawyer at Prescott & Talbott, too."

"Is she still alive?" Larry asked.

"Yes," Sasha and Naya answered in unison.

Sasha turned to Caroline for confirmation. "She is, right?"

"Yes. I mean, as far as I know."

Sasha pulled her eyes away from the picture.

"You gave this to Cinco?" she asked.

"Yes. I ... well, I was shocked and sickened when I saw it. I stuffed it back into the envelope and took it in to Mr. Prescott."

"Did you talk about it with him?" Naya asked.

Caroline shook her head. "No. He must have known I'd seen it; the envelope had been opened. But he didn't mention it to me, and I was feeling queasy about it. I didn't want to bring it up. I guess I assumed he wouldn't want to discuss it."

She finished in a soft voice and stared down at her hands.

"What did he do after you gave it to him?" Sasha asked.

"He met with the management committee again. After that, he told me to get Will Volmer for him."

"And then?" Sasha asked.

Caroline looked up. "And then, Will came out of Mr. Prescott's office and asked me to find your phone number."

Everyone was silent while that sunk in.

Then Caroline cleared her throat. "I need to use the ladies' room."

Naya showed Caroline to the bathroom and returned with a pitcher of water and an armful of glasses. While they waited for Caroline, Larry and

Naya bent their heads over the picture and spoke in low tones. Sasha stood at the window, looking out over the tops of the low buildings across the street.

Her heart thrummed in her throat. Prescott & Talbott was using her to cover something up. Sasha wanted to scream. Run wind sprints until she wore herself out. Or unleash a flurry of fists on a heavy bag. Instead, she focused on breathing deeply and deliberately.

She had to keep her anger in check and gather information. And she had to take care of her clients. She'd deal with Prescott & Talbott later.

She returned to the table as Caroline entered the room.

Caroline walked them through the rest of it. How she'd arrived at work Thursday morning to find a second envelope, identical to the first, on the floor inside the door. How she had resisted the urge to open it.

She paused and retrieved the second envelope from her bag. Inside was another defaced copy of the photograph. This time, both Ellen and Clarissa were covered with red Xs and the chilling message read "TWO DOWN."

They stared at it while Caroline explained that she'd given it to Cinco, who told her to have Clarissa see him when she got in.

"But of course," Caroline said, her voice shaking, "Clarissa never made it to work yesterday."

"Did Mr. Prescott tell the police about either of these photographs?" Larry asked.

"No," Caroline replied immediately. Then, her years of working at a law firm kicked in and she corrected herself. "I mean, not to my knowledge. I suppose he could have. I doubt it, though, considering they were in the stack of the documents he told me to shred."

Naya raised an eyebrow and pursed her lips. Sasha read the look to say Naya wasn't surprised by Cinco's behavior. Sasha had to admit she was surprised. Not shocked, but surprised. Cinco had to know the consequences for destroying evidence. His secretary certainly did.

"How did that all go down?" Sasha asked. "The shredding, I mean."

Caroline poured herself a glass of water from the heavy pitcher. Her hands were steady.

"Yesterday, after he met with the police in the garage, he came back to the office and started rifling through the filing cabinets. He was obviously looking for something but he wouldn't tell me what it was." She paused and took a sip of water. "Finally, he gave up and told me he needed some old personnel files. They were so old that they were archived in off-site storage. I had them sent up and he took them into his office."

"Was it unusual that he would want to see old files?" Sasha asked. Cinco was the chairman of the firm. Presumably, he would need access to all sorts of historical information.

Caroline took another long drink and considered her answer. "I take no pleasure in denigrating Mr. Prescott. We've worked together for a long time, and he's a fair boss and a decent man. He's not what I would call a detail person, though. He's never gone digging around in the files before. He reads his mail, holds meetings, and that's pretty much it."

"Fair enough," Sasha said.

"Yesterday afternoon, he came out of his office with a redweld stuffed full of documents. He told me to shred them. At first, I assumed he wanted me to do what I always do: leave them in the tray for the office services team to pick up and shred, but then he explicitly said he wanted me to shred them personally." Caroline traced a circle with her finger on her drink coaster around the outside of her water glass. "He'd never done that before. We send everything to shredding—salary information, draft settlement agreements, all sorts of sensitive documents. But he wanted me to handle this myself."

"Did he tell you what the documents were?" Naya asked.

"No." She looked up. "But the two Tyvek envelopes were on the top of the pile. I could see them sticking out of the redweld. I took them out to see if it was just the envelopes, but the picture of Ellen with her face crossed out was inside the first envelope. So I looked inside the second one and saw the other picture."

"And you knew you shouldn't destroy them, right?" Larry said, trying to prompt her gently.

She was silent for a long time. Then she said, "They're important, right? They could be evidence of a crime, right?"

Sasha nodded.

"And that gave me pause. Why would he have me shred pictures that would be helpful to the police?" She tapped the edge of the glass with a polished fingernail. "I didn't want to distrust him, but I thought I should look through the rest of the documents."

"And?" Sasha asked.

Caroline met her eyes with a steady gaze. "There were three complete associate personnel files—Ellen's, Clarissa's, and Martine's. All of their professional development plans, self-assessments, annual evaluations and performance reviews for their years as associates. There was also an entire official client file. I'm not sure how he got that, because it was very old, too, but I hadn't ordered it for him."

Sasha knew that, with few exceptions, Prescott & Talbott's document retention policy specified that official client files were maintained indefinitely. Destroying an archived client file might not be a crime, but it was certainly a breach of firm policy. Presumably the same was true of human resources records.

"What was the client matter?" Naya said.

"It was a pro bono family law matter. *Vickers v. Vickers.* I flipped through the correspondence file. It appears that Ellen, Clarissa, and Martine all worked on it together as first year associates."

"Who was the supervising attorney?" Sasha said.

Caroline just shook her head. "I didn't see a partner's name on the signature block. But that can't possibly be right, can it?"

No, Sasha thought, it couldn't possibly. A large international law firm like Prescott & Talbott was built on layer after layer of management, supervision, and oversight. New attorneys were paid extraordinary sums, but they weren't permitted to cross the street without someone more senior holding their hands to make sure nobody was hit by a car. A junior associate at Prescott was forbidden to sign a letter without having a partner review it. Sasha couldn't imagine a scenario where the firm permitted three first year associates to run a case with no oversight.

"It's certainly highly unusual," Sasha told her.

Caroline reached once more into her shoulder bag and pulled out a heavy redweld. Its accordion bottom was stretched to the limit. She heaved it onto the table.

"Well, it didn't sit right with me, either. So I didn't shred them, but now I don't know what to do with them. I guess that's where you come in."

43.

ICH HURRIED FROM THE KITCHEN to the laughably small living room area of his cramped apartment. He carried his lunch in one hand and his Ziploc freezer bag in the other. One perk of working for Andy was that he didn't care if Rich drove home for lunch.

The way Andy put it, it was no skin off his dick if Rich wanted to burn his time driving back and forth on the Miracle Mile all day. Rich didn't know why old-timers called Monroeville's William Penn Highway, where Andy had his office, the Miracle Mile. The highway was a stretch of ordinary retail stores, strip malls, big box stores, and chain restaurants that sat just outside the city limits. Maybe back in the day the availability of so much commerce in one place had seemed like a miracle, Rich often thought to himself when he was inching along in the brutal bumper-to-bumper, stop-and-go traffic that had become the highway's claim to fame. As far as he was concerned, the only miracle available on that road was catching a wave of traffic that actually flowed.

But Rich gladly braved the bottlenecks so that he could escape to his apartment and eat his turkey and cheese sandwich with the local news for company instead of sitting in the break room at Andy's office listening to the secretary gripe about her lazy husband while she microwaved her disgusting salmon cakes, curried rice, or popcorn. It seemed to Rich that she deliberately chose the most noxious foods available for her lunches.

Rich arranged his plate and the bag on his snack tray and hit the power button on the remote. He checked the time. The broadcast had already started. While his ancient television roused itself to life, he unzipped the bag and removed the picture from its envelope. He stared at Martine's face until a picture developed on the screen, then he set it aside and picked up his sandwich.

He ate with his eyes glued to the set. The new lunchtime anchor, Maisy Farley, was his favorite. She had a softness and an innocence under all her blonde beauty that was a nice contrast to the sharp, overly toned anchors on the other stations. He'd always been drawn to her. He used to get up early and turn on the Channel 11 morning news just to watch her do the weather.

Rich thought she seemed tense today. Her green eyes looked worried and her smile was distant. She leaned forward and said, "And now, let's go to Seth Champerton, for an exclusive interview with the attorney representing both of the Lady Lawyer Killers."

The anchor's face was replaced by a shot of the field reporter hustling after a girl in a parking lot. Rich turned his attention to his sandwich.

When he looked up again, the reporter had caught up with the person, who was not a girl after all. According to the caption across the screen, the tiny figure was Sasha McCandless, attorney to the two men accused of killing their lawyer wives. Rich leaned forward and listened to her tell Seth Champerton that her clients were innocent. Something about the way she said it chilled him, like she *knew*.

But she couldn't know. She was just being a lawyer, lying and tricking everyone, he told himself. She couldn't know, could she?

Rich pushed his half-eaten sandwich away. He stared at the picture of the three lawyers and tried to think of what mistakes he might have made. What did she know?

44.

SASHA'S OFFICE WAS BLESSEDLY QUIET. Larry had left, hurrying to get home in time to help Bertie prepare their evening meal before the Shabbat's prohibition on working kicked in. He'd promised to stop by the office on Sunday to help out. Caroline was also long gone, with instructions to put the whole mess out of her mind and spend the weekend gardening with her husband—advice that Sasha knew she would disregard, judging by the worry lines framing her eyes.

And Naya was behind her closed door with a copy of the picture of Nick and the girl, working the phones. She was going through the phone book calling local modeling agencies. It was a long shot, but the girl was a knockout and, if Nick's story was true, Sasha suspected the killer had hired the girl to trap Nick. Then he'd stolen Nick's hammer and bludgeoned his wife. If they could find the girl, they could find the killer.

Sasha stared at her laptop screen, scanning the newspaper articles her search had returned. Although a preliminary hearing was not typically the time to defend a case on the merits, it had been, and could be, done in Pennsylvania. That's what she was going to have to do—convince the Municipal Court Judge to throw out the District Attorney's case against Nick right then and there. And, then, with that concession in her pocket, she would oppose Greg's bail revocation as being part and parcel of a failed investigation into the Lady Lawyer Killers.

It was a plan. Not a good one, she knew. But it was something.

She checked her to do list. She'd crossed off 're-search news articles, case law, and procedure.' She'd also already called and broken the news to Greg about both Nick's weekend accommodations and Greg's own upcoming hearing. He'd taken it about how she'd expected him to: badly, with a lot of yelling. All she had left to do was 'come up with brilliant plan.' That was all.

She clicked the button to power down the computer. Then she stood to stretch her tight back and get some oxygen flowing to her overtaxed brain.

She moved through a series of yoga asanas to clear her mind and relax her body. She finished in Child's Pose and stayed there, kneeling on her floor, stretched forward, waiting for inspiration.

Think.

Larry's parting words to her were to resist the urge to be Perry Mason. After Googling Perry Mason, she'd decided Larry'd meant that she didn't need to prove who *did* kill Ellen and Clarissa; she just needed to convince the judge that the District Attorney couldn't prove it, either. But how?

Think.

Before she could have an epiphany, her phone rang. She caught herself wondering if it was Connelly calling, as she unfurled herself and raced to answer it.

"Sasha McCandless," she said, hoping her voice didn't sound breathy.

"Sasha, ah've been told you're representin' the Lady Lawyah Killers. Tell me it's not true, darlin' girl?"

Maisy's syrupy accent did nothing to sweeten her words. Sasha's neighbor across the hall was a television journalist who had made the jump from early morning weather girl to noontime anchor in record time. She'd then parlayed that into the anchor job on a competing station. Her Southern belle act had evidently lulled her colleagues into making the fatal conclusion that she was not a threat.

"Hi, Maisy."

"Sugah', you didn't answer my question," Maisy prodded.

Although Sasha knew not to be taken in by Maisy's soft exterior, she also knew that her neighbor's love for hard-hitting journalism was tempered by a wide romantic streak. Sasha decided to let the truth work for her, even though it was manipulative.

"Oh, I was hoping you might be Connelly calling," Sasha said. She waited for Maisy to take the bait.

"And how is sweet Leo?" Maisy asked.

"Gone."

"What do you mean, *gone?*"

Sasha exhaled. "He's taking early retirement from Homeland Security to become the chief security officer for some pharmaceutical company outside D.C."

"Y'all are movin'?"

Sasha blinked at the assumption that she'd just pick up her life and follow Connelly.

"He's moving. Or ... I guess, he's moved. He was supposed to go down for the weekend to look for a place to live, but he's decided to stay."

Maisy was silent for a moment. When she spoke, her sweet tea and magnolia accent had disappeared, replaced by an accusation. "Why? Sasha, what did you do?"

"Mom? Is that you?" Sasha asked.

Maisy laughed, a lilting noise, and the accent returned. "I'm sorry, honey. That wasn't fair. Did you do sumthin' to upset him?"

"I guess so," Sasha admitted.

"Which was?"

"He asked me to come with him. And then he tried to give me this ring, but I had to leave—"

A squeal rose from Maisy, and she interrupted, "An engagement ring?"

"I don't know. Anyway, he left without saying goodbye, so I just thought you might be him."

"Oh, sweetpea. We're gonna get some supper tomorrow and talk."

Sasha shook her head, as if Maisy could see her. "I can't. I have to work."

"You have to eat, too. Let's do Ibiza. We can drink too much sangria and pick at tapas. Seven o'clock?"

Sasha was about to resist, but thought about the weekend of drudgery and solitude that stretched out in front of her. A dose of Maisy would break it up nicely.

"Sure. That sounds good."

"Perfect," Maisy said. "And, Sasha?"

"Yeah?"

"Don't you go thinkin' I'm gonna forget you didn't answer my question."

Maisy hung up with a laugh before Sasha could respond.

Sasha added dinner with Maisy to her calendar then wandered across the hall to see if Naya was making any progress.

Naya swiveled her desk chair around when Sasha opened the door.

"Any luck?" Sasha asked.

Naya shrugged. "I have feelers out with all the agencies. I told everyone the girl might be a witness in a murder case; most places told me to go ahead and email a copy of the picture over and they'd see if anyone recognized her. I gave everyone my cell number and yours, just in case something pops on Sunday, but I wouldn't hold my breath if I were you."

Sasha knew she was right. But they just had to keep moving, keep turning over rocks, and eventually they'd find something. Or they wouldn't, but then at least she'd have the certainty of knowing there was nothing to find.

The relentless search for answers was one of the most useful things she'd learned as a young attorney at Prescott & Talbott. The answers were usually out there somewhere. And the victor in any courtroom showdown was generally the person who kept looking for something that helped her case—a published decision, a witness, a piece of evidence—long after it seemed futile. Prescott & Talbott taught its attorneys that whoever was willing to sacrifice more time to the pursuit of an answer won. It really was that simple.

"Huh."

"What?" Naya asked.

Sasha hadn't realized she'd spoken aloud.

"Oh, I was just thinking, Ellen, Clarissa, and Martine were first years when they handled that pro bono case, right?" She said, moving across the room to sit in the chair across from Naya.

"Right. So?" Naya put down her pen and looked closely at her. "What are you thinking?"

"What's the first thing new attorneys learn at Prescott & Talbott?" Sasha said.

"To answer a question with another question, apparently."

"To leave no stone unturned. Research everything, brief everything, review everything."

Naya nodded. "Sure. But the second thing they're taught is to rein it in." She laughed and went on, "After the first month, when some chucklehead bills three hundred hours to researching some exceedingly minor issue, Marcus gathers all the baby lawyers in a conference room and roars at them that they're being paid for their judgment."

"True," Sasha conceded. "But one of the reasons Prescott would never let three first years run a case together is that there'd be no seasoned attorney with judgment on the matter."

"You think they did something stupid?" Naya said.

"Come on," Sasha responded, "if there was no one reviewing their work? I'm sure they did *something* stupid. The question is, did it get two of them killed?"

Naya cocked her head toward her windowsill. "File's over there. You wanna split it up?"

"Yeah. Are you hungry?" Sasha asked, checking the time. It was just past six o'clock.

"I can hold off for another hour or two, if you can," Naya answered.

"Sounds good."

They both knew the longer they waited to break for dinner, the shorter their night of work would seem. It wouldn't *be* any shorter, but it would *seem* shorter. And when a woman was staring down the barrel of a twenty-hour workday, she'd play all the mental games she knew to make it less painful.

Sasha stood and retrieved the file. "Let's take it to my office. We can use the conference table to spread out."

Naya walked around the desk and held the door for her. As Sasha walked through it, Naya said, "What are we going to do about Martine?"

"I don't know," Sasha said, because she didn't.

They'd touched on the issue with Larry before he'd left, but they hadn't reached a consensus as to whether they should contact Martine or not. Sasha didn't want to rehash the discussion. She figured she didn't need a consensus: if it became apparent to her that she should contact Martine, she would. For now, the main reason she wanted to hold off was, unless she had reason to believe that Martine was in imminent danger, Sasha didn't want to scare her.

The secondary, and less charitable, reason was Sasha didn't want Diana Jeffries to get wind of the existence of the photographs until she sprang them on her at the preliminary hearing on Monday, when it would be too late for her to concoct a story to explain them away.

45.

Saturday

ASHA ARRIVED TWENTY MINUTES EARLY for dinner with Maisy. Even with the sun setting, the October evening was unseasonably warm, so Sasha gave her name to the hostess, procured a glass of Chilean red wine from the bartender, and escaped to the brick patio nestled between Ibiza and its more formal sister restaurant, Mallorca.

After spending the entire day poring over the ugly details of the unraveling of Jessa and Malcolm Vickers's marriage, Sasha's nerves were raw. The buzz of the last happy hour stragglers shouting to make their plans over the music inside had felt like an assault. She sat at a wrought iron table, watched the headlights of cars flowing over the Birmingham Bridge, and let the sounds of the city wash over her.

She pushed thoughts of the Vickers, Nick, and Greg from her mind so she could enjoy the evening air while she had the chance; Maisy would never agree to sit outside and let the exhaust from cars and the grime from the street wreak havoc with her perfect porcelain complexion. Her face was, after all, her business.

Besides, Sasha knew the hostess would take one look at Maisy and seat them in the dead center of the giant window in the front of the restaurant. There was no better advertising for an establishment that catered to urbane sophisticates than having a beautiful local celebrity on display in what amounted to a light box.

Sasha sipped her wine. She was tired. Once she got past the next few days, maybe she'd take a long weekend. Visit Connelly in D.C. and try to figure out what they were doing. The thought of that conversation made her even more tired.

She turned her head toward the couples scattered across the small courtyard at tables for two. She passed the time until Maisy arrived playing "Married or Working It?"

It was a game she and Naya had invented during a two-week trial in Hoboken, New Jersey, back when they'd worked at Prescott & Talbott. Most nights, they worked through dinner, getting the testimony for the next day ready, but every so often they'd find themselves in good enough shape that they could take a break and go to a restaurant.

Unimpressed by the cuisine at the hotel restaurant and the surrounding establishments, they focused, not on the food, but on their fellow diners. They'd surreptitiously watch the couples and try to catch snippets of their conversations to determine if they were married or dating. Checking the ring finger was not allowed.

Eating in silence? Married. Talking about dreams of joining an international humanitarian organization? Working it. Sitting side by side instead of across from one another? Working it. Using a coupon? Married. They got so good at it that they could also reliably spot same-sex couples, long-term cohabitators, newlyweds, and married-but-about-to-be-divorced couples.

Tonight's crowd was heavy on dating couples, Sasha decided, at least on the patio.

She smiled to herself and picked up her glass. Maisy came rushing in, a filmy pink scarf trailing behind her and the beaming hostess at her side.

"Am I late, sugah'?" Maisy asked, her bright white smile turning into a small frown.

Maisy was big on punctuality.

"Nope, right on time," Sasha assured her, draining her glass.

The blinding smile returned. "Oh, thank goodness. Look at you! Have you lost weight?"

Maisy, who had been blessed with curves and cursed with a sweet tooth, didn't seem to understand that Sasha's natural weight was ninety-seven pounds, most of it muscle, and was forever trying to get Sasha to share an imaginary diet secret.

"Nope, it must just be the lighting," Sasha told her.

Maisy gave her blond curls a shake. "Well, you look fantastic. And, guess what?" she said, turning her body to gesture toward the hostess. "We've got a *fabulous* table!"

As Sasha stood to follow them inside, she was distracted by a guy in his early twenties who was negotiating the crowded sidewalk outside the low brick wall with a beach cart loaded with dirty laundry. He was headed, no doubt, to one of the laundromats that sat on the end of East Carson Street.

He had apparently recognized Maisy and must have been a fan, because he was walking with his head twisted over his neck to look at her, not where he was going, and crashed his cart into the pole for a streetlight.

Sasha swallowed her laugh as he turned to meet her eyes. He seemed to be unhurt, but his faced reddened and he hurried away.

46.

RICH SHOVED HIS WHITES INTO the over-sized washing machine with shaking hands. He couldn't believe what he'd just seen. Maisy, the adorable noon news anchor, at that hipster tapas bar. A shiver of electricity had run up his spine when he'd realized it was *her*. Right around the corner from his apartment.

But the thrill had turned into a jolt of fear when he'd seen her companion. It was the little lawyer representing Lang and Costopolous.

He slammed the door shut and fed his coins into the slots. Took large, gulping swallows of air to try to quell his panic.

Why was Maisy talking to that lawyer? She had to be investigating the murders for a story. And that lawyer seemed to know something, something that could prove her clients were innocent.

Rich shook his head at himself. He shouldn't get distracted from his goal. He needed to follow the rest of his plan. Kill Martine. Deliver the third envelope. Finish what he'd begun.

The soapy water whirled in the window on the door of the machine. Rich felt like his thoughts were whirling just as fast. It couldn't be helped. He had to find out what Sasha McCandless knew.

He pounded his hand against the top of the washer, which earned him a look from the tired, bald guy manning the snack cart.

The squirrelly Hispanic kid who seemed to be on the same laundry schedule as Rich week in and week out looked up from playing Angry Birds on his phone. "You okay, man?"

Rich gritted his teeth. He was drawing attention to himself. That was not good. Not good.

He exhaled, "Yeah, I'm cool. I forgot the dryer sheets, is all."

The guy had already turned his focus back to slinging birds at pigs.

Rich forced himself to sit in one of the aluminum chairs that lined the wall and be still. He just had to stay calm. He'd figure out a way to find out how much McCandless knew and would take whatever steps were necessary to stop her from screwing up the rest of his plans.

47.

"**H**OW'S MAISY?" Naya asked, lifting her head from a stack of performance reviews, as Sasha walked into the office.

"Appeased. I told her she'll get an exclusive interview with me if and when Nick and Greg are both found not guilty." Sasha handed Naya a styrofoam takeout container. "Here, it should still be hot. Eat."

"Thanks, Mac."

Naya pushed the files to the side and opened the container. She fetched a set of silverware from her top desk drawer and started to work on the chicken.

"Mmm, this is good. Stuffed with crabmeat?" she said between mouthfuls.

"And spinach, I think," Sasha answered absently, flipping through the personnel files. "Are you finding anything interesting?"

Naya dabbed at her mouth and took a swallow of water before answering. "Not really. All three of them got uniformly high marks, which is what you'd expect. All three made partner, after all."

Sasha nodded. "Did any of the reviews specifically mention their work on Vickers?"

"No. And that's kind of odd, because they billed a ton of hours to it their first year. It was the bulk of their work, and they got a good result, right?"

"If you call terminating a father's parental rights a good result," Sasha said.

Naya put her fork down. "Okay, point taken. But I mean from the firm's point of view, that's a good result, right? They were representing the mom. She believed it was in her child's best interest to have no contact with dad, and her lawyers made that happen."

"That's true," Sasha conceded.

It had been clear to Sasha from reading the client file that, from the very beginning, Jessa Vickers's goal had been to have the father's rights terminated. The divorce and alimony were almost secondary. She was adamant Malcolm could not have partial custody or even visitation.

As every lawyer well knew—even three newly minted first years—that was a tall order. Family court judges were required to make decisions based on what would be in the best interests of the child. As a general rule, courts typically found it in a child's best interests to have a relationship with both of his or her parents. Even going so far, as Clarissa had noted in one early letter to Jessa, to rule that it was in a child's best interests to have visitation with his father, who had murdered the boy's mother. Jessa had been unimpressed with the difficult road ahead and had insisted they could find a way.

Ellen, Clarissa, and Martine had written research memo after research memo, summarizing cases and analyzing various strategies. All of the memos were to the file, rather than to a partner. In addition, The Terrific Trio, and not a partner, had signed all the pleadings and client correspondence.

Somehow, with no apparent guidance from a senior lawyer, after devoting nearly one thousand hours of free legal services to the case, the associates had managed to convince a judge that Malcolm Vickers was such a malevolent force in his young son's life and such a danger to his estranged wife that the court awarded Jessa full custody, with no visitation for the father.

Buoyed by her victory, Jessa pressed for more. She instructed her attorneys to file a petition to have Malcolm's parental rights terminated. Ellen, Clarissa, and Martine dutifully filed, briefed, and argued the petition. And, again, after several hundred hours, they won.

Malcolm, who had been represented by competent, if outmatched, counsel at every stage of all proceedings, wrote a letter to The Terrific Trio after the order terminating his rights had been issued.

Sasha flipped to the page she'd flagged in the correspondence file and re-read it while Naya finished her chicken.

Dear Attorneys:

I hope you can sleep at night knowing what you've done to me and my son. By peddling that sack of lies Jessa fed you, you've ruined my life. And his. A boy needs his father's love and support as he grows, but Richie will become a man with no one to guide him.

My lawyer tells me the court's decisions to give Jessa full custody and to terminate my rights were bad law and I should appeal.

I wish I could. But I've lost everything in the divorce, thanks to you, and I owe my lawyer tens of thousands of dollars that I don't have.

Someday, I hope you get to feel the pain of having your child taken from you, tears streaming down his face, and being powerless to stop it.

God have mercy on your souls, if you have them.

Malcolm Vickers

She couldn't imagine what her reaction would be if she ever received such a raw, wounded letter. Even fifteen years after the fact, she could feel the man's anguish. She looked up to see Naya watching her.

"That letter is hard core," Naya said.

"Yeah, I can't believe it found its way into the official file," Sasha said.

"And, there was no mention of it in anyone's performance review," Naya reminded her.

They'd both logged enough years at Prescott & Talbott to know that something was seriously wrong with this picture.

"Do you think Cinco sanitized the file?" Naya said, finally giving voice to what they'd both been thinking.

"But why? Why take out references to the supervising partner if he was just going to have Caroline destroy the whole file? It makes no sense," Sasha said.

Her frustration level rose. They were missing something.

Naya shook her head, equally peeved. "No, you're right. So the supervising attorney just ... didn't? And, don't forget, Ellen wasn't a litigator and, really, neither was Clarissa. There's just *no way* the firm gave them this case and told them to run with it."

Just then, Naya's cell phone rang. They both started.

"Naya Andrews," she answered.

Sasha stood and cracked her back. Naya was listening intently to the person on the other end of the phone; she squeezed the phone between her ear and neck and scribbled notes.

"Not at all," Naya said to the caller. "I'm glad you called tonight instead of waiting."

She must have felt Sasha watching her, because she looked up. Sasha pointed to the empty coffee mugs, and Naya nodded then returned her attention to the call.

Sasha carried the dirty silverware and empty mugs downstairs to the closed coffee shop. Using the key Jake had given her, she unlocked the door to the retail space and walked through the shadowy room toward the kitchen. Her path was lit by the soft glow of the light from the refrigerator cases filled with expensive fruit-flavored waters and bottled teas.

The trip through the dark room reminded her, as it always did, of her run-in with an undercover agent in the space when it had been vacant. She wondered fleetingly whether Agent Stock would have put in a good word for Connelly, if he'd asked. Seeing as how she and Connelly had helped Stock with an investigation that had led to a promotion, he likely would have supported Connelly. Had Connelly even tried to save his job?

She dumped the dirty dishes in the tray beside the sink and stretched onto her toes to pull two clean mugs down from the stainless steel rack on the wall. Then she grabbed the plastic white coffee carafe that Jake filled with fresh coffee for her each night before he locked up.

She took the coffee into her office and waited for Naya to finish her call. While she waited, she poured Naya's coffee. As she was stirring in sugar and cream, Naya burst into the room.

"Here." She handed the cup to Naya and poured her own. "Well?" she asked.

Naya's eyes shone. "We caught a break. Sort of."

They sat at the conference table.

Naya put down her coffee and flipped back to the first page of her notes, while Sasha waited. She took a long drink of coffee. It was still hot. In another hour or so, the carafe would be providing

warm coffee, at best. But lukewarm coffee was better than cold coffee, and cold coffee was better than
no coffee.

"Okay, that was the booking manager for Three
Rivers Models and Actors. She was working late,
catching up on paperwork, and she opened my e-
mail with the girl's picture," Naya said.

"She recognized her?"

"Yep. She had been one of their models. But
about a few weeks ago—this lady was fuzzy on the
exact date—she called in and said not to book her
on any more jobs because she was moving to New
York."

"Does she have a name and contact information?" Sasha asked, trying to keep her excitement under control until the story checked out.

"Her stage name is Tawny Truitt. The booking
manager, Amanda, said she doesn't know her real
name because she hadn't been modeling with them
very long. The agency only files tax forms when
their talent hits a reporting threshold, which
Tawny had not. And she didn't have a forwarding
address. She told Amanda she'd call when she was
settled to give her the address for her last check,
but no one's heard from her yet." Naya shrugged.

"Did this move to New York come out of the
blue?" Sasha asked, moving on for now. They could
figure out how to track down Tawny later.

Naya nodded, looking down at her papers. "Yeah, Tawny said she'd gotten a job on her own, freelance, that had paid well enough that she could move up to the big leagues and take her shot."

"Did she mention what the job was?" The timing worked, Sasha thought.

"I'm getting there," Naya told her. "Amanda said she didn't ask. She assumed the girl had turned a few tricks or stripped at a fraternity party or something. She said it's not an unusual occurrence in their line of work. But Tawny volunteered that she'd been approached at the laundromat by someone who offered her a PG-rated acting gig and an enormous sum of money for about an hour's work. Amanda said she'd warned Tawny that was a dangerous way to live, but the girl insisted she had been smart about it. The work was all done in public. The guy who hired her met her back at the laundromat when she was done to pay her in cash. He didn't know where she lived or her real name and she didn't ask his."

Sasha forgot about her coffee. "So we think our killer saw Tawny at the laundromat, realized Nick wouldn't be able to resist her, and set him up. Then used the pictures to create marital discord for the Costopolouses and a motive for murder?"

Naya looked at her for a long time.

"What?" Sasha asked.

"The killer. Or someone at Prescott. They stink to high heaven in this."

Sasha looked back at her. "Or someone at Prescott is the killer."

"Or that," Naya agreed.

"We need to talk to Martine Landry," Sasha said.

Talking to Martine proved to be easier said than done.

It had started out well enough. Although Martine had left Prescott & Talbott before Sasha had started, she knew Sasha's name. On the basis of their shared lineage, Martine had been inclined to talk to Sasha, even though she was calling her at home at close to eleven p.m. on a Saturday.

Once Sasha got past the condolences on Ellen and Clarissa's deaths and mentioned that she was representing their husbands, Martine's goodwill had evaporated.

Martine's last words, before she slammed the phone down in Sasha's ear had been both cutting and strangely familiar.

"I hope you can sleep at night, Sasha, doing what you do. I know as well as anyone that everyone's entitled to a defense, but that doesn't mean *you* have to provide it. And, I'm certainly not going to help you. Do what you have to do, and may God have mercy on your soul," Martine had hissed.

Afterward, Sasha had rubbed her forehead and waited for it to come to her. Martine's rant had echoed the letter Malcolm Vickers had sent to her and her dead friends fifteen years previously.

Sasha told Naya to go home and get some sleep. Then she fired up her laptop and started the outline for her argument at the preliminary hearing.

The good thing about being crushed with work, she thought, was that when she hit a brick wall on one front, there were plenty of other equally pressing tasks waiting for her.

48.

Sunday

CINCO TURNED AWAY, but it was too late. Marco had already seen him.

It irritated him to no end that Marco, who was neither Episcopalian nor a resident of Fox Chapel, crossed two bridges every Sunday morning to worship at St. Peter's. Couldn't he have one day a week when he didn't have to deal with anyone from the firm?

But every time Cinco complained to Greta, looking for just a smidgeon of understanding from his spouse, she shushed him. Marco's wife, Lidia, was a Daughter of the American Revolution and a dyedin-the-wool WASP. Her pedigree trumped her Italian-American husband's Catholicism as far as Cinco's wife was concerned.

"Cinco," Marco bellowed now, hurrying across the narthex to give him a hearty handshake, which Cinco returned without enthusiasm. "Greta," Marco said, "you look lovely. Wasn't Pastor Mark's sermon particularly inspiring and thought-provoking today?"

"It was," she agreed, offering her cheek for a kiss.

Cinco wondered if either of them had listened to it. He knew he hadn't. He'd passed the time the way he did every week, marveling at the craftsmanship in the elaborate stained glass windows that gleamed like jewels when the sunlight hit them, imagining the painstaking care that the artists had used to highlight the gold-leaf halo around Christ's head in the painting over the altar, and admiring the detail work apparent in the marble baptismal font. If there was a God, Cinco often thought, his glory and majesty were in the careful acts that had created such beauty.

Lidia extracted herself from her conversation and moved their way, the picture of old money in her pale pink suit and skirt and perfect blond helmet of hair. After their squealed greetings, Lidia and Greta wandered away, babbling about the up-coming ladies' auxiliary luncheon.

Marco pounced immediately.

"What's the status?" he asked in a low voice.

Cinco ignored the flare of disgust that filled him. It was Sunday morning, for chrissakes.

"Sam Davis had found Vickers's son. But other than that, nothing," he said.

"That's something," Marco said. "What are you going to do about it?"

"Nothing right now," Cinco answered. He sup-posed it was too much to hope that Marco would drop the subject.

He was right. Marco grabbed his arm just below his elbow and squeezed it hard.

"What do you mean, nothing? This implicates your old man as much as anyone else, Cinco. Go see the kid and offer him money. Jesus."

Cinco wrested his arm away. "Get your hands off me. And watch your language. Have you forgot-ten where you are?"

Marco dropped his hand, chastened, for the mo-ment. Cinco continued, "First of all, I'm not going to make an offer. How many settlements have you negotiated? If the kid's behind this, and money's what he wants, he'll make a demand. I'm not bid-ding against myself."

"Of course he wants money," Marco exploded, "what else would he want?"

"Keep your voice down," Cinco warned him. "Believe it or not, not everyone is motivated by filthy lucre. And second, don't bring up my father's name again. Are we clear?"

Marco rolled his eyes but held his tongue as their wives drifted back toward them.

Cinco gave the women a wide smile and offered up a silent prayer that this ugliness would just vanish, somehow. Before Marco cracked.

49.

SASHA DIDN'T BELIEVE IN GHOSTS—or zombies, for that matter. If she had, she'd have been certain that Malcolm Vickers had killed Ellen and Clarissa.

She'd woken before dawn and had turned on her laptop before she'd even poured her first cup of coffee. She'd spent the morning working at her dining room table in her pajamas. Her Googling had revealed that after losing his son, Vickers had turned to advocacy. He'd been a pioneer in the fathers' rights movement and in various male-bonding fads that had long since faded from public view. His early posts in online forums and chat rooms made it clear his anger hadn't dissipated over time but, instead, had hardened into a steel rage.

For years, he'd urged fathers to use "any means necessary" to keep their children in their lives. But he seemed to have stopped posting and organizing rallies after a widely publicized kidnapping by one of his followers had ended in tragedy. The father, fleeing the police with his fourteen-month-old daughter in the backseat of his Taurus, had crossed the median at an estimated eighty-seven miles an hour, smashed into an eighteen-wheeler, and flipped the car. Father and child were both declared dead at the scene, and Vickers fell off the map.

The next mention of his name that she'd been able to find was his obituary. After detailing his advocacy on behalf of fathers and his battle with cancer, the piece ended on the plaintive note that "he is believed to be survived by his only son, born Richard John Vickers, current name and whereabouts unknown, but held in his father's heart every day of his life."

Sasha ran several searches on Richard John Vickers, but he had no electronic footprint. She made a note to have Naya try the databases used by private investigators and debt collectors and closed her browser. She couldn't spend her entire day going down Internet rabbit holes; she still needed to work on her opposition to the district attorney's motion to have Greg's bail revoked. Once she had her argument roughed out, she planned to shower and then head to her parents' house.

Her family would gather there after attending Mass together at Saint Theresa's, where, as Martine Landry would have been glad to know, they would all have prayed for Sasha's soul. Given that she was the only lapsed Catholic in a large family, her soul likely garnered more than its fair share of prayers.

Ordinarily, she would skip the McCandless family Sunday dinner on a day before not one, but two, court appearances. Not today. Despite her long to do list, she'd decided to make the time. She recognized her motivation was, at least in part, to prove she wasn't emotionally stunted and she did value her family, despite what Leo Connelly might think.

She exhaled. She didn't have time for this distraction. She pushed thoughts of Connelly and his cutting words from her mind and padded barefoot to the kitchen to refill her coffee.

She watched as the face painted on the side of the mug turned from black and sleeping to white and wide awake as the heat from the coffee activated the paint. Connelly had surprised her with the mug one random weekday morning over the summer. He said he'd seen it and had immediately thought of the way she switched from sleepy to alert with her first sip of morning coffee. Hot tears pricked her eyes at the memory. *Damn him.*

She abandoned the mug on the counter, coffee untouched, and went into the bathroom to turn on the shower. The opposition would be there later.

50.

RICH TURNED THE HAMMER OVER in his palm. It was cold and hard. He needed to be the hammer. Cold, hard, and impervious to outside forces.

The Clarissa situation was still eating at him. He tried not to blame himself. How could he have known she was pregnant when he'd plotted her death? Of course, he wouldn't have wanted to harm an innocent baby—a fact he'd readily conceded to her.

When he'd popped up from the backseat of her car after she'd parked in her office garage, her screams had pleased him at first. But when she'd broken into sobs and told him she was carrying a baby, his satisfaction had vanished. Gone in an instant. Replaced by uncertainty.

A baby.

He hadn't wanted to believe her, had wanted her to be lying. But she'd fumbled through her purse with shaking hands and pulled out one of those pictures of the fetus. A sonogram. The thin filmy paper had curled up into a scroll, and the grainy gray blob had looked like, well, a blob, but the computer-generated information at the top of the picture confirmed that this was a blob living in Clarissa's womb.

Clarissa had looked up at him through wet, black eyes and had pleaded with him to spare her baby. He'd smacked Nick's hammer against his palm, deliberating while she'd begged.

He smacked it again now, remembering.

He'd had to make a snap decision about this unforeseen circumstance. He'd done the best he could, he told himself. He'd handled it the right way.

And after that hiccup, he'd simply continued on with the rest of his steps as predetermined. He had already dropped off the envelope with the photograph at Prescott & Talbott the night before, because he'd thought it would be too risky to venture into the offices after her body had been found in the garage.

In retrospect, he realized that had been a mistake. If Clarissa hadn't died, he would have looked like he was bluffing when Prescott opened the picture.

This time, he needed to do everything in the proper order: tear Martine and Tanner apart; wait until she took steps to divorce Tanner; then kill her; and, finally, drop off the third picture.

He hit the hammer against his palm once more with a dull thud.

No surprises this time.

51.

"WHERE'S LEO?" Sasha's mother asked, enveloping Sasha in a hug and a cloud of Clinique Happy as soon as she walked through the door.

The scent meant Sunday to Sasha. Valentina McCandless loved perfume, but she saved it for church, her birthday, and her anniversary. One year, Sasha had given her a large bottle for Mother's Day, so that she could wear it whenever she wanted. The bottle had lasted six years.

"Hi, mom," Sasha said, kissing her mother's cheek and ignoring her question.

Her brother Sean stepped through the doorway between the dining room and the family room carrying a tray of nachos and cheese dip. Jordan, his wife, followed with the beers.

"Hi, Squirt," Sean said, nodding his head toward her. "Where's your boy? He's going to miss kickoff."

"Hi, Sean, Jordan. He's out of town," Sasha answered.

She hurried to the kitchen in the back of the house to avoid further questions about Connelly.

Riley, her brother Ryan's wife, sat at the table, chopping vegetables for the salad.

"Hi, Sasha," she said in her soft voice. She sliced the mushrooms in a quick, precise rhythm. Her uniform pieces would have made Connelly proud.

"Hi. How are you feeling, Riley?" Sasha asked. Riley was, as usual, pregnant.

"Pretty good. A little tired, but that could be from chasing the hooligans around, too. Hey, I saw you on the news yesterday! You were being interviewed about the men who killed their wives," Riley said, her eyes wide.

"Allegedly," Sasha said.

"What?" Riley blew her long bangs out of her eyes and kept slicing while she talked.

"Nevermind. Nothing. So what did you think?" Sasha said as she walked to the refrigerator and looked inside, out of habit more than hunger.

"I liked your suit," Riley said.

Sasha's mother walked into the kitchen and closed the refrigerator door. "You'll ruin your appetite," she told Sasha. Then she turned to Riley. "What suit?"

"Sasha was wearing this really cute dress and jacket on television," Riley explained, waving the knife for emphasis.

"You were on television, and you didn't tell your mother?" Sasha's mom said. "Dad and I would have recorded it, honey."

"It wasn't a scheduled thing, Mom. I just got nabbed by a reporter who had some questions about a case. It was no big deal, really," Sasha explained. She gave Riley a long, meaningful look.

Riley nodded, wide-eyed, to let Sasha know she understood. She'd been married to Ryan long enough to know that Valentina would not view murderous husbands, alleged or otherwise, as appropriate pre-dinner conversation.

"Where's Ryan?" Sasha said to change the subject.

"Out back with your dad and the kids," her mother answered, turning her attention to the two plump, naked chickens destined for the roaster.

Sasha watched through the small window as her father threw the ball in the general direction of the knot of grandchildren at the far end of his backyard and they tumbled after it like puppies.

Ryan caught her eye and waved. She waved back.

"Do you need any help, Mom?" Sasha asked.

"From you? Heaven forbid. I wish Leo were here, though. I wanted to get his recipe for the potatoes. You don't happen to know it, do you?" her mother said over her shoulder, with her hands inside a chicken.

"Uh, the roasted ones? Rosemary, sea salt, and olive oil," Sasha said, impressed with herself for remembering.

"Amounts? Temperature? Time?" her mother responded.

"Oh, yeah, I don't know," Sasha answered.

Behind her, she heard Riley swallow a giggle.

Valentina just shook her head and said, "Go outside and get some sun. You look pale."

Sasha didn't argue. She stepped out on the big back deck and settled into the teak glider.

"Hi, doll," her father called from the yard.

"Hi, Dad," she answered, rocking the glider back and starting its gentle motion.

Her oldest nephew, Liam, turned at the sound of her voice.

"Aunt Sasha!" he whooped and took off running toward her.

Siobhan, Colin, and Stefan were right behind him, squealing and laughing as they raced across the yard. Daniella lagged behind, pumping her chubby toddler legs as fast as she could. They thundered up the stairs and piled onto the glider in a tangle of arms and legs.

"Hello, five little monkeys," Sasha said, reaching to tickle five bellies.

Ryan and her dad stayed in the yard and gave the football a few last throws. Even at sixty-four, her dad's arm could still send a bullet whizzing through the yard. Padric McCandless had quarterbacked the Central Catholic high school football team. He'd handed each of his three sons a pigskin as soon as they'd been able to stand without assistance and, to his wife's dismay, had seen no reason to treat their peanut-sized daughter any differently. Sasha had a framed picture in her office of the two of them. She couldn't have been much older than a year, dressed in a lacy pink dress and white shoes. Her father crouched beside her, correcting her form as she tried to throw a regulation-size football to one of the boys.

Sasha watched them toss the ball and listened to the kids talk over one another in a rush to fill her in on school, sports, and the eight-and-under social scene. With their excited voices in the air, the sun on her skin, and Daniella snuggled on her lap, she took in the moment and gave no thought to dead lawyers, broken marriages, or demanding boyfriends.

Then Sean appeared in the doorway.

"Dad, Ry, come on! Game's about to start," he called.

"Go, Steelers!" Colin yelled, and the entire mass of wriggling children slipped off the glider and swarmed into the house.

Sean stepped down onto the deck to let them pass. He looked at Sasha and took a swig from his beer.

"How's Leo feel about your representing the Lady Lawyer Killers?" he asked in a deliberately neutral voice.

Sasha glanced up at him, shielding her eyes from the sun with one hand. His face was blank.

"I wouldn't know. I don't consult him about my work," she answered, matching his tone.

Ryan and her father clomped up the steps and stood beside Sean.

"No Leo?" Ryan asked her.

"Not today," Sasha said.

"Maybe he doesn't approve of Sasha's choice of clients," Sean said.

Don't take the bait. De-escalate.

"He's out of town on business," she said, looking at Ryan and her dad.

"Oh? Did he decide to take that job in D.C.?" her dad asked.

Sasha stared at him. Connelly had talked to her father about his job offer before he'd mentioned it to her? She felt betrayed by two of the men she loved.

Finally, she said, "Yes."

Ryan looked at her closely. "You gonna move there?"

Sasha shook her head. "No. Maybe. I don't know."

Sean said, "He's a good man. He'll take care of you."

"I don't need to be taken care of, Sean," she said, forcing herself to speak calmly. She reminded herself that Sean was trying to fill a role he was neither born to play nor particularly well suited for. When their oldest brother, Patrick, had been killed at age thirty, Sean, two years his junior had tried to step into his shoes. He seemed to think he had a responsibility for his youngest sister, despite the fact that Sasha was, herself, well into her thirties now.

Ryan, ever the pacifier, stepped in. "Of course, you don't. We all know that. It's just, Leo seems to make you happy. You've kept him around longer than all the rest. And, plus, I'm sure mom and dad would like you to give them some grandchildren at some point."

Sasha cocked her head at him. "I think you guys have the grandkids pretty well covered, don't you?"

Her father laughed and said, "Boys, leave your sister alone. Go in and save me a seat in front of the TV." He tossed the football at Sean and sat next to Sasha on the glider.

Sean and Ryan walked into the house. Their sister's romantic situation already forgotten, she could hear them arguing over the point spread for the game.

Sasha and her father sat and moved the glider forward and back on its rockers, not speaking. Finally, he said, "You want to talk about it?"

"No."

"Okay."

They rocked some more. Sasha stared at the sturdy deck rails directly in front of her. The deck wrapped around the side of the house and then down into a second level. It was massive, impressive, and functional.

"Remember when you and the boys built the deck?" she said, still looking straight ahead.

"Sure," he answered. "Summer of '98. All the boys helped. Patrick, the most."

"I was home from college, working the dinner shift at The Colony. I'd wake up every morning to the sound of hammering. And every day, more deck would appear. I remember thinking it was amazing that you guys could create *this* out of nothing but a pile of wood and nails and your effort," she said, sweeping her arms wide.

Her dad smiled.

She went on. "I can't do that. But I can take a pile of words, nothing but a jumble of good and bad facts and good and bad law, and create an argument that will convince a judge."

"You sure can," he agreed.

Sasha turned to face him now. "But for some reason, that's not worth anything. I should just stop what I do and follow some guy?"

"You should do what makes you happy," he said, putting an arm around her. "Whatever that is."

Sasha looked down for a moment, then she said, "Do you think I'm broken inside?"

Padric smiled again. "No, you're not broken, Sasha. You're just different from them." He nodded toward the house.

"Connelly thinks I'm broken," she said.

"Leo's probably hurting, honey," her father said slowly. "You aren't broken, but you sure are ... self-contained. It seems to me he opened up to you and was expecting you to do the same. But that doesn't mean there's something wrong with you, baby. You've always been that way. Serious and closed off."

Serious and closed off?

"That *sounds* broken," she said.

He laughed. "No, that sounds like a small girl who decided to take on big things. You're just careful, is all. Not as careful as I'd like, with all the flitting around and beating up bad guys, but careful about letting anyone in who might try to distract you from your goals. That's all."

"You make me sound like a robot," Sasha said. Maybe she was emotionally stunted.

"You can't make yourself crazy over something some boy said in the heat of the moment, Sasha. Come on, let's go watch the game."

Connelly wasn't some boy. He was a man. And she wasn't a high school girl, either. She had no business moping around her parents' house like a hormonal teenager while a killer ran around Pittsburgh, knocking off female lawyers and framing their husbands.

She hopped off the glider. "I can't. I'm sorry, Dad. I shouldn't have come today. Can you tell Mom I'm not feeling well, and I'll sneak out through the garden?"

He looked at her.

"Please?"

He nodded. Then he kissed the top of her head. "Go on."

~ ~ ~ ~ ~

Sasha had the windows down and the music up as she headed back into the city. The combination of cool air and loud music drove thoughts of Connelly and her brothers from her mind.

The Vickers case was like a splinter in her foot, though. It needled her with each step. She needed to talk to someone who'd been at Prescott & Talbott when the case had been active. Someone who knew everyone. Someone who liked her and would help her. She needed to go see Lettie.

At the last minute, just before the road fed her into the Liberty Tunnel, which carved its way through Mt. Washington and onto the Liberty Bridge, she jerked the car into the far right lane and wound up and around, climbing the steep backside of the hill that sat above the city.

At the top, she slowed and eased the car onto a narrow, hilly side street then made a quick, sharp right onto a narrower, hillier side street. During her eight years at Prescott, she'd driven her secretary home a handful of times. Lettie took the Incline down to Station Square and then transferred to a bus to the office each morning, reversing the trip at night, unless she worked late. Lettie's husband or son would pick her up if she worked overtime. But on a few occasions, when they'd gotten an early evening snow, Sasha had taken her home so that her husband wouldn't have to put out a folding chair and fret that someone might move it and steal his parking spot. Mt. Washington had an exquisite view of the city and its rivers. What it lacked was off-street parking.

Sasha turned onto a narrow street and squeezed her Passat into the first spot she found. She grabbed her purse and started the climb to Lettie's townhouse near the top of the street. Shouts and cheers floated out through open windows, as families sat in their dens and living rooms rooting for the Steelers.

Lettie wasn't watching the game. She was working in the small garden bed in the front of her townhouse. She was, however, wearing a Steelers jersey.

"Hi, Lettie," Sasha said as she drew near.

Lettie turned toward her voice, a spade in one gloved hand, and squinted to see who was calling her. A wide smile spread across her face when she realized it was her former boss.

"Sasha, this is a nice surprise," Lettie said. She put down her spade and peeled off her gloves, placing them in a neat pile next to the garden tool.

"I'm sorry I didn't call first. I was on my way home from my parents' place and just stopped, kind of on a whim," Sasha said. *Kind of on a whim, and kind of out of desperation,* she thought.

Lettie laughed. "Don't be silly. It's great to see you. Do you want to come inside, have a cup of coffee? Gene and Justin are watching the game."

As tempting as the idea of coffee was, Sasha declined. "Thank you, but no. I really can't stay. I just wanted to say hi and, to be honest, I was hoping to pick your brain."

Lettie frowned and said, "I hope you aren't planning to ask me about Ellen or Clarissa. I heard you're representing their husbands." Her tone left no doubt as to what she thought of that.

Sasha considered pointing out that it was Lettie's employer who had engaged her, at least for Greg, but there was no upside. She needed Lettie's help. Getting her hackles up about the murders wasn't the way to get it.

"Of course not, Lettie. I wouldn't do that. I just have a question about an old pro bono case from the nineties—*Vickers v. Vickers.* Do you remember it?" she asked, although she knew Lettie would remember. Lettie was Prescott & Talbott's unofficial historian.

Lettie nodded. "Sure," she said, her voice still cautious. "It was a messy divorce that came to us through a Neighborhood Legal Services referral. Ellen and Clarissa cut their teeth on that case."

"And Martine Landry," Sasha said.

"Right," Lettie agreed without elaborating.

Lettie enjoyed a well-deserved reputation as a chatterbox; the very fact that she hadn't yet launched into a detailed explanation of the matter was evidence that she didn't trust Sasha with whatever information she had.

Sasha tamped down her impatience and looked straight into Lettie's gray eyes. "Listen," she said, "we worked together for a long time. You know me, and I hope you know how I practice law. This isn't some lawyer trick, Lettie. I think Ellen and Clarissa's murders might be related to that case. And, if I'm right, Martine's in danger. But she refuses to talk to me, so I need your help. Please?"

The older woman blinked. "Of course."

"Thank you," Sasha said, relieved. She trusted Lettie, but telling her about the files Caroline had smuggled out of the office could put her in a vulnerable position, so Sasha didn't mention them. Instead, she asked, "Do you remember who acted as the supervising partner on that matter?"

Lettie sighed and said, "There wasn't one."

"How was that possible?" Sasha asked.

Lettie walked over to her front stoop and sat on the bottom step; she folded her hands in her lap like a schoolgirl. Sasha joined her on the cold concrete and waited.

Lettie took her time, gathering her thoughts, then she said, "I guess you could say there was ... an oversight. The firm has done pro bono work forever, of course, but in the nineties, the bar association rolled out an initiative. There was a pro bono challenge of some sort, and Prescott signed a pledge. As part of all that, the Management Committee created the Pro Bono Program Director position, which, of course, still exists. But now it's a permanent administrative position. Back then, it was a rotating assignment. From what I recall, the idea was to assign a junior partner to the position for a one-year term. It would allow the partner to demonstrate his management skills and put him in line for the more coveted committee assignments."

Sasha nodded. It sounded like Prescott & Talbott's typical approach: the more layers of management, the better. "So what happened?"

Lettie chewed her lower lip while she thought. "Okay, if I recall correctly, the first year, the directorship went to John Porter. He did a fine job, as far as I could tell. Some of the other junior partners resented that he had the power to assign them to cases, but that was part of his responsibility, so they had to accept it. At the end of that first year, the partners voted to give the Pro Bono Program Director the authority to assign *any* partner in the firm a case to supervise. The thinking was that giving the director that authority would signal to the legal community that Prescott & Talbott was truly committed to public service."

"And it would also signal to the junior partners that they should stop their bellyaching," Sasha observed.

Lettie gave a wry a smile. "That, too," she agreed. She rubbed her forehead with the back of her hand and then continued. "So, the second year, Marco DeAngeles was named the director. If you think he's a firebrand now, you should have seen him back then. The very first case in the door after he took over was the Vickers divorce. The three girls volunteered to work it together, and Marco assigned none other than Mr. Prescott to supervise."

"Cinco?" Sasha asked.

"Oh, no," Lettie said, "the fourth Mr. Prescott. His father. He was still the chair of the firm back then, but he was getting up in years and was starting to make arrangements to hand things over to the fifth Mr. Prescott."

"That was a bold decision by Marco."

"It was. And, as I understand it, it did not sit well with Mr. Prescott. His secretary, Barbie Roman—she's retired now, of course—said at the time that they had an ungodly row about it. She told me she could hear Mr. Prescott through the door just roaring at Marco that he had overstepped. But Marco wouldn't back down. And the Management Committee had to support him, however reluctantly, because it was within his power." Lettie shook her head at the memory.

"So what happened?" Sasha asked.

"Nothing happened," Lettie answered. "Mr. Prescott simply ignored the case. Marco refused to assign another partner. So those poor girls were just set out to sea with no paddle. They worked their tails off with no guidance. But as I recall, they got a very good result for their client. I think we had champagne in the Mellon Conference Room after the decision came down."

She searched Sasha's face. "Does any of that help? Because I really don't know any details."

Sasha patted her hand. "It helps a lot, Lettie. Thank you. Now, I'd better get out of here and let you get back to your weeding."

They stood, and Sasha gave her former secretary a quick hug. As she walked away, Lettie called after her, "Now, you tell Leo I said hello."

Sasha turned and waved.

52.

ICH'S SHOULDER THROBBED, heat radiating down his arm and up his neck. His right arm hung limp and awkward by his side while he ran down the stairs from the law office, taking them two at a time. He kept his face averted as he passed by the entrance to the coffee shop and shouldered through the front door with his good side.

Out on the sidewalk, he raced across the street and cut through the parking lot, running on a diagonal, trying to put as much distance between himself and the building as he could. He'd cut a wide circle and backtrack for his car without getting close to the Law Offices of Sasha McCandless, P.C. If that crazy old coot was conscious, Rich had no interest in a rematch with him and his damned cane.

He shouldn't have risked it anyway, he thought. He was so close to completing his plan. Letting Sasha McCandless distract him had been a mistake.

He'd gone to her office, just to see if he could find some hint of what she knew. He'd come prepared to have to break in, but to his surprise the door had been ajar. Just inside, on a small round table, someone had left piles of files, spread out across the surface, with no apparent organization. He'd spotted the picture of Costopolous making out with the model on top of a stack of printouts of legal cases. Two piles over, he was surprised to see the pictures he'd delivered to Prescott & Talbott: the fact that she had copies could only mean that someone was feeding her information from inside. That thought had made his stomach cramp up with fear.

He'd clenched his stomach with one hand and pawed through the papers with the other, searching for more documents from Prescott & Talbott. Suddenly the back of his shoulder had exploded in pain and he'd pitched forward, smacking his jaw against the table.

He had turned his head to see an old man standing in the doorway behind him, raising a thick wooden cane to crack him again. He'd twisted out of the path of the cane just in time, and it had come down hard on the table.

Then Rich had crouched like a running back and had run low and hard at the man blocking the door. Just before he'd reached the man, he'd deepened his crouch and rolled his shoulder forward. Then he'd plowed into the old guy's belly and had kept going. The contact had knocked the man out of his path and to the ground. As Rich had run past him, the guy's face had bounced off the corner of the doorframe, knocking his glasses off. They skittered into the hallway, and Rich's shoe had crunched down on them as he sped toward the stairs.

It had happened so fast, Rich thought now, as he prowled through the side streets, anxious to get out of the neighborhood. He cradled his aching shoulder and ran.

53.

"DO YOU WANT TO TAKE a tea for Larry up with you?" Ocean asked, handing Sasha her coffee mug. She'd filled it to the very top.

"Larry's still up there?" Sasha asked. She checked the time; it was after three. Larry's plan had been to work until early afternoon and be back home by halftime, so he could catch the second half of the game. He should have been long gone.

Ocean shrugged. "I think so? He stopped in this morning for a mug of red rooibos and a bear claw. I didn't see him bring the mug back down, and he always does, you know?"

"Okay, well, I'll bring his mug back down for a refill if he wants one," Sasha said.

Mounting the stairs, Sasha wondered if Larry had stuck around because he'd had a breakthrough. *A girl could hope,* she thought.

When she reached the top of the stairs, she glanced down the hallway and spotted a flash of white on the floor near the open door to her office. It was an arm. Her hope drained away, replaced by cold fear. She ran. Coffee sloshed over the rim of the mug and burned her hand.

She stumbled, tripping over a piece of twisted metal as she neared the doorway. She reached the doorway and sunk to her knees beside Larry.

He lay sprawled across the threshold, one arm extended forward into the hallway and the other tucked under his body. A gash on his temple had bled down the side of his face and dried, leaving a crust of black blood. His eyes were closed.

"Larry?" she said. Her own voice sounded distant.

He opened his eyes. "Hi," he croaked.

"Are you okay? Can I move you?" she asked.

"Just having a rest," he cracked. He tried to push himself onto all fours.

"Wait." Sasha put an arm across his chest and around his shoulder and helped him stand.

He looked around. "Have you seen my cane? Or my glasses?"

Sasha stepped into the office and retrieved his cane. Jumbled papers were strewn across the floor under and beside the table. She didn't see his glasses. She handed him the cane and went out into the hall. She crouched by the metal that had tripped her.

"I'm sorry," she said, holding up his mangled glasses.

He waved a hand. "Eh, I have a spare pair at home."

Sasha led him inside the office and settled him into her guest chair. She sat across from him in the chair's mate. He took a handkerchief from his pants pocket and dabbed at the cut on his head, then winced.

"It's dried," she told him. "Wanna tell me what happened?"

Larry returned the cloth to his pocket and shrugged. "I was reading those bail revocation cases you'd found. I needed to relieve myself, so I went to the restroom. I left the door ajar. My mistake, I admit. I didn't see a need to lock it just to run to the bathroom."

"I don't generally lock up to go to the bathroom or pop downstairs for a drink, either," Sasha told him.

"Well, you should start," he said. "I returned to see a man pawing through the papers on the table.

He had his back to me. I stepped into the doorway and cracked him with my cane."

"You hit him?"

Larry looked at her. "Don't you lecture me about avoiding the fight. I've practiced Krav Maga since you were in diapers. Sometimes the principles aren't practical."

Sasha raised an eyebrow but wasn't about to argue with him. "Okay, go on."

"I belted him good. His shoulder has got to feel like hell. Anyway, I reared back to hit him again, and he charged me. He knocked the wind out of me and I crashed into the door." Larry shook his head, a forlorn, wistful look on his face. "Ten years ago, I'd have managed to at least trip him when he ran by."

"He take anything?" Sasha asked.

"No."

"Did you get a good look at him?"

"Eh, white kid, early twenties. Completely nondescript. Not much to go on," Larry said.

Sasha rubbed her eyes with her palms and tried to think. After a moment, she said, "Okay. I need to make two phone calls. Then, I'm going to drive you home, unless you'll agree to let me take you to the hospital to get checked out."

Larry threw her a look. "Home, Jeeves."

She surprised herself by laughing. "You stay here. I'm going to get you a cup of tea and a wet cloth for that cut."

She patted his shoulder and headed toward the door. When she reached the doorway, she turned and said, "Just in case I run into this guy again, which shoulder do I want to go for?"

He smiled at her. "The right one."

~ ~ ~ ~ ~

While Sasha waited for Larry's tea, she pulled out her phone. She actually had three calls she needed to make, but Larry couldn't know about this one.

Daniel answered on the third ring. "Hello?"

"Daniel, it's Sasha," she said, turning away from the counter and speaking in a low voice.

"I was about to call you," he said. "I'm at my folks' place, and dad never came back from your office. Is he with you?"

"He is," she said. "And he's fine. But before I got here, we had an intruder. Your father apparently tried to beat him with his cane, but the guy knocked him over and took off. Your dad hit his head when he fell. He had a nasty cut on his fore-head and his glasses are broken, but other than that, I think he's mainly embarrassed."

Daniel was quiet for a second, then he said, "That old coot won't accept that he's aging. Sasha, promise me you'll stop with the Krav Maga before you're in a nursing home."

She laughed, relieved that Daniel was taking the news so well. She knew Bertie would be a different story.

"I promise. Listen, he doesn't want to get checked out. But I have a friend, a gerontologist, who I'm sure will come to the house as a favor and just give him a once over. Will you be there to make sure your dad submits?"

Daniel let out an exaggerated sigh. "I'll be here. Your doctor friend should bring restraints, though. You don't know my dad."

She went on, "I hate to do this, but I am going to have to drop your dad off and run. I need to get back here and figure out what the guy was looking for."

"No problem. It's probably for the best if you don't come in. I'm sure my mom's going to be on the warpath," Daniel said. "Just pull into the drive-way and I'll come out to get my dad. And Sasha?"

"Yeah?"

"Don't skip class tomorrow. Sounds like you need to be on alert."

She ended the call and thanked Ocean for the refill.

Back in the office, while Larry cleaned up his cut and drank his tea, she dialed Dr. Kayser's number.

"This is Al Kayser," he answered.

"Dr. Kayser, it's Sasha McCandless."

She glanced up at Larry to gauge his reaction to hearing her address the doctor. He was frowning at her, but his shoulders were slumped. He looked resigned to what was about to happen.

"Sasha, how are you?"

"I'm well, thanks. How have you been?" she asked.

"Good, good. Too busy, as always. I've just returned from a conference in San Diego and digging out from under all the paper that accumulated while I was away has been quite a chore. But I assume you're not calling me on a Sunday afternoon to chat. Is there something I can do for you? Do you have another case?"

Dr. Kayser was her late grandmother's physician; he was also a well-regarded testifying expert in the area of geriatric medicine—a fact that had helped Sasha immensely in her representation of an elderly man up in Clear Brook County back in the spring. Dr. Kayser had determined that the old guy wasn't incompetent, but, rather, was being drugged by his treating physician.

"Not exactly," Sasha said. "But I do have a favor to ask of you."

"Anything for you, dear."

"I appreciate that. I have a colleague who ... took a bad fall. He says he's fine, but I'd feel much better if you could have a look at him."

Dr. Kayser didn't hesitate. "Certainly."

"Thank you. I really appreciate it. Larry lives around the corner from you, on Shady Avenue. Do you think you could meet him at home?"

"Not Larry Steinfeld?" Dr. Kayser said.

"As a matter of fact, it is Larry Steinfeld," she said.

Dr. Kayser chuckled. "Took a fall, my left foot. You tell Larry I told him at his last visit, it's time to retire from the hand-to-hand combat."

"Don't you worry, I certainly will."

"Is Larry at the house now?" Dr. Kayser asked.

"No, we'll be leaving here in just a minute," Sasha said.

"Okay, then I'll leave now and try to butter Bertie up before you get there," Dr. Kayser said with another soft laugh.

Sasha hung up and looked at Larry. "It appears we have a mutual friend. Al Kayser's going to meet you at home and check you out," she said.

Larry grumbled something indistinct.

"He said to tell you ..." she began.

"Bah, move on," Larry cut her off with a wave of his hand.

She was delighted to see him acting so brusquely. It helped confirm her belief that his pride hurt worse than his body.

"We've got one more call to make and then we're out of here," she said.

Larry hoisted himself from the chair and leaned on his cane. He started to walk toward the table.

"I'll just pack up these cases and take them with me, then," he said.

Sasha came around to the front of the desk.

"Larry, listen to me. I've got this. Please, just rest. Do what Dr. Kayser says. If he tells you not to come to court tomorrow, listen to him. If he says it's okay, you can come to keep me company. But don't worry about the cases. I've got it."

"I'm fine. You really shouldn't worry about me," Larry said.

"I'm not worried about you. I'm worried about what Bertie will do to me if you don't take it easy," she said.

Larry laughed but made his way back to the chair and eased himself into it. Sasha gathered up the files while she waited for Naya's answering machine to pick up. She'd do the rest of her preparation from home. Just in case their visitor decided to return.

"Hi, Naya, it's me. When you get home, please hop on the people search databases and find out what you can about Richard Vickers. Google is a dead end. And, stay away from the office tonight. Larry had a run in with an unwelcome guest. Call me at home if you have any questions." Sasha said to the machine.

She took one last look around the room to make sure she had everything.

"Let's get out of here," she said to Larry.

54.

Monday

SASHA SHOULD HAVE BEEN TIRED, but instead she was wired, filled with anticipation and energy. She drank her morning coffee standing in the kitchen and then was out the door while the sky was still dark.

She watched it turn from black to indigo to pre-dawn gray as she ran up the hill from Shadyside and through the sleeping business section of Forbes and Murray (up street, as the locals said) to her Krav Maga class. The storefronts were still dark and the commuter traffic was light.

For class, Daniel paired her with Corey, a shy teenager. He was a junior at the high school around the corner and a wrestler. He was quiet and intense. He blistered her with punches and held nothing back.

After the session, he offered her a sweaty fist bump. He hurried off to shower before his homeroom bell summoned him. Daniel nodded at her and excused himself from his conversation with an eager student.

"How's your dad?" she asked as he walked toward her.

"Still smarting from the blow to his pride and the browbeating from my mother and Dr. Kayser, but otherwise fine. He's planning to meet you at the courthouse later," Daniel said.

"That's great," Sasha said.

"Yeah, I suppose. Listen, this guy, you think you know who he is?" Daniel asked.

Sasha looked closely at his face. She saw no anger or thirst for revenge. "I do," she said. "Why?"

Daniel shook his head. "Don't worry, I'm not going to take the fight to him. And my dad is refusing to report the attack to the police, but what's your plan?"

She wasn't sure. Naya had found Rich Moravian, born Richard John Vickers. She'd called after midnight with an address on the South Side and an employment history. Rich worked for none other than Andy Pulaski. The Big Gun himself. He was the killer, she was certain. But the issue was when to spring it on Diana Jeffries, and how. She wanted to consult with Larry.

She looked up at Daniel. "The plan is fluid right now, just know he's going to pay for what he did, Daniel."

Daniel considered her for a moment. Then he put a hand on her shoulder and gave her a gentle squeeze, almost a half-hug. "Be careful, Sasha. Don't be brave."

~ ~ ~ ~ ~

Sasha's focus was on her upcoming court appearances as she left class. She ran mindlessly, her attention on her arguments. Her pace felt good, fast, and easy. But when she tuned into her surroundings, she realized she was headed toward Point Breeze. Instead of continuing straight down the hill from Squirrel Hill into Shadyside, she'd apparently hung a right somewhere.

She slowed her pace, bemused at her wrong turn. At the corner, she jogged in place to read the street signs. She was two blocks from Martine

Landry's house. She checked her watch. It was almost seven-thirty. Close enough to a civilized hour in a household full of kids, she decided. She turned right and ran toward Martine's street, trying to decide what she would say when she arrived.

Four houses down from the Landrys' yellow brick two-story home, she slowed to a walk to catch her breath. At the end of Martine's driveway, a boy of about ten stood, pulled slightly backward by the oversized backpack on his shoulders, with his head bent over a handheld game.

"Hi," Sasha said loudly as she approached.

He raised his head. "Hi." Then it was back to the game.

"Is this your house?" she asked.

He looked up again, curious now. "Yeah," he said, taking in her running clothes.

"Is your mom home? I'm an attorney. I used to work at Prescott & Talbott, too," Sasha said, giving him a smile.

"Oh," he said, his tone conveying disappointment that she was just another boring old lawyer, "yeah, she's in the kitchen, cleaning up breakfast. I'm waiting for the bus."

"Thanks. Have a great day," Sasha said.

He was already done with her, his thumbs flying over the controls on his device.

Sasha walked up the wide front stairs and crossed the porch. She pressed the bell and heard the chime sound deep within the house. She waited. She was raising her hand to ring the door-bell again when she saw a figure walking from the back of the house.

A pale, round face ringed by strawberry blond curls appeared in the window.

"May I help you?" Martine said, polite but cautious. She looked past Sasha to check that her son was still at the end of the walk.

Sasha had decided that a direct approach would be best. "I don't know, but I think I can help you."

"I beg your pardon?"

"I'm Sasha McCandless," she said, putting her foot up on the threshold to stop the door when Martine inevitably tried to shut it in her face.

Martine pushed the door forward to close it. It hit Sasha's sneaker and stopped.

"I think you're in danger. I have reason to believe that Ellen and Clarissa weren't killed by their husbands," Sasha continued.

"Of course you do," Martine said in a harsh voice. "You represent them." She pushed hard on the door, trying to force Sasha's foot back so she could slam it shut.

"I think Richard Vickers killed them," Sasha said in a rush.

"Who?" Martine said.

Sasha felt the pressure lessen on the other side of the door. "Jessa and Malcolm Vickers's son. He goes by the name of Rich Moravian now. And he works for a divorce attorney named Andy Pulaski, who was representing both Ellen and Clarissa." Sasha saw Martine's eyes spark with recognition at the name.

Martine swung the door open. "I know, but, I'm not getting a divorce," she said.

"Not yet," Sasha said, "but you're the last living member of The Terrific Trio, and I think you're next on his list."

Martine stared at her and pursed her lips, thinking. She looked back at her son, the sunlight reflecting off the top of his tousled hair as he played his game. "Come on in," she said and stood to the side to let Sasha pass.

"He's okay out there, right?" Martine asked, gesturing toward the boy. "His bus should be here in three or four minutes."

"I don't see why not," Sasha said. "If Vickers follows his pattern, step one is going to catch your husband engaged in some behavior that's a deal breaker in your relationship. He's methodical."

Martine laughed as she shut the door. "Well then I wish him all the luck in the world. Tanner's a saint. Do you want a cup of coffee or something?"

"I have a personal policy to never refuse an offer of coffee," Sasha said, following her to the kitchen.

"What makes you so sure Vickers killed them? I'll grant you that it's a pretty big coincidence that he works for that divorce attorney, but it could be just that: a big coincidence," Martine said over her shoulder as she pulled a red ceramic mug out of a glass-fronted cabinet above her coffeemaker.

"It could be, but it's not. Vickers figured out Nick and Greg's weaknesses, set them up, and snapped pictures of them in the act. What I can't work out is how he steered them to Pulaski," Sasha said.

The mug landed on the counter with a bang. Martine turned to her wide-eyed. "I know how he did it. Clarissa told me that the day the pictures were delivered to the office, she ran into a messenger for Andy Pulaski in the lobby who gave her Pulaski's card. She checked him out and he seemed like an aggressive attorney, so she called him and recommended him to Ellen."

"They got the pictures at work?" Sasha asked.

"That's what Clarissa told me. Why?"

"Because those aren't the only pictures that were delivered to the office," Sasha said.

She was steeling herself to tell Martine about The Terrific Trio photos, when they heard the scream.

55.

RICH HADN'T BEEN ABLE TO believe his eyes when he'd seen Sasha freaking McCandless walk up to the boy and start talking to him. Then, to make matters worse, she'd gone up to the front door, and a few moments later, Martine had let her in.

"Are you kidding me?" he mumbled aloud from his position in the bushes. Now what was he supposed to do? Over the weekend, he'd considered and rejected grabbing the kid and holding him somewhere, hoping to cause disharmony between his parents, maybe instigating a big, public fight. Or worst case, killing the kid and pinning it on Tanner. But he had to stay true to his father. And he knew his father would never have approved of that.

He'd finally decided to wait until the boy had gotten on his bus. Then he was going to put on his mask, force his way into Martine's house, tie her up, and ransack it, telling her that Tanner owed him money for drugs. It was weak, he knew. But he hoped it would cause a rift. Then, he'd call from Andy's office on a pretext about Ellen's will. In a stroke of luck, Ellen had bequeathed some volume of legal books to her. Then ... then, his plan got fuzzy. He had to hope she'd be angry enough at her husband that he could lead her into a conversation about divorce or something. It was important to follow the pattern: problem in the marriage, divorce, murder.

Now, this McCandless wench was messing up everything. What was she in there telling Martine?

Rich could feel his panic rising in his chest. He had to get in there and stop her. He half-rose from his crouch. Cold metal touched his ear.

"Stay right there," a husky female voice said from behind him.

The woman patted him down one-handed. Then she said, "Turn around, nice and slow."

Rich turned. He faced an older woman with silver hair in a sleek bob. She wore a black pantsuit and held the gun with authority. He'd never seen her before.

"Who are you?" he croaked. His throat felt tight and dry.

"What's it matter, Moravian?" She answered. "It's over now."

Those words turned Rich's fear to rage. *No, it's over when Martine's in the ground, and not until then.* He felt a red wave rushing through his body and he rode it, charging her like he'd charged the old man.

She stumbled and went down on one knee but kept her grip on to the gun.

As she pushed herself back to standing, he took aim and kicked her wrist. The gun popped out of her hand and clattered to the gravel.

He reached it first and grabbed it. The woman jumped on his back, clawing at his face with one hand. The other was wrapped around his throat, squeezing. He flailed at her, tried to shake her off, but she hung on.

He couldn't breathe. Black dots pricked at the corners of his vision. He started to feel hot and dizzy. He wanted to huddle on the ground and surrender to sleep.

And then he thought of his dad. Of the boxes and boxes of letters and packages marked "return to sender" that his executor had sent to Rich when he'd finally tracked him down. They'd dated back through the decades, but his father had kept sending them. A letter each month, a gift on Rich's birthday and Christmas. Year after year. Even though they came back to him each month, Malcolm hadn't given up.

How could Rich give up now?

He shook his head, digging at the woman's claws around his neck. Then he smacked her knuckles hard with the gun. She loosened her grasp, and he threw her off his back. He kicked her as she fell, then he took off running through the hedgerow down to the sidewalk and the boy, who hadn't even noticed the struggle taking place in his parents' bushes; his head was still bent over his game, thumbing away.

Rich grabbed the boy and started to drag him along the sidewalk. That's when the boy screamed.

56.

SASHA AND MARTINE RAN TO the front of
the house and out onto the porch.

"Carlton!" Martine wailed.

"Mom!" he called back, tears streaking his face.

The boy was being jerked by his backpack straps
along the sidewalk, away from the house. A young
guy was doing the jerking. There was nothing
memorable about the guy. Except for the gun in his
free hand. It was a big, evil looking thing.

Sasha stepped off the porch and crossed the
front lawn on a diagonal, heading straight for Rich
and the boy.

A trim woman in her late fifties came limping
out of the bushes.

"Who the hell are you?" Martine demanded.

Good question, Sasha thought.

"Sam Davis," the woman answered, resting her hands on her knees and sucking in air. "Chief Security Officer at Prescott & Talbott. I was sitting on Moravian's apartment this morning and followed him here. He's been squatting in your bushes since a little before seven."

"Mom!" the kid cried again, his voice high and desperate.

Martine stepped down from the porch then stopped, hesitating in front of the stairs, unsure what to do to save her son.

"Stop right there!" Rich said, walking backward, with the boy in tow.

Sasha kept walking.

"I said stop!"

"Make me," she said.

"I'll shoot him," Rich said, jabbing the gun at Carlton's head. He whimpered.

"No you won't," Sasha told him. "Your dad wouldn't like that."

His face curled into an angry mask, and he snarled. "Don't talk about my father. You don't know anything about him," Rich said.

"I know enough. I know he wanted to be with you more than anything in the world and it burned a hole in him that he couldn't. I know he wouldn't want you to do that to Carlton's dad," Sash said in a soft voice.

Rich locked eyes with her and swallowed hard.

Behind her, Sasha heard Samantha explaining what happened to Martine.

"I jumped him in the bushes, but he got his hands on my weapon. I was choking him out, when he flipped out, knocked me to the ground and took off after the kid," Samantha said.

He hadn't come with a gun, Sasha reasoned. He'd disarmed Samantha. So he probably hadn't planned to hurt the boy.

"Think of how scared he must be," Sasha said to Rich, nodding at the boy. "Think of how scared you would have been at his age."

"Please," the boy begged, "please, don't hurt me."

Rich dropped the backpack straps abruptly, and the boy stumbled. Then he took off running and didn't stop until he was in his mother's arms.

Rich pointed the gun at Sasha and started walking toward her.

"C'mon," he said, "we're going back to the house."

She walked backward, keeping her eyes on the gun and watching for an opening to disarm him.

When she was halfway up the driveway, he told her to stop.

He glanced over to Martine and her son, who was still clinging to his mother, sobs wracking his thin frame.

"Send the boy inside," he said in a low growl.

"Go ahead, honey. Go in the house," Martine said in a too bright, cheerful voice.

"Mom, no," he cried, his arms around her waist.

She smoothed his hair. "Honey, please do as I say."

The boy didn't move.

Rich kept the gun trained on Sasha with one shaky hand and pointed at Sam with the other. "You, get him out of here."

Sam hurried over and peeled Carlton's hands off Martine, gently but quickly. Martine whispered to him and kissed his head.

Sam led him to the door and pushed him inside. Sasha watched him disappear down the hall.

"Get on your knees!" Rich shouted, shaking Sam's gun at Sasha. His face was red and his arms were trembling.

Sasha heard Daniel's voice in her head telling her to stay on her feet at all costs. But her gut told her to comply, so she slowly lowered herself and knelt on the driveway. She faced Rich and the front of the house. Rich had his back to the house. He stepped close and pointed the gun between Sasha's eyes. Too close. His first mistake.

"Listen, you don't want to do this," Sasha said. She kept her voice low and slow. Her brain seemed to have divided in half: the trained part clicked in and took over, calculating and talking; the other part was panicking, thinking about Connelly, thinking about bleeding out on a driveway on a beautiful October morning.

"Shut up!" Rich said, his eyes bulging. He waved the gun, bobbling it, then righted it and aimed it at her head again.

Surely the boy was old enough to know to call 911. If the neighbors hadn't already. Point Breeze was not the sort of neighborhood where a woman kneeling on the pavement with a gun to her head at seven-thirty in the morning would go unnoticed. She hoped.

Her other hope was that the gun wasn't loaded. Ordinarily, she had to assume it would be. Asking the assailant wouldn't be productive. But here she could ask Sam. She suspected it was. If Sam had been concerned enough to carry it, she probably had been concerned enough to render it useful.

She could tell by the way Rich handled the gun, clumsy and unsure, that he wasn't familiar with firearms. That wasn't to her advantage, though. He didn't need to be a proficient marksman to hit her at point-blank range. And, he was likely to shoot her by accident, just fumbling around with the thing.

Sasha locked eyes with Sam over his shoulder.

"Is it loaded?" she asked.

Sam nodded a quick yes, then she said, "As a matter of fact, it's not. But this one is."

Rich twisted his neck to see if Sam had a second gun.

Sasha knew his movements were at normal speed, but everything seemed to be moving in slow motion. She reached forward and grabbed the barrel of the gun with her left hand. She wrapped her right hand around the butt. At the same time she jerked the gun to the right, redirecting it from her forehead to the space over her right shoulder. She tensed her biceps and gripped it hard.

Rich's eyes registered surprise, then panic. When he pulled back on the gun, trying to get it away from her, she was ready for the movement and leaned into it, allowing the force to pull her forward. She used the upward momentum to get her feet under her.

She drove her right knee forward and snapped her foot out, smashing her lower shin into his groin. He shuffled backward and she wrenched the gun from his hands.

She recoiled and drove again with her right shin, pulling from her hip and remembering to breathe out on impact with his groin. She hit him with a satisfying crack.

Rich yelped and collapsed in heap on the driveway, curled in the fetal position. Sasha pulled her foot back a final time and kicked him square in his exposed right shoulder blade. For Larry.

Rich jerked his arm and cried out. Curled up, rocking and mewling, with his eyes closed, he looked like a defenseless child. She turned away.

Sam hurried down the driveway.

"Good work," she said, clasping Sasha on the shoulder. "Martine's inside calling the police."

Sasha handed the gun to her gingerly. "Thanks. Here."

Sam checked the clip, then tucked it in her jacket pocket.

"What do you want to do with him until the cops get here?" Sam asked.

They both watched Rich whimper and squirm on the ground.

"I might have crushed his pelvic bone," Sasha said. "I don't think he's going anywhere. Why were you at his place this morning?"

Sam brushed her bangs back before she answered. "I'm former FBI. When Mr. Prescott asked me to run down Malcolm Vickers, I found this clown. I told Prescott where he lived and noted the extreme coincidence that Ellen Mortenson and

Clarissa Costopolous had both worked his mother's divorce and had both been brutally murdered. Prescott's reaction was, I don't know ... off? Hinky? Whatever, I figured I'd check this guy out. He came over here, skulking in the bushes. So I had a friend run the address. When it came back as the Landry residence, I knew our boy had something naughty planned."

"Why didn't you call the police?" Sasha asked.

"Why didn't you?" Sam countered.

"What do you mean?"

"Am I supposed to think you just happened to drop by Martine Landry's out of the blue? I'm sure you turned something up while you were preparing your case. Or cases."

Sasha shrugged. She wasn't going to tell Sam Davis that Caroline had helped her.

"Look, I haven't been at Prescott long enough to know who's clean and who's dirty. If you know something, tell me. Please," Sam said.

"All I'll say is you need to take a long look at Cinco. And his cabal."

"The Management Committee?" Sam pressed. Sasha nodded.

"Can you tell me who I can trust?"

"Volmer. And Caroline Masters," Sasha told her. "Can you deal with the police? I have to be in court in an hour."

She left Sam standing over Rich and walked up the driveway to Martine's front door. She rapped softly, but no one answered. She eased the door open.

Martine and Carlton sat in the front room, which looked to be used as a family room. Martine cradled the boy on the couch. She looked up at Sasha over his head.

"Is he okay?" Sasha asked.

"Scared. But he's fine. Thank you for what you did," Martine said, tears shining in her eyes.

Sasha nodded. "Listen, I have to go. When the police get here, give them my contact information and send them my way, okay?"

"Okay, sure," Martine said. Her voice got soft and she added, "I can't believe he wanted to kill us. Because of a sixteen-year-old divorce?"

Sasha told herself to leave it alone, but she heard her voice ask, "Why did you terminate his father's rights, Martine?"

"It's what the client wanted," Martine answered. "And we didn't know any better. We were gung-ho: we thought we should win at any cost. We didn't understand parent-child dynamics. Hell, we didn't understand anything."

"And nobody guided you?"

Martine shook her head slowly. "No. It was the strangest thing. You know how Prescott is, every case has layer upon layer of supervision, but it was just the three of us, without a net. At the time, we were terrified of all the responsibility, but we didn't want to complain. We figured we had to prove we had what it took. And, until now, I would have said we did an outstanding job, all things considered."

Sasha let herself out. Martine sat, staring blankly at her fireplace and stroking her son's hair.

57.

SASHA WALKED BACK TO HER apartment, her blood still buzzing in her ears from the adrenaline rush of the attack. She showered, changed, and raced to the Municipal Court Building with still-damp hair.

Naya and Larry were waiting for her on a bench outside Magistrate Judge Foster's courtroom. They both popped up when they saw her coming.

"Where the dickens have you been?" Larry asked. "They're bringing Nick up now."

"I went to see Martine. Vickers was there. He grabbed her boy. He's in custody now. I'll fill you in later." She looked around. "Where's the district attorney?"

Naya and Lara stared at her. Finally, Naya jerked her thumb toward the courtroom. "She's inside already. And, yes, it's *her* again."

"That's okay. She'll need to approve the dismissals anyway, I imagine." Sasha said.

She headed into the courtroom and walked straight over to Diana Jeffries, who was laughing with her assistants.

"Excuse me," Sasha said.

Diana turned. "Oh, there you are. Good morning, Sasha."

Sasha stared. Could she really not know?

"You did hear that Richard Moravian was picked up this morning, right?" Sasha said, cocking her head in confusion.

"The name sounds familiar," Diana said with a smile that revealed a berry smudge of lipstick on one front tooth.

She'd reapplied in a hurry, with a not-too-steady hand, Sasha thought. Her casual lack of concern was a bluff.

"Good," Sasha said. She turned to walk over to the table where Naya and Larry waited.

"Wait," Diana said, "don't you want to talk about a deal?"

"Nope," Sasha said over her shoulder without turning around.

The bailiff stood and announced the judge, as everyone in the room hurried to their feet.

"Take a seat, ladies and gentlemen," Judge Foster said. She looked down at Sasha and then the district attorney. "Are you ladies ready for me to bring in Mr. Costopolous?"

Sasha stood back up. "Your honor, if I may?"

"By all means," the judge said.

"Counsel for Mr. Costopolous wants to ensure that the Court is aware of a very recent development. Earlier this morning, an individual by the name of Rich Moravian, also known as Richard John Vickers, was taken into custody at the home of Martine Landry, a third female attorney who had previously worked at Prescott & Talbott. It appears that when Mr. Moravian was a child, Ms. Mortensen, Ms. Costopolous, and Ms. Landry represented his mother on a pro bono basis in a very contentious divorce and custody matter. So contentious, in fact, that Mr. Moravian's biological father's paternal rights were terminated, which has not sat well with Mr. Moravian. He apparently devised a scheme to drive wedges between the three women and their respective husbands and then, once divorce proceedings had been instituted, murder the women and frame their estranged spouses." Sasha finished her spiel and then looked up at the judge, expectant and preternaturally calm.

The judge's eyebrows shot skyward. "My, my. That's what I call a dissatisfied client." She paused to let the audience sitting in the gallery titter, then she turned to the district attorney. "Do you have anything to say, Ms. Jeffries?"

Diana took her time standing, then shuffled her papers and smoothed her hair before responding. "Yes, thank you, your honor. I was told by the homicide detectives that, earlier this morning, Mr. Moravian did, in fact, confess to the murder of Ellen Mortenson. Accordingly, I have prepared a motion to dismiss the charges against Mr. Lang."

The judge squinted at her and said, "Do I hear a *but* coming, Counselor?"

The district attorney gave her a small smile and continued, "However, Mr. Moravian has denied any connection to Ms. Costopolous's murder. He claims he did hire a model to flirt with Mr. Costopolous and sent photographic evidence to Ms. Costopolous. And he did, in fact, accost Ms. Costopolous in her car in the parking garage on the morning of her death with the intent to kill her." She paused and cleared her throat. "But upon being informed by Ms. Costopolous that she was with child, he realized he could not go through with it, and he fled the scene."

Sasha shot to her feet. "Your honor!"

Judge Foster put up a hand and said, "You'll get your turn."

"The People are investigating that story, your honor, but, at this time, intend to proceed with its case against Mr. Costopolous," Diana explained.

The judge shook her head. "Are you sure about that?" she asked.

"Yes, your honor."

"Well, then, bring in the defendant," Judge Foster said to the bailiff.

He picked up the phone.

Sasha leaned over to Naya and whispered, "Give me the pictures."

Naya passed her a manila folder.

"Your honor? May we approach while we're waiting?"

The judge shrugged and then waved them up with her hand. Sasha, followed by Larry, approached from one side; Diana and her lackey from the other. The judge flipped a switch and turned on a white noise machine. Its whooshing sound filled the small courtroom.

She leaned forward over the bench. "What's up?"

"Your honor, I came into possession of these photographs after court on Friday. I don't know if the District Attorney has seen these yet, but I think they'd help inform her decision," Sasha said, holding up the folder.

The judge reached down and took it. She flipped it open and grimaced at the first picture. She turned it over and looked at the second one, with two Xs, one obliterating Ellen's face, the other Clarissa's.

"Two down, huh?"

"Exactly, your honor," Sasha said. "The women in these photographs are, from left to right, Ellen Mortenson, Clarissa Costopolous, and Martine Landry. The evidence is overwhelming that the same person killed Ms. Mortenson and Ms. Costopolous *and* that he intended to kill Ms. Landry."

The judge passed the folder to Diana Jeffries, who opened it and stared. Then she turned to the second photograph.

Diana turned to Sasha and said through clenched teeth, "Where did you get these?"

"I'll be happy to have a witness come in and explain in open court, if the District Attorney's Office insists on moving forward with this farce," Sasha said, addressing the judge and not her adversary.

The judge said, "Diana, don't do this. If I have to dismiss these charges from the bench, it's going to destroy your campaign. Obviously, Mr. Moravian or whoever he is realizes that copping to murder of an unborn child will sign his death warrant, so he concocted this ... story. But you don't have the goods on Costopolous. Drop it now and save yourself. Build a case against this Moravian guy and nail his hide to the wall for killing that young woman and her baby."

For a long moment, the only sound was the white noise. Then the door from the hallway swung open and banged against the wall with a loud thud.

Judge Foster glanced up and frowned. Sasha turned and saw a uniformed police officer standing in the doorway.

"Can we help you, officer?" the judge asked, flipping off the white noise machine.

The police officer looked young to Sasha. Possibly even younger than Judge Foster's interns.

She gripped her patrol cap with both hands and cleared her throat. "Yes, ma'am. I mean, your honor. I'm sorry to interrupt but I need to speak with the District Attorney, ma'am. Detective Gilbert sent me. It's urgent," she said. She stood ramrod straight and waited for an order.

The Judge waved a hand at Diana. "Go talk to her, but make it quick."

"Yes, your honor." Diana bobbed her head and hustled down the aisle to the waiting police officer.

They whispered loudly for a few moments. Sasha could tell from the district attorney's posture that she was growing irritated. Finally, she nodded and put up a hand to cut off the patrolwoman. Diana stormed back toward the bench, frustration flashing in her dark eyes.

When the district attorney reached her spot next to Sasha, the judge flicked a switch and white noise filled the courtroom again.

"Well?" Judge Foster demanded.

"Well," Diana said, smoothing her features into an approximation of a smile, "the murder weapon does not appear to be from Mr. Costopolous's tool set."

Sasha hid her surprise.

"Is that so?" the judge asked.

Diana looked sideways at Sasha then nodded.

"Yes. It seems Mr. Costopolous has a Craftsman Professional toolset, and the hammer found at the scene was a DeWalt. I am also told that the hammer found at the scene appeared to be brand new, save for its use in the attack."

The judge looked from Diana to Sasha and then back to Diana. "Ms. Jeffries, it's time to make a decision. Fish or cut bait, as they say."

Diana Jeffries smiled a broad politician's smile, but anger stained her cheeks beneath her freckles and she said, "In light of the totality of the evidence, the People will withdraw the charges against Mr. Costopolous."

"Go back to your tables," the judge instructed, then she nodded to the bailiff.

They returned to their seats as the sheriffs arrived with Nick. He'd aged over the weekend. His eyes were dull, his skin gray. Sasha felt a twinge of pain when she looked at him.

Larry clasped him on the back. "Did they treat you okay, son?" He'd called his friend and had extracted a promise that Nick would be protected.

"As well as could be expected, I guess," Nick answered. His voice was like his eyes, lifeless and flat.

Sasha leaned over. "It's almost over, Nick," she whispered close to his ear.

He didn't respond.

The judge moved her microphone close and said, "Good morning, Mr. Costopolous."

"Uh, good morning, your honor."

"Ms. Jeffries?" The judge said.

Diana stood. Sasha saw her chest rise as she inhaled deeply, perhaps thinking about the upcoming election. She exhaled slowly, then she said, "May it please the court, the Commonwealth of Pennsylvania moves to drop the charges against Mr. Costopolous in light of new evidence that has come to the attention of my office."

A murmur of surprise shot through the audience.

Nick grabbed Sasha's arm. "Is she serious?"

"Yes," Sasha answered, removing his hand and patting it.

"What new evidence?" he asked.

"They found the man who killed Ellen and your wife. He grabbed Martine Landry's son this morning," she whispered.

"What? How?"

"I'll fill you in later." Sasha turned her attention back to the judge.

"Mr. Costopolous, the charges against you are dismissed. Sir, you are free to go," Judge Foster said, giving Nick a warm, genuine smile.

Diana started to pack up her bag. Her assistant cornered Larry. Sasha heard him promise that he'd send papers over before lunchtime dropping both the motion to revoke Greg's bail and the charges against Greg.

They were done. She had two free clients, and a killer was in custody.

"That's it?" Nick said.

"That's it," she answered.

58.

STILL FLUSHED WITH THE EXCITEMENT
and adrenaline that came with victory, Sasha
wandered around her office, straightening
stacks of paper and otherwise wasting time until
Maisy showed up for the promised exclusive.

She picked up the phone, thought about calling
Connelly, then dismissed the idea. What would she
say? *How's the house-hunting? By the way, I caught a
killer, saved a woman's life, and got my clients' murder
charges dismissed; wish you were here to celebrate with
me?*

She was returning the phone to her desk, when
Naya walked in, a bounce in her step and a bottle
of champagne in her hands. She noted Sasha's
hand, still on the phone.

"Did you call Connelly?" she asked.

"What? No. Why?"

"What do you mean, why? Sasha, call him."

Sasha jerked her head toward the bottle and changed the subject. "Where'd that come from?"

"Prescott & Talbott," Naya answered, placing it on the conference table and giving Sasha a long look.

"Are you serious?" Sasha couldn't believe the balls on Cinco.

"Well, Will Volmer, specifically," Naya clarified.

That was less creepy. Will had already left her a message congratulating her and letting her know he'd do what he could to protect Caroline. Sam had also left a message. As had Detective Gilbert. She supposed she should start returning them.

Larry came through the door with Nick and Greg in his wake. "Look what I found on my way in."

Greg shook Sasha's hand. "Thank you. From my heart, Sasha, thank you."

"You're welcome," she said.

Nick enveloped her in a tight hug. He'd showered and smelled like cologne. "Thank you," he murmured into her hair.

She freed herself and tugged her jacket down. "And you're welcome, too."

"We came to invite you to my place for a sort of combined wake and celebration. We're going to remember our wives and give thanks for our freedom," Nick said. "Will you join us? All of you?" he said, including Naya and Larry with a wide smile.

"Sure," Naya shrugged.

"One drink to toast freedom, of course," Larry said.

"I have a meeting in a few minutes," Sasha said, "but maybe I'll catch up with you after."

"Please do," Nick said.

"Let me grab my purse. I'll meet you guys downstairs," Naya said and walked over to her office.

The men trooped out of the office, Larry in the lead, waxing poetic on freedom and the criminal justice system.

Naya popped her head back in. "You are coming, right, Mac?"

"I'll try," she said.

"Call Connelly," Naya said and withdrew her head before Sasha could respond.

~ ~ ~ ~ ~

The empty offices were too quiet, and Sasha was too fidgety to stay there alone until Maisy arrived.

The glow from the win had worn off and something was nagging at her, tugging on the back of her brain.

So she headed downstairs for a wholly unnecessary cup of coffee.

Ocean and Kathryn were huddled by the cappuccino machine, giggling and whispering. She walked over to the counter.

"Hi, Sasha," Kathryn said, unable to hide her grin.

"What's so funny?" Sasha asked.

"Nothing." More giggles.

Ocean burst out laughing, "Kathryn just saw her crush."

Sasha looked around. The shop was empty.

"A customer?"

"Not one of ours. Yours." Ocean said.

Kathryn poured Sasha a coffee and said, "A client, I guess. He was with Naya and Larry and some other dude. He's old. But he's cute in a swarthy way."

The girls dissolved into more laughter. Sasha realized they were talking about Nick and shook her head.

"Thanks for the coffee," she said, turning to leave.

Kathryn elbowed Ocean, and they pulled themselves together. "Don't be mad," Kathryn said, "I would never hit on one of your clients; he's just so smoldering."

"I'm not mad, but he's way too old for you. And, he's a widower. They both are," Sasha said, in case the girls didn't follow the local news.

Ocean gasped. "Like, they had wives? And now they're dead?"

"Just like that," Sasha said.

"Oh, that's so sad," Kathryn said. "Especially for the cute one."

Ocean turned to her friend and said, "You know he's not *that* cute, Kath. And he's kind of creepy."

Kathryn rolled her eyes.

"Well, he creeped *me* out," Ocean insisted.

Sasha was curious. "What did he do that creeped you out, Ocean?"

Ocean hesitated, then she said, "I mean, it wasn't a big deal. It was just kinda odd. One day last week, the sink in the back was leaking, so Jake sent me over to Home Depot to get some washers right after the lunch rush died down, you know?"

"Sure."

"Well, that store is just totally confusing. So I wandered around and finally ended up at the tool area in the middle. I was just gonna ask someone. The guy was busy with a customer. It was your guy. The cute one. Anyway, this Home Depot guy was trying to help him pick out a hammer, going on and on about, um, DeWalt, I think it was, and how it was such a great brand, but cute guy did *not* want any help. Finally he grabbed a hammer off the pegboard then stalked away. Creepy," Ocean finished with a dramatic eye roll.

Sasha's stomach roiled.

"You okay?" Kathryn asked. "You look … green."

"Yeah, I'm fine. Ocean, can you remember what day it was? It's really important," Sasha said. She put down her coffee and gripped the edge of the counter with both hands, willing herself not to vomit.

"Uhm," Ocean thought, "it had to be Tuesday."

"You're sure?" Sasha said.

"Positive sure."

On Tuesday, two days before his wife's murder, Nick had purchased a DeWalt hammer, the same brand that had been used to kill his wife, even though he claimed to have not needed a hammer that day and to have not known his had gone missing.

"Do me a favor," Sasha said.

"Sure," they said in unison.

"A woman named Maisy Farley is going to come in looking for me. She's a very pretty blonde with a Southern accent. Please tell her an urgent personal matter come up and I had to leave. Will you do that?"

"Uh-huh," Ocean said.

"Got it," Kathryn added.

Sasha could barely hear them over the blood rushing in her ears. She smiled a weak thank you and left. In the hallway, she took deep, gulping breaths, but it felt as if her throat were blocked. She tripped up the stairs and locked up the office. She put her head down and walked out to her car as quickly as she could on shaking legs. She had to get home.

Rich Moravian might have stolen Nick's hammer, but Nick had dealt the blows that had stolen Clarissa's life.

EPILOGUE

On the twelfth day after Sasha learned that Nick Costopolous had played her for a fool, she came home from work and changed out of her suit. She pulled on her yoga pants, and they promptly puddled into a heap around her ankles.

A quick inspection in the bathroom mirror revealed that her rib cage was visible in both her chest and her back. Although her appetite had disappeared twelve days earlier, replaced by a persistent nausea and low-level panic, she decided it was time to eat a meal.

Sasha wondered if the recipes Connelly had left for her included his white chicken chili or the country-style mushroom and lentil stew that made her think she was at a chateau in Bordeaux every time she smelled it. She wasn't certain he'd deem either dish appropriate for her skill level, but if she had to eat, she wanted homemade comfort food—something warm and filling—and she had no desire to visit her parents.

So the only option was to make it herself. Preferably with ingredients she already had on hand, which was going to add to the difficulty level, considering she hadn't been to Trader Joe's since she realized that she'd freed a murderer. Buying groceries had seemed frivolous and somehow indulgent, despite Larry's daily call to remind her that she had simply being doing her job.

She fired up her laptop and queued her music play list. Train filled her kitchen, singing soulfully but soothingly, while she dug out her striped apron and twisted the cap off a beer. Tackling a meal was exactly what she needed to take her mind off the mess she'd created.

She pulled the recipe box down from its spot on the pot rack. The box, with its country kitchen motif, was wildly out of place in her sleek kitchen of polished bronze and recycled glass. But it had earned its prominent spot: back in the spring, the secretary to a murdered judge had used the box to conceal a mini-cassette that the judge's killer had desperately wanted to get her hands on. The recipe box had stayed, and Connelly had gradually filled it with detailed recipes he'd written specifically to be Sasha-proof.

She carried the cardboard box and her Yuengling over to the island. Something rattled around inside the box. She leaned against the island and, as Train sang to her about that one night and promised it wasn't a drive by, she put down her beer and opened the box.

In the front was a recipe card with a hole punched in the top left corner. She removed the card. A piece of kitchen twine was threaded through the hole and the dazzling ruby ring Connelly had tried to give her their last night together dangled from the twine.

She stared at the deep red stone for a few seconds before she took a pull on her beer and read the card. In his messy scrawl, Connelly had written *"A Starter. Serves Two. Ingredients: You. Me. Telephone. Directions: Pick up the phone. Call me."*

AUTHOR'S NOTE

I've heard from lots of readers about this book's ending. Some people seem surprised to learn that Pennsylvania's Rules of Conduct (the ethical rules governing lawyer conduct) really would prevent a lawyer in Sasha's position from reporting what she learned to the authorities. *I know!* Other people want to know whether Sasha and Leo are going to get back together. I'm happy to report that *Lovers and Madmen*, a bonus novella set after the next full length-novel in this series provides some closure regarding both the ethical issue and the personal one.

ABOUT THE AUTHOR

Melissa F. Miller is a *USA TODAY* bestselling author and a commercial litigator. She has practiced in the offices of international law firms in Pittsburgh, PA and Washington, D.C. She and her husband now practice law together in their two-person firm in South Central Pennsylvania, where they live with their three young children. When not in court or on the playground, Melissa writes crime fiction. Like Sasha McCandless, she drinks entirely too much coffee; unlike Sasha, she cannot kill you with her bare hands.

57999651R00302

Made in the USA
Lexington, KY
30 November 2016